DRAGONRIDER LEGACY
Book 1

BESTSELLING AUTHOR OF THE DRAGONRIDER CHRONICLES

NICOLE CONWAY

Month9Books

Trade Paperback ISBN: 978-1-946700-46-9
EPub ISBN: 978-1-946700-44-5
Mobipocket ISBN: 978-1-946700-45-2
Hardback ISBN: 978-1-946700-47-6

Published by Month9Books, Raleigh, NC 27609
Title and cover design by Danielle Doolittle
Cover illustration by Tatiana A. Makeeva
Map illustration by Nicole Conway

Month9Books

To William H. and Ethan I.
A few dragonriders in training.

ONE

The jungle was quiet. Every fern frond, leaf, and flower petal dripped with cold dew. The first rays of morning sunlight bled through the canopy overhead, turning everything a surreal shade of green and sparkling through the clouds of mist that drifted between the tree trunks. The thick air smelled of rich, damp soil and the faintly sweet fragrance of the vividly colored flowers.

My bare feet squished on the damp moss as I crept along the tree limbs. I squeezed my bow tightly in my fist. My heartbeat throbbed in my ears and my palms were already slick with sweat. I clenched my teeth to stop them from chattering. Now was not the time to lose my nerve.

Out of nowhere, a brightly-colored parrot burst from the foliage and fluttered across my path. I slipped, losing my footing and rocking back on my heels as I flailed to get away. My stomach lurched. I opened my mouth to yell.

Someone grabbed my belt from behind.

Enyo dragged me down into a squat, hiding amidst the leaves. Together we watched the bird disappear into the distance while I struggled to catch my breath. So much for being stealthy.

Enyo's eyes sparkled like aquamarines in the dim light and the brightly painted beads woven into her dark hair clattered as she turned and shot me a hard look. I scowled back at her. It wasn't *my* fault. That stupid bird had come out of nowhere.

I wrenched out of her grip and slung my bow over my shoulder, crawling down a steep turn in the limb and leaping over into the next tree. That was how you moved in Luntharda— scurrying from tree to tree like a squirrel. The ground wasn't impassable, but it was extremely difficult terrain. Not to mention it was practically writhing with things that would have been happy to make breakfast out of a pair of novice scouts.

Technically, we weren't supposed to be this far away from the city without a senior scout to escort us. But today was different—today I had a mission. And it didn't include falling to my death from fifty feet in the air.

"This isn't going to work, you know," Enyo muttered as we scaled a network of thick vines that snaked up a tree trunk.

I ignored her, but couldn't outrun her. Even if I was taller, she was much faster. Together, we ran along the boughs, leaping, dodging, and climbing until I knew we had to be within earshot. I stopped first, and Enyo skidded to a halt beside me with a broad grin on her lips.

I glanced around for the perfect spot right above the narrow, well-beaten trail that zigzagged through the underbrush below. Faundra left those trails when they moved between their favorite grazing spots. My father had spent years teaching me how to track them, hunt them, and kill them. I could do this—by myself.

I smirked when I found it; the ideal spot where an overgrowth of giant lichen made a great place to hide and watch the trail below. I slipped my bow off my shoulder and took out an arrow, making sure to check the fletching and the shaft for damage before setting it in the string.

"Say you do actually kill one this time. Say we even manage to field dress it and get it back to the city. Do you really think Kiran is going to be okay with you running off without him?" Enyo whispered as she tucked herself into the lichen beside me. I could feel the heat off her skin when her arm brushed mine.

"Well obviously, if I did it without him, then I don't need him in the first place, right? I'm not a kid anymore," I growled under my breath. "He's holding me back on purpose."

Okay, so that was debatable. Gray elves went through puberty around fifteen. Their hair turned from black to as white as frost and their bodies matured to look more adult. After that, they were considered adults and could choose a profession, get married, and basically do whatever they wanted. I was sixteen. I *should* have been treated like an adult, too.

There was just one problem—I wasn't a gray elf.

To make matters worse, my adoptive father, Kiran, didn't want me trying to make my first kill yet. He didn't want me going anywhere without his permission. He still treated me like a little kid.

"Maybe because you never listen," Enyo muttered under her breath.

I narrowed my eyes at her. "Just shut up. Why did you even come?"

She glared back. "Well if you die, someone should at least be able to explain what happened."

"Pfft" I snorted and looked away. "Just keep out of my way."

Enyo pushed some of her long, coal-black hair behind one of her pointed ears. "And stay here—I know, I know."

A twig snapped.

We both fell silent. My heart raced, making my fingers throb and my body flush. This was it, the chance I'd been waiting for.

One-by-one they emerged from the morning mist. The herd of faundra traveled quickly with their littlest fawns grouped in the center to shield them from predators. The does were as big as horses, some even seven feet tall, with their white pelts flecked with soft gray markings. They had long, powerful legs and one kick to the face would crush your skull like an egg. But they weren't the ones you really had to watch out for.

The stags were even bigger. Their shaggy pelts had stark black swirls and a blaze right down the front of their snout. Their heads were crowned with sweeping white antlers with ten razor sharp points. You definitely did not want to be on the wrong end of those.

"Beautiful," Enyo whispered faintly.

I smirked.

Then I saw him—the alpha male. He stepped from the shadows, an impressive beast much larger than the other members of his herd by far. He had a single black stripe that ran from the end of his snout, down his back, and all the way to his tail. He was older, so his pelt was thicker around his neck like a mane, and all the other black marks along his hide had faded away. His horns sloped back to almost touch ends with four extra points on each side.

My stomach fluttered and swirled with excitement. I could barely breathe. When I drew my bow back, my hands shook. It made my arrow point bounce all over the place.

Enyo placed one of her palms on my back.

I closed my eyes for a moment and tried to remember everything Kiran had taught me. I took a deep breath. I listened to the jungle. Then, slowly, I opened my eyes again and took aim straight for the alpha male's heart. My hand was steady and my bowstring taut.

All I had to do was let go.

Something caught my eye. It was fast, like a flickering shadow darting through the underbrush.

I hesitated. My eyes searched, tracking through the underbrush for more movement. A snagwolf? Or maybe a wild shrike?

A sinking sensation rose in the pit of my stomach. It made all the tiny hairs on my arms and neck stand on end.

Oh no. Not this—not now.

Clenching my teeth, I tried to ignore it, to push it out of my mind, to fight it.

A cold chill hit me suddenly, making my body jerk beyond my control. The bowstring slipped, and my arrow went flying. It zipped through the moist air, grazing leaves and lodging deep into the side of a doe. She bucked and bleated, sending the rest of the herd into a frenzy. They bolted in every direction, disappearing like ghosts into the jungle.

But the doe I'd shot was badly wounded. She couldn't run far. Without thinking, I ran for the trunk of the tree and started my descent, jumping down from branch-to-branch.

"Reigh! Stop!" Enyo screamed.

No. There was no stopping now. When my feet finally struck the forest floor, I went to the spot where I'd shot her. There was blood on the ground and more droplets speckling the leaves and ferns, leading away into the undergrowth. She wouldn't last long. Running would make her bleed out faster.

Enyo seized my wrist suddenly. Her face was pale and her eyes as round as two moons. "We can't be down here. It's too dangerous." Her voice trembled.

"I can't just leave a kill lying out there. Stag or not it's still a—"

"Reigh! Don't be stupid. Something will have heard them," she pleaded and pulled on my arm. "Something will smell the blood!"

"Go back to the tree and wait for me, then." I snatched away from her and pointed. "I'm finishing this, with or without you."

Her expression faltered. She looked back at the tree, then to me, with her eyebrows crinkled and her mouth mashed into a desperate line.

"I said go!" I yelled.

Startled, Enyo backed away a few steps. She blinked at me, lips parted as she took in a few quick breaths. Then she turned and ran.

I tried not to think about all the rules I was breaking as I dove into the foliage, alone, to track down my kill.

Leaving the city without telling Kiran—that's one. Going into the jungle unsupervised was another. Taking Enyo with me was worth at least two more because we hadn't told her parents about it, either. And then there was the whole "hunting alone before I'd been officially marked a scout" thing. So yeah—basically, Kiran was going to be furious.

My only salvation was finding this doe. At least then, when I returned, he wouldn't be able to argue that I wasn't ready. The stag would have been much more impressive, but a kill was a kill. This was proof I could handle myself. I deserved to get my scout's mark.

The blood trail wasn't hard to find even among all the towering fronds and enormous leaves of the plants. I'd never stood on the jungle floor alone like this before. I felt insignificant, like a tiny insect, as I looked up at the giant trees. Everything seemed bigger now that I was this close to it. The air seemed cooler, too. The canopy was so far away, like a distant sky of endless green leaves. It gave me chills.

Or maybe that was just my *problem* acting up again.

I crept through the undergrowth, traveling fast and trying to stay out of sight as I followed the blood trail. The drops were getting bigger and closer together. She was slowing down. It wouldn't be long.

And then I saw her.

The doe was lying in the middle of a small clearing between two big ferns. She was motionless, but I could see her side rising and falling with the shaft of my arrow sticking straight out. She was still alive.

I quickly shouldered my bow and drew my hunting knife. As I got close to the edge of the clearing, I paused. I did a quick glance around, waiting to see if anything or anyone else was nearby. Enyo was right—the smell of blood might draw the attention of other predators.

Everything was quiet and still.

The doe bleated loudly when she saw me. Her legs kicked, eyes looking around with wild anxiety. Standing over her, I could feel my hand begin to shake again. I had to kill her, end her suffering—preferably before she gave away my position to every dangerous creature in a five-mile radius.

I put my knee over her snout to hold her head still. She was too weak from blood loss to fight me off. Her milky brown eyes stared straight ahead as I drew back, ready to plunge my dagger into her heart.

A deep, heavy snort broke the silence.

I froze, slowly raising my gaze just in time to see him stride free of the underbrush, his white horns gleaming in the morning light. The alpha male had come back for her.

Our eyes locked. His ears flicked back and he stamped a hoof. I tightened my grip on my knife, and tried to think of what to do—any fragment of a lesson Kiran had given that would help me right now.

There wasn't one.

The stag lowered his head, pointing those deadly horns straight at me, and charged.

I scrambled to my feet and ran for the nearest tree. His thundering hooves on the ground got closer and closer. I wasn't going to make it. I was fast, but he was faster.

The second before I could grab onto the lowest handhold, I heard a bowstring snap. The alpha bellowed. I dared to look back, just in time to see him fall and begin rolling. An arrow was sticking out of his haunches. He tumbled toward me, rolling like a giant furry boulder.

The massive stag smashed right into me.

The impact knocked the wind out of my lungs. Something popped and one of my arms went numb. Not good.

When everything stopped, I realized I couldn't move at all. Was I … dead? Dying? No—I was pinned. Crushed between a tree and a very angry faundra stag, I couldn't escape. Something sharp, probably one of the stag's horns, sliced right across my face. Warm blood began running down my face.

"Reigh!" Enyo's voice was calling my name, but I couldn't see her.

The stag staggered back to his feet, shifting his weight off me. I sucked in a desperate, wheezing breath as I crumpled to the forest floor in a daze.

"Don't just sit there! Climb!" Enyo yelled again.

What?

I looked up, my vision still spotting, to see the stag charging straight for her.

Even with the arrow sticking out of his flank, he galloped at full speed. She clumsily drew back another, eyes stuck on the shaggy monster thundering straight for her. Her whole body trembled with terror. She was hesitating, trying to decide if she should fire or flee.

She wasn't going to make it either way.

Something inside me burst, like the last raindrop before the dam broke.

I screamed her name at the top of my lungs. The chill came over me again, a coldness that rushed through every vein, making my body jerk and my eyes tear up. This time I didn't fight it. I clenched my fists and let it take me.

Time seemed to slow down and stop altogether. My pulse got slower. My skin went cold. I could see my own breaths turning to white fog in the air. Before me, darkness pooled, amassing into one dark, inky puddle on the ground. It rose like a flickering column of black flames, and took the form of *him* …

The black wolf I called Noh.

He looked at me with a smiling canine mouth and red, wavering bog fire eyes.

"Kill it," I commanded.

"*With pleasure*," his hissing voice replied.

TWO

I couldn't remember a time in my life when Noh hadn't been there. Ever since I was a little kid, he'd always been hiding in the back of my mind, like a memory from a former life that refused to fade. Almost as soon as I'd noticed his presence, Noh had absolutely terrified me.

Nothing about that had changed.

It wasn't that he'd ever tried to hurt me. Somehow, I didn't think he could even if he wanted to. But I could feel his presence just as clearly as I could sense his intentions—and they weren't good. He thrived on my anger, sadness, and confusion. Whenever Kiran and I had an argument, he would start creeping around the corners of the room, slipping soundlessly from shadow to shadow, almost like he was waiting for me to finally lose it.

I didn't know what he would do. Frankly, I didn't want to

know. Kiran had warned me over and over that I had to keep myself under control, and make sure not to go too far. The repercussions could be severe. Noh might hurt someone, and it would be my fault. I was the only one who could see and hear Noh, and the only person he listened to. I could control him—for now. But who knew how long that would last. There was always a chance that one day, when I let him off the chain, I might not be able to get control of him again.

Then no one would be able to stop him from doing whatever he wanted.

The worst part was knowing that eventually it was going to happen. Somehow, someway, I was going to mess up. I always did. That's me—Reigh—Luntharda's number one screw up.

I couldn't move. Lying on my back with my arms and legs spread wide, my whole body was numb except for the cold pinpricks on my skin. The dull, constant sound of my heartbeat droned in my ears. Maybe that meant I wasn't dead.

Suddenly, there was a voice. Someone was shouting above me. "Reigh? Reigh!"

A strong hand smacked my face.

My eyes popped open. I bolted upright and choked, sucking in a deep breath.

"It's all right. Breathe. You'll be fine." Kiran knelt next to me, studying me with a concerned furrow in his brow.

"E-Enyo … " I tried to speak, but I was barely able to catch my breath. My head wouldn't stop spinning.

"She's fine." Kiran put a hand on the back of my head and leaned in close, poking experimentally at the open wound on my face. Pain shot through my nose, making my eyes water.

"You'll need stitches," he decided aloud. "One of the stag's horns had blood on it. I feared the worst."

That's right. The stag had nicked me.

I looked past Kiran to the place where the doe should have been lying, but she was gone. There was no trace of her or the stag anywhere. Across the clearing, a few other gray elf scouts were checking Enyo. She was unconscious, but her cheeks were still flushed with color. She was alive.

My body sagged with relief. I met Kiran's knowing gaze. The hard lines in the corners of his mouth grew deeper as he frowned.

"Is he still here?" he asked quietly so that no one would hear.

I glanced around. There were no dark shapes or creeping shadows anywhere that I could see. Noh was gone, for now.

I shook my head slightly and winced. My arm—no, my whole shoulder—felt like it was on fire. I couldn't even stand to move it.

"Good. Now get up." He patted the top of my head; a gesture that passed as his gruff, awkward effort at parental affection.

I struggled to stand, and Kiran had to help me to my feet. He dusted the leaves, moss, and twigs off my clothes and picked up my bow. Across the clearing, one of the other scouts picked up Enyo and carried her back with the others toward the nearest tree-path.

I followed with Kiran walking right behind me. I could feel his gaze burning at my back. Anyone else would have thought he was just lurking back there to make sure I didn't stumble and fall to my death because of my injured arm. I guess that could have been part of the reason, but that wasn't all of it. He was worried about Noh showing up again. I was worried about that, too. Worried—and confused about what had happened to the doe and the stag.

Kiran managed to keep his temper in check as we made our way back into the city. We split off from the group when we reached the first market square. I craned my neck, watching them carry Enyo off toward her house. She still wasn't awake yet. My stomach soured and guilt squeezed at my chest like a cold fist around my heart.

I wanted to know she'd be okay.

With Kiran still right on my heels, I made my way back to the small medical clinic where we lived and worked. Kiran was a healer by trade—something he'd also been teaching me since I was a little kid. He ran the best Healing House in the whole city, caring for the sick and wounded while I served as his apprentice.

The clinic wasn't a fancy place by any stretch. Kiran wasn't big on decorating. But it was home—where I'd spent my entire life. The house stood at the end of a street lined with other shops, on crest of a small hill. It was a narrow, plain looking building with three levels—most of which were rooms for patients. A general clinic room where Kiran treated minor illnesses and injuries took up most of the first floor. There was also a kitchen and a living room with a fire pit that was just for us. The rooftop garden was where Kiran grew the herbs and plants he used to make medicines, and where Enyo and I sometimes practiced sparring.

My heart was hammering as we climbed the steps to the

front door. Not even the familiar smell of the drying herbs comforted me. This was going to be bad. Like an angry specter, Kiran haunted my steps as I went inside.

Then he let me have it.

"Have I taught you nothing? Did you ever hear a single word I said?" Kiran stared me down, expecting an answer.

I couldn't decide what was more terrifying, that he was about to pop my dislocated arm back into its socket or that he was using the human language to scold me. He only did that when he didn't want anyone to overhear what we were saying—usually when we were talking about Noh.

Kiran hadn't said much while he cleaned the wound on my nose. The gash was deep, and it took fifteen stitches to close it. I was going to have a brutal looking scar from one cheek to the other, right across the bridge of my nose. Painful? You bet. And I had a feeling Kiran had intentionally taken longer than usual to close it. That was part one of my punishment.

Now it was time for part two.

I swallowed, my entire body tense as his fingers probed my shoulder. Whenever he poked too hard, my vision swam and a whimper tore past my clenched teeth.

"And this time you took Enyo with you," he went on. "You

risked her life, as well. She is not yet fifteen, Reigh. A *child*!"

I looked away. "I told her to go back. She didn't listen."

He gave my shoulder a sudden, violent jerk. It snapped, and I screamed. But the tingling numbness in my joints was gone. I could move my arm again.

"You do not listen, either. You are a reckless, thoughtless boy," he growled as he began to rotate my arm, testing to see if it was set properly. Then he sternly wrapped my whole shoulder in a bandage. "Everything you do, every decision you make, has consequences. Why don't you understand this? You only think of yourself. And that is exactly why I do not let you take your place as a scout."

I glared at the woven grass mats on the floor. "So, is that why you're ashamed of me? Or is it because I'm human?"

Kiran stopped. "I am not ashamed of you."

"Then it's because I'm a monster?"

"You aren't a monster, Reigh."

I raised my burning gaze up to him. "Then what am I? Do you know anyone else who can feel when someone is dying? Who else has a bad spirit living in their head? Noh killed the faundra didn't he?"

When I started to shout, Kiran raised a hand. I closed my mouth and glowered back down at the floor. Right. I wasn't supposed to get angry. We wouldn't want my dark friend showing up again.

"Is that why you won't let me call you 'father?'" I asked.

He didn't answer. He never did. We'd had this argument before—lots of times already. And that was where it always stopped.

Kiran wasn't my father—not my biological one, anyway. He was a full-blooded gray elf who had taken me in when I was a baby. According to him, I'd been abandoned, left lying on a rock just inside the boundary of the jungle, alone and vulnerable. Luckily, he heard me crying before a hungry tigrex or snagwolf could make an easy meal of me. Kiran took me in and raised me like a son, although I wasn't sure why. Clearly parenting wasn't his thing. He avoided people like others avoided the plague. And while he did try to be warm to me sometimes, it was like he didn't know what to say, so instead, he didn't say much at all.

And never once allowed me to call him father.

He was plenty old enough to be my father. He'd earned his scars almost forty years ago, fighting in the Gray War. Of course, he never talked about any of that. He was strange, even by gray elf standards. He'd never married, never had any biological children of his own, and he didn't have many friends. Not that he wasn't well thought of in our community—his reputation from the war made him a local legend. He was regarded as a hero. But that didn't seem to matter much. He seldom smiled, rarely laughed, and he never talked about his past.

But sometimes I overheard others telling stories during the great feast. They talked about how he'd ridden on the back of a dragon, fought to end the war, and stood alongside the King of Maldobar. Some said he'd even called the lapiloque by name.

I didn't know if any of that was true, although sometimes Kiran would sit for hours in front of the fire pit, completely silent, watching the flames slowly die. Those were the nights when I saw the darkness in his eyes.

And sometimes, when he didn't think I was paying attention, I would catch him staring at me that way, too.

"Drink this," he muttered, pushing a cup of strong smelling tea into my hands. It was an herbal remedy to treat swelling and pain, and it tasted so bitter I could barely swallow it. But every awful sip made the soreness in my shoulder subside.

"Enyo's okay, isn't she?" I dared ask once his back was turned. "I didn't hurt her, too, did I?"

Kiran paused. He let his hands rest on top of the chest where he stored all of our medicines. When he turned around, his expression was wrinkled with a sour frown. "She was unharmed," he replied. "But her mother will break her bow for this. She will have to start her training over to earn another one."

My head sagged toward my chest. Great. She was alive, but she was going to hate my guts from now on.

"Did she see what I did?" I couldn't make my chin stop trembling so I bowed my head lower, hoping Kiran wouldn't see. "It's just, you know, I don't have a lot of friends and Enyo is the only one who … " I couldn't finish.

"No. I don't think she knows what happened."

A sniffle escaped before I could choke it back in. With a sigh, Kiran sat down next to me and put his arm around my shoulders, pulling me over to lean against him. "I found you before the others did. You were right. Noh did kill the doe and stag. But I disposed of the carcasses. No one will find them. No one will know what happened. You'll be fine, but this *cannot* happen again. We were very fortunate."

I nodded shakily. Yeah, we'd been insanely lucky. Noh had

never killed before. I'd always been able to stop him. "I just couldn't control it. I just—I didn't know what else to do. I had to save her."

He patted my head. "I understand."

"It's getting stronger. I see him almost every day. He won't leave me alone."

Kiran didn't answer.

"What's wrong with me?" I asked quietly. "What am I?"

His answer was barely a whisper. "I don't know."

It was close to midnight when I gave up trying to sleep.

My mind spun over the memories of what had happened in the jungle. I couldn't stop thinking about the faundra, the feeling of letting Noh go, and how the wound on my face was making my whole face throb. Kiran had smeared it with a thick salve that would keep it from getting infected, but it still made my eyes tear up if I touched it.

Finally, I couldn't stand it anymore. Between my aching face and overwhelmed brain, sleep was not going to happen. I got up and peeled the bandage off my shoulder to stretch and flex my arm. It hurt, too, but the herbal remedy helped a lot. By tomorrow it would be as good as new.

Pulling on a long, silk tunic with baggy sleeves, I buckled

my belt and dagger around my waist. I carried my sandals downstairs, careful to hold my breath when I crept past Kiran's room. He had ears like a fox, and I shuddered to think of what he'd do if he caught me sneaking out again.

I grabbed my bow and quiver off the hook and slipped out the door of the clinic. Above me, hung a wooden sign with the words HEALING HOUSE painted in green elven letters. It was a little faded, and if I wasn't careful it would rattle when I shut the door and wake Kiran up.

Outside, the market square was dark and quiet. Up and down the street, all the shops were closed and the streets were empty. From where I stood on our doorstep, I could see a long way because of where our clinic was perched on the crest of that small hill. All around the lights of the city twinkled in the night. Oil lamps flickered against colored glass windows and towering buildings made of cool alabaster stone. It was a sight I knew well.

Mau Kakuri was the largest gray elf city rebuilt after the war. Some called it the "City of Mist" because it stood against a steep mountainside where a curtain of waterfalls poured down into a shallow river that ran through the middle of the garden district. The falls provided a constant haze of cool, crisp mist that hung in the air, trapped beneath the dense jungle canopy. Sometimes, if the sunlight broke through the trees just right, it made dozens of shimmering rainbows. And on nights like tonight, when the moon was full and bright, its silver light managed to bleed through the canopy and make the mist shine like a floating sea of diamonds.

With a deep breath, I started down the steps and out into the street. Nothing and no one stirred this late at night. The streets, arched bridges, tall stone buildings, and elegantly spiraling palace towers were all built atop the mossy boulders surrounding the plummeting water. The water from the falls made canals, pools, and streams that filled the air with the sound of running water. It also divided the city into districts along the canals—the market district where craftsmen ran their shops, the garden district where the orchards and vegetable gardens were kept for public use, and a few residential districts where most everyone lived. Kiran and I were one of a few exceptions because being the prominent city healer meant sometimes he had late night emergencies. It made more sense for us to live where we could be on call all the time.

Mau Kakuri was where the royal family had chosen to live, where the ancient archives were kept in caverns behind the falls, and where I had lived my entire life. I was one of only two humans living there, and we were so far from the boundary of Luntharda and Maldobar, so deep within the dense jungle, that odds were I'd never see another human … ever. Not that the gray elves were hostile to them, but making the journey through the dangerous jungle to reach it wasn't for the faint of heart. According to Kiran, humans didn't spend much time learning to climb and walk along the tree paths. This jungle—our world— terrified them.

I took the quiet back road to the edge of the city. I wasn't sure she'd be there. After all, Enyo was probably furious with me. She might never want to speak to me again. But I was willing to take that chance.

At the end of a long, narrow path that zigzagged treacherously up the side of the cliff face behind a few of the falls, I found her. She was sitting in our usual spot, her bare feet dangling over the edge of the mossy rocks. The water poured over the edge before her, a constant veil from the city below.

It was tricky to get to her. The boulders were slick and the edge was steep. But I'd come this way so many times I could have done it with my eyes closed.

"Did you come here to apologize?" Enyo wouldn't look at me as I sat down beside her.

"Would it help?" I hesitated and studied her profile. She didn't look thrilled to see me.

"No. And I'm not sure I would believe it, anyway."

I chewed on my lip.

"Your nose looks awful."

I poked at the fresh stitches gingerly. "Hurts, too."

"Good."

We sat in uncomfortable silence for what seemed like hours. Then, I took my bow off my back and placed it gently on her lap.

She stared and ran her fingers over it, then slowly raised her eyes to meet my gaze. "You're giving it to me?"

I nodded.

"But you'll lose your place to become a warrior and scout. You'll have to start all your training over."

"Yeah, well, I'll probably have to do that anyway." I shrugged. "Kiran doesn't think I'm ready. He thinks I'm selfish and probably stupid, too."

Enyo smirked and nudged me playfully with her elbow. "I kind of agree."

"As long as you don't hate me, that's all I care about." I sighed and sat back, resting my weight on my hands. "But I am sorry, you know. I shouldn't have brought you along."

She snorted sarcastically. "I saved your life! You'd be dead without me."

"As if."

"You're such an idiot, Reigh." She socked me in my sore shoulder.

I whimpered and rubbed my arm.

After a few seconds of sitting there, watching the falls and listening to the constant rumbling of the water, she looked my way again. She was still rubbing her hand along the bow I'd given her as though she were anxious about something.

"Do you remember what happened? After the stag charged for me?" she asked at last.

I tried to avoid her probing stare. "Do you?"

"No," she said quietly. "Everything got hazy. I was so afraid I must have fainted. I just remember feeling so cold. When I woke up, I was home. No one would tell me where you were. I thought you were dead, Reigh."

I swallowed hard.

"Was Kiran angry with you?"

"No more than usual."

She nibbled on her bottom lip. "My mother was furious. She said that we both should have died. It doesn't make any sense, does it? Why would the stag just decide to let us go? And what happened to the doe?"

I didn't want to answer any of her questions. Lying had never been one of my finer skills.

"My mother said it was a miracle," she said softly, like it was some kind of secret. "The spirit of the lapiloque saved us."

I stared at her. Seriously? I couldn't help it. I laughed out loud. "You think the ghost of some dead god saved us?"

Enyo pursed her lips, her cheeks flushed and her eyes narrowed. "Don't say it like that. He's real."

"Right." I rolled my eyes.

"He's not dead, Reigh. I know it."

"How? How can you possibly know that?"

Her expression became dreamy, like she was lost in her own private fantasy. "I can't explain it. I just do."

"That's ridiculous, even by your standards."

She glared at me. "Haven't you ever just believed in something, Reigh? Even though you couldn't see it or touch it?"

I thought about Noh and my body instantly got chilled.

"He's not just a myth. He *is* real." She spoke with such conviction; I almost wanted to believe her. "And he's coming back, just like he promised."

I cleared my throat. Maybe it wasn't such a bad thing to let lapiloque take the credit this time. After all, I didn't want Enyo to find out about Noh. "Right. Well, be sure to thank him when you meet him."

She socked me again. "You better thank him, too! We both should have died. My parents were furious. Father won't even speak to me."

"You think it would help if I apologized to them?"

"No." Her shoulders sagged some and she looked back down at my bow resting in her palms. "Besides, I … I'm not even sure I want to be a scout anymore."

My jaw dropped. "What? Because of today?"

Some of her wavy black hair fell from where she'd tucked it behind her pointed ear, blocking my view of her face. "That's not the reason. I've been thinking about it for a while now. I know Mother will be upset. She's spent a lot of time training me. But there's something else—something I've wanted to try for a long time."

I leaned in closer, a little afraid she wouldn't tell me. Enyo hadn't hit the gray elf version of puberty yet, so by their standards she was still a child. Even so, I could tell she was starting to change. Things were different. Growing up, she'd always told me what she thought about everything. Now she was keeping secrets, even from me. I tried not to let it faze me. It was bound to happen, sooner or later.

Still, I didn't like feeling like I was losing her trust.

Enyo turned a thin, forced smile back at me. "It's not a big deal. I haven't made up my mind yet, anyway."

"Don't lie. You're just trying to make me feel better," I grumbled and crossed my arms.

"No I'm not!" She giggled and tugged playfully at the rounded top part of my ear. "If I wanted to do that, then I'd say something like 'having a big scar on your nose will look so good!'"

I scowled. "Maybe it will."

That only made her laugh harder.

THREE

Things were quiet for a while and life got back to its normal rhythm for Kiran and me. I kept a low profile, following his orders to stay in the city and out of trouble. He didn't want me out of his sight. This was part three of my punishment, I guess. Part four was when he took the stitches out of my nose.

I spent long days working the clinic with him, tending to patients, washing linens, making medicines, and treating some of the minor injuries. It was easy work that kept me indoors and my mind occupied. But at the same time, it was smothering. Being trapped behind the walls of the clinic day in and day out was beginning to drive me crazy. I was safer, and yet I was aching for something more.

It didn't help that our little mishap had the city buzzing. Rumors swirled through the crowded markets and bustling public baths about how Enyo and I had miraculously escaped being mauled to death by a faundra stag. Some of our local friends even came by the clinic to ask me about it and check out my battle scar, although Kiran forbade me to tell them any details. Most people agreed with Enyo's theory that the spirit of the lapiloque had somehow intervened and protected us.

Only Kiran and I knew differently, and that was how it had to stay.

But Kiran didn't act like anything had happened. He went on running the clinic, treating patients for snake bites, broken bones, cuts, and all the usual daily ailments. He must have sensed my restlessness because he doubled my load of chores—probably to make sure I didn't have any spare time to do anything else stupid. After that, I didn't even have time to visit Enyo.

Early in the mornings, I ran errands on foot through the city squares, buying ingredients so I could spend the evenings grinding herbs and making medicines. Then I changed bed sheets, washed bandages, scrubbed Kiran's surgical tools, and helped him make the delivery kits for the midwives. Kiran was the best healer in the city, so his schedule was always packed and there was rarely a day when we didn't have a line of patients going out the door. We worked till sundown, ate our last meal of the day in awkward silence, and then I dragged myself upstairs to collapse into bed. That was it—my life in a nutshell.

On rare occasions, before the sun rose, Kiran left me in charge while he went out with the other warriors to lead scouting parties that kept a close watch on the city's outer perimeter. Every able-bodied warrior had to take a turn doing that. Well, everyone except for me.

For extra money, Kiran tutored some of the younger warriors, too. He taught them to fight and to shoot a bow, throw a dagger, or wield a scimitar with deadly accuracy. And all I got to do was watch him leave from the clinic doorway.

Being left at the clinic was beyond unfair. Before the incident, he'd at least let me be a sparring partner. I was his best student with a blade. But without a bow, I was going to have to wait until he decided I was trustworthy enough to be trained again.

Never, basically.

"Everyone else my age has already gone on their first hunt or done a patrol. They've brought down graulers, battled tigrex, and I'm just sitting here," I moaned.

Kiran was ignoring me, crouched at our fire pit stoking the coals so he could cook our dinner of roasted fish and potatoes.

"It's embarrassing. They're making fun of me, you know. All those warriors you're training call me names sometimes."

"I'll ask them to stop," he answered calmly.

"Right. Because getting my father to tell them off is really going to make them not treat me like a little kid," I scoffed.

Then I realized what I'd said.

Kiran pointed a harrowing glare in my direction. "I am *not* your father."

I cringed and bowed my head slightly. "I know."

My jaw clenched and I swallowed against the hard knot in my throat. Didn't he know how that made me feel? Or did he even care? Sure, I knew the gray elf culture and traditions. Bloodlines were traced through the mothers, so being a father was considered an immense honor and privilege. It's not a word they used lightly. It was basically the pinnacle of any man's entire life to earn that title.

But Kiran refused it—even if I had no one else to call father.

He went on working quietly, almost as though he were trying to ignore me. At last, he got up to shove a few small silver coins into my hand. "Go and buy bread. No wandering. Come straight back."

I managed to keep it together until I got outside.

As soon as I was a safe distance from the door, I kicked the crap out of the first small tree I came across. I wailed at it hard, breaking the trunk and stomping it into the ground over and over until I was out of breath.

When I stopped, my face was flushed and my heart was racing. I raked my long, dark red hair out of my eyes and sat down a step to cool off. I squeezed the coins in my fist and thought about all the things I could do with them instead of buying bread.

Maybe I could pay a seer to tell me who I really was. But as enticing as that seemed, I was terrified of what a mystic might see if they looked at me too closely. Nothing good, that's for sure. Good people didn't have bad spirits following them around.

Besides, Kiran didn't have to say it. I already knew why he didn't want me calling him father. I was the kid no one wanted. My own parents had left me to die—probably because someone had tipped them off about the monster I was destined to become. It was bad enough Kiran was stuck with me now, if he claimed me as his son, then every stupid, horrible thing I ever did would reflect badly on him. He didn't want a monster as his only progeny.

"*A spider is only a monster to a fly,*" a familiar, whispering voice echoed through my mind. It sent shivers over my skin.

"Go away, Noh," I muttered. "Leave me alone."

I saw his red, glowing eyes smoldering in the shadows nearby. He materialized from the gloom and began to approach me, the edges of his pitch-black body wavering like licking black flames. He always appeared as a wolf-like creature with tall pointed ears and a long bushy tail, but I knew Noh wasn't an animal at all. He was something else entirely.

"*I cannot leave.*" He padded over to lurk cautiously nearby.

"Why not?"

"*Because we are one, you and I.*"

"What is that supposed to mean?"

His toothy maw curled into a menacing smile, before he vanished into a puff of black mist without answering.

"Reigh?"

I looked up and saw Enyo climbing the steps toward me. She had a confused frown on her face.

"Who are you talking to?"

I shook my head and grumbled, "Myself."

Her expression became sympathetic. "You had another fight with Kiran?" she guessed.

I nodded.

Enyo stood over me, tapping my foot with hers. "Come on. I want to show you something." There was an excited edge to her voice I couldn't resist.

I got to my feet, cramming Kiran's coins into my pocket, and followed Enyo into the sleeping city. Moonlight broke the canopy, casting eerie shadows over our path as we ran along the narrow passes between buildings, scaling garden walls, darting over bridges, and climbing terraces to get to the rooftops. Enyo was light on her feet, springing the gaps from one roof to another like a cat. It was fun, and I couldn't keep from grinning as I landed and kicked into a roll, leaping immediately to my feet to keep running.

For an instant, I truly felt free.

Enyo darted ahead, her legs pumping faster and faster until she sprang, arms up to grasp a low hanging limb. She whirled over, using the branch like an acrobat to flip herself over and land on top of it. My attempt at the same trick wasn't as graceful and she giggled as I flailed to get my balance again.

"You're still so clumsy," she laughed as she crouched next to me. "Maybe that's why Kiran won't make you a scout."

I pretended to sulk—right up until she grabbed one of my ears to pull me in closer so she could plant a kiss on my cheek.

"Aw, Reigh, don't pull that face. You know I'm just teasing."

I blushed, unable to come up with a good comeback.

We lingered there for a minute or two, watching the moonlit mist sparkling like a swirling shower of diamonds over the city. Well, that's what she was looking at. I was looking at her. I wondered what she'd be like after she went through that gray elf change. Her hair would turn white and she'd look more mature, sure. But would she still like going running with me? Would she even want me around?

Before I could come up with the nerve to ask, Enyo took off again. I sprang down to chase after her, gulping in deep breaths of the cool, earthy jungle air. We dodged through the nearly empty market district. A few merchants were still closing down their shops. The blacksmith's forge still glowed in the gloom, his hammer making a rhythmic *clang-ping-clang-ping* sound and sending up a spray of sparks as he worked. A few shepherds shouted us as we startled the flock of faundra yearlings they were carefully herding through the street. Oops.

I followed Enyo up the side of another building, through someone's rooftop courtyard. Happy sounds of laughing and lively conversation came from inside the house—along with the smell of something delicious. The farther we ran, the brighter the air seemed. Skidding to a halt at the edge of the last residential rooftop, the palace loomed before us with its slender spires bathed in silver light. Behind it, the waterfalls made a constant roaring sound.

Enyo sat down and began taking off her sandals.

"What are you doing?" I squatted down next to her.

"Shh! We have to be quiet. Now hurry and take yours off, too," she whispered.

I left my shoes next to hers and followed as she started climbing down the side of the building. There was a high, white stone wall separating the palace from the rest of the city. It only had one gate, and I didn't think we were going to just go waltzing through it.

Enyo had found her own way inside.

Between two young trees was a place where the roots had cracked the stone, breaking it just enough for a small person to slip through. She'd obviously been here before, because she'd taken the time to dig out the ground around the hole so I might be able to squeeze through.

"You first," she whispered, grinning from one pointed ear to the other, as the moonlight shimmered brightly in her multicolored eyes.

Okay; I had a bad feeling about this.

As I wriggled and squirmed my way through the hole, I prayed to whatever god might be listening that I wouldn't get stuck.

My body came to a screeching halt.

Yep. Definitely stuck. The gods hated me.

I tried to turn and flail, but it wasn't any good. My shoulders were wedged in tight. I could imagine the look on Kiran's face as he dragged me out by the ankles. I'd never hold another bow as long as I lived. Behind me, I could feel Enyo trying to help. She was pushing on my rear as hard as she could. This was a new low.

Suddenly, with one great push from behind, my shoulders popped free and I launched out of the hole and onto the soft grass right on my face.

I sat up sputtering and brushing my hair out of my eyes. Then I got a good look around. I was sitting in what appeared to be a garden. Before me was a small pond surrounded by willow trees. Through the wavering fronds, I could see stone archways and open hallways leading away into the palace. There were statues everywhere carved into the shapes of different animals, and beautiful flowering water plants grew in the still water.

Voices echoed from across the pond. I saw a fluttering of white fabric. And then Enyo grabbed me from behind, dragging me into a hiding place behind one of the statues. She pressed a finger to my mouth as a warning. We had to stay quiet.

"She is so fragile, Jace. We must do something. She won't survive on her own," an old woman's voice pleaded. "If we take her to the temple, perhaps he will hear our prayers. I can't just sit back and do nothing."

"Araxie … I'm just as worried about her as you are," a man's deep voice answered. "But it's been so long. Nothing has changed. I think we need to look to our own medicines and methods—the things your people have relied on all these years. Or perhaps Kiran learned something about this when he studied in Maldobar."

"You don't believe, then?" The woman stepped into view, her long white gown billowing around her, a golden crown nestled in her snowy white hair. Her features were crinkled with age, and yet she stood with her shoulders back and her head held high.

The man moved in closer and took her hand. He wore dark green and silver robes with a circlet of silver on his head. He was an older man, too—but he was no gray elf. His features were rugged and his ears were like mine ... round and undeniably human.

I sucked in a sharp breath.

I'd never seen the king and queen this close before. They didn't make many public appearances and were much older than I expected. The king had a stubborn looking cut to his jaw as he considered his wife. Age hadn't bent him or made him frail, probably because he'd been a dragonrider before leaving the human kingdom of Maldobar. At least, that's what everyone said whenever they told the old stories.

With a square-cut white beard and long hair that was salt-and-pepper colored, he walked like a warrior as he moved to put his arms around the queen. The way his eyes sagged at the corners made him look exhausted, though.

"I can't lose another one. She is my only grandchild, Jace. The last of our bloodline. I can't bear it." The queen's voice weakened. She started to cry as the king held her close at his side, slowly walking with her back into the palace.

Once they were gone, Enyo and I exchanged a glance.

"Is that what this was all about? Eavesdropping on the royal family?" I whispered.

Enyo scowled. "Of course not. I want to show you something." She grabbed my wrist and dragged me out of our hiding place.

Across the garden, on the other side of the pond, stood a large, flat stone tablet made of bone white marble. It had been polished until it was completely smooth and engraved with an intricate picture. It was a scene depicting a young man in strange armor holding a round object in the air over his head. I'd never seen him before, but I immediately knew who he was.

I'd heard the stories, after all. Everyone had. With his distinctly-human stature and pointed ears, wearing a carved pendant around his neck and the cloak of a dragonrider—it could only be one person.

Jaevid Broadfeather. The lapiloque.

The rest of the scene carved into the stone was just as detailed. There was an elven maiden on one side of him, and a human king on the other. Both were kneeling in great respect while their armies placed their weapons on the ground.

"It's from the end of the Gray War. When the lapiloque took up the god stone and destroyed it so it could never fall into evil hands again." Enyo was smiling again, her expression that of dreamy-eyed wonder. "You see? He was real."

"Just because someone carved it on a piece of rock doesn't make it true."

"And just because you don't believe in him doesn't mean it's not," she countered.

I pursed my lips. "What is it with girls and falling for these hero types, anyway?"

Enyo's cheeks turned as red as ripe apples. "I never said I liked him like *that*!"

"You didn't have to," I teased. "Just look at those rippling arms he's got, eh? I bet you dream about him."

"I do not!" She started after me with her fists tight.

I backed up and laughed, darting out of the way as she took

a swing at my face. "I bet you can't stop thinking about what it would be like to get whisked away on the back of his dragon."

Enyo dove at me again, rearing back and trying to land a punch wherever she could. Then suddenly, she stopped short. I saw her face go pale and her eyes grew wide, focusing on something—or someone—behind me.

I felt the chill a second too late. My breath turned to white fog in the air. Slowly, I began to turn around.

Noh was standing right behind me, his red eyes smoldering like coals against the night. Only, this time he didn't look like a wolf. He looked like a human teenager with long, unruly hair, a squared jaw, thin frowning mouth, and the same long scar across the bridge of his nose that I now had.

He looked *exactly* like me.

Only, instead of dark, muddy red hair his was black. His skin was a strange ashen gray color, and his eyes had no center—just bottomless pools of vivid red light.

For an instant, I was captivated. I stood there marveling at the sight of him, totally unafraid. Why did he look like me? Was this something he'd always been able to do? I resisted the urge to reach out and offer him my hand, just to see what he would do.

Then I saw his attention shift. He stared at Enyo, and I could sense the change in his mood before a wicked smirk curled across his features. He licked his lips hungrily.

"No," I shouted and stumbled away from him. "You can't have her. Leave now!"

Noh tilted his head to the side slightly. He studied Enyo for a second longer and then looked back to me. His smile widened, showing slightly pointed canine teeth.

"I mean it! *Leave!*" I shouted louder, throwing my arms out as I planted myself between him and Enyo. "I won't let you touch her. You don't get to hurt anyone unless I say so!"

"*As you wish, my master.*" He chuckled, his whispering voice sending chills over my skin. With a flourish of his hands, he bowed at the waist and swiftly began to dissolve, vanishing into fine black mist.

The sound of his laugh was still hanging in the air even after he was gone. I tried forcing myself to calm down, but I was angry and panicked. I couldn't think straight. Enyo had seen him. No one else had *ever* been able to see him before—not even Kiran.

The situation was changing from my private problem with one random bad spirit to something I didn't even have a name for.

"R-Reigh?" Enyo's voice trembled.

"It's fine! It's nothing!"

"Nothing? Are you insane?"

I bit down hard on the inside of my cheek.

"Reigh, who was that?" She grabbed onto my arm so I would look at her. "What's going on?"

I jerked away and started for the hole in the garden wall. "Nothing! You didn't see anything! Just forget it ever happened!"

Enyo darted in front of me, planting her hands on my shoulders and forcing me to stop. "No! Tell me what's going on!"

I wanted to. I really did. But as often as we argued, there was one thing Kiran and I both agreed on: no one could ever know about the things I could do. I was dangerous. And while he called me master, Noh was becoming more and more difficult to control.

I couldn't risk it—I couldn't let him hurt Enyo. I'd let this thing, whatever it was, tear me apart before I ever let anything happen to her.

"No," I growled at her fiercely. "Get away from me. Never come near me again."

Her eyes widened and her mouth opened, but no sound came out. Slowly, she took her hands off me. "You don't mean that. I know you, Reigh. You're my best friend. Please, just talk to me. You can trust—"

I shoved her out of my way hard enough she fell back onto the grass. "You're wrong. You don't know anything about me. I'm not your friend. You're annoying and … a waste of my time. I can't even stand the sight of you. Stay away from me, Enyo. I mean it."

When she didn't answer, I started running.

I dove for the hole in the wall and crammed myself back through it as fast as I could. I staggered to my feet on the other side and began sprinting through the city streets, past the empty market squares with gurgling fountains and down dark alleys crowded with wooden crates. I didn't bother going back for my shoes.

I ran for home.

FOUR

He knew.

As soon as I burst through the door, barefooted and without any bread, Kiran knew something bad had happened. In an instant, he was on his feet and racing to shut and bolt the front door to our clinic. He grabbed the collar of my shirt, dragging me into the living room before he went around dousing all the lamps in the house. The glow from the embers smoldering in the fire pit gave off just enough light that I could see him blur around me, his expression grim as he shut all the windows and closed the drapes.

Our home became as dark as a tomb. Long shadows climbed the walls, taunting my frazzled nerves as I stood, wringing the hem of my tunic between my sweaty fingers. I was too afraid to look at them closely—afraid they might begin to move or take the shape of *him* again. My heart drummed in my ears and my whole body was numb. Whether it was because of Noh or just pure terror, I wasn't sure.

"Tell me what happened," Kiran commanded in a quiet, eerily calm voice. He was standing in front of me, holding my shoulders so I couldn't turn away.

I tried. But when I opened my mouth, nothing would come out. Questions whirled through my brain. Was I losing control? What if I couldn't get Noh to leave? What if he hurt someone? Would Kiran abandon me, too? Where would I go? What would I do? Would I ever find a home again?

My throat grew tight. I squeezed my eyes shut and bowed my head, trying to silence the whispering doubts.

Suddenly, Kiran pulled me in and wrapped his arms around me tightly, holding me like I was a small child.

"It's all right, Reigh," he said. "Whatever happened, I'll fix it. You're going to be okay."

I buried my face against his shoulder. Regardless of what he said, he couldn't fix it—not this time. And when I told him what had happened, I think he began to realize that, too.

Whatever I was becoming, I wouldn't be able to hide it for much longer. Noh was getting stronger, and for better or worse, he and I were bound somehow. I didn't know how or why, but he was here because of me. I couldn't get rid of him.

Kiran sat across the hearth from me, quiet despair creeping into his features as he stared at the flames. For a few minutes, he didn't say a word. We sat in heavy silence, watching the flames hiss and dance in the darkness. Dinner was finished and while it smelled good, neither of us had touched it.

A sound echoed through the house.

Knock, knock, knock.

Someone was at the door. My stomach did a frantic backflip and my heart hit the back of my throat. Kiran jumped up and snatched his scimitar off the hook by the door. I started to get up, too, but he snapped his fingers and gestured for me to stay put. I did—at least, until I heard him open the front door. Then I crept to the doorway. It was a long way down the hall, past the examination room to the front door, but sound bounced off the stone walls of our home like a cave.

"W-we apologize for the late hour, master. We bring word, an urgent request from Her Majesty the Queen," a young man's voice stammered with nervousness as he addressed Kiran.

My stomach did another backflip. Had Enyo been caught on the castle grounds?

"What is it?" Kiran demanded.

There was a rattling commotion and the sound of the door shutting. Whoever it was, Kiran had let them inside.

"News from the border. Maldobar is under siege. Northwatch burns and a company of human soldiers has retreated into the jungle. They are headed this way, but they travel with many wounded and no supplies. It is doubtful they will survive to reach the city," the young man reported. "Her Majesty would like you to lead a rescue mission to intercept them with supplies and guide them safely here. Your knowledge of the human language and customs would be essential."

"Leaving when? I have responsibilities to my patients here,"

Kiran spoke sharply.

"Immediately. The errand is most urgent. It's believed that one of these men is a member of Maldobar's royal family."

There was a tense silence. I waited, holding my breath, until at last I heard Kiran let out a growling, frustrated sigh.

"Very well. I'll need some time to arrange for my boy to stay with someone. Bring shrikes. We leave at dawn," he answered.

There were a few mutterings of gratitude and the retreating sound of footsteps. The front door snapped shut and I heard Kiran coming back down the hall. Quickly, I slipped away, up the stairs, and into my bedroom. I left the door cracked and flopped down onto my bed, jerking the blankets up to my chin.

I pretended to be asleep when I heard Kiran push the door open in a bit further. He sighed again, whispering something under his breath that I couldn't make out. Then he pulled the door closed and I heard his footsteps fading away down the hallway toward his own room.

Minutes passed and I waited until the house was quiet. Kiran hadn't come back out of his room. I figured he was either busy packing or stealing a few hours of sleep before he had to leave.

I got up and opened my closet, digging through my stuff until I unearthed a backpack made from soft, tanned leather. It was stocked with a few basic supplies, two days' worth of rations, and something else—something Kiran didn't know I had.

I pulled the long, curved blades out of the bag and held them firmly in my hands. The soft leather grips felt at home there, as though they'd been made especially for me. They hadn't, of course. These blades were a lot older than I was. Each pommel was plated with silver and set with chips of mica to make the shape of a snarling snagwolf's head.

The gray elves called these weapons "kafki," and only the finest fighters for the royal family had wielded them. Each blade was twelve inches long and curved, like a pair of small shotels or scythes. But that wasn't what made them unique.

The blades weren't made of metal. They were made of wood that was as white as bone and harder than iron—wood from the most dangerous predator in all Luntharda. Greevwood trees were legendary, even among the gray elves. They were subtle monsters, not something you'd think twice about until one had its roots around your neck and was slowly digesting you.

Gruesome? Oh yeah. But their wood was as prized as it was hard to gather. Once you cut away the bark and exposed the white meat of the tree beneath, you only had a short time to cut and mold it. After that, it became harder than iron. The elves liked making knives, swords, and scimitars from it because they couldn't be broken and they never went dull.

I'd come across these purely by chance, and Kiran didn't know anything about them. I was afraid that if he ever saw them, he'd take them from me and insist on giving them back to their rightful owner—whoever that was.

I'd found them during one of my many outings with Enyo, several years ago. After all, that encounter with the stag wasn't the first time we'd been out in the jungle alone. That day, we'd ventured farther than either of us had ever been before, out to one of the burial groves. That was where gray elves traditionally buried their dead and planted a new tree atop the gravesite—something else they'd begun doing in honor of the lapiloque. We were exploring when I'd gotten one of those familiar, harrowing chills. Only, this one hadn't involved Noh. As soon as I stopped to look back ... I saw these. They were lying in a clear area between two of the trees, placed carefully on a patch of green moss like someone had left them there especially for me.

Only, there was no one else in sight.

Enyo thought they were a gift from the lapiloque or maybe even the foundling spirits. Whoever left them there, I wasn't about to turn down a free pair of Greevewood blades. All I had to do was keep them out of sight until I became an official scout—then it wouldn't matter where they came from.

It wasn't that weapons were forbidden to me. After all, Kiran had given me my first bow and taught me everything I knew about how to handle a blade. He'd trained me to wield a spear, a scimitar, fire a bow, how to throw daggers with lethal proficiency, and even how to fight with a human-styled sword. But I doubted if even he had any experience with kafki. They were considered an ancient weapon, used more for decoration now than anything else.

Maybe I'd bring them back into style.

I dug through my wardrobe for my scouting clothes—the best thing for traveling in Luntharda when you didn't want to be spotted. Since I wasn't a scout, I'd never worn them before, so they were still new and creased. They'd been waiting for me at the bottom of the drawer for a year.

Quickly and quietly, I took off my casual clothes and put

on the black undergarments. I tucked the sleeveless black silk shirt into the matching long black pants, and bound each of my legs from my ankle to my knee with a strip of thick, black canvas, making sure to tuck my pants down into it snugly. It was padding for running, skidding, rolling, leaping, and climbing through the trees. Then I did the same with my arms, binding from my wrists to my elbows with several layers.

The outer tunic was made of something thicker, and it was midnight blue with a silver border stitched into the elbow-length sleeves and around the base. It came down to my knees and was split up the sides so I could move easily. Over it, I buckled a light, black leather jerkin and a belt with sheaths for the two Greevwood kafki. I laced up my nicest pair of sandals, the ones with soles made especially for gripping even the slickest of tree limbs, and threw my pack over my shoulders.

The night air rushed in when I opened my bedroom window. Cool, sweet, humid, and delicious—I breathed it in deeply and climbed out onto the ledge.

A twinge of pain pinched in my chest. Crouched on the windowsill, I looked behind me at my childhood bedroom.

I had two choices.

Kiran was going to leave at dawn. He was going to strike out into the jungle, leading a group of warriors to help those human soldiers. And once again, I was going to get left behind. No way he'd take me with him, especially after what happened with Noh today. So, either I could stay here, hiding in the clinic like a coward and trying to keep my dark companion at bay while pretending there wasn't something seriously wrong with me.

Or I could do what Kiran didn't have the guts to do:
I could kick myself out.

He was probably hoping this would all blow over, that I'd regain control of Noh, or that he might even leave altogether and I'd get to finish out my life as a normal person. But deep down, the truth wasn't something either of us could change. Noh had killed once. He would do it again, and whether I liked it or not—whether it was fair or not—I would be the one to blame.

No one here would be safe from Noh unless I was gone.

Clenching my teeth, I looked out across the sleeping city of Mau Kakuri and knew I couldn't stay here anymore.

It was time to break free.

This was my only chance. I had a few hours to get a head start before Kiran figured out I was gone. He wouldn't be able to look for me, not right away. He'd gotten orders from the Queen, so he was obligated. I had to be long gone by the time he wrestled with his better sense and decided to ignore it and come looking for me.

First challenge—leaving the city. At least that was one I knew I could pull off. Enyo and I had done it dozens of times already. Despite having fairly tight security protecting the city perimeter, I was confident I could slip out without having to work too hard. The scouts on the ground rode on trained faundra, patrolling every five minutes to make sure no ground-based predators wandered in. The scouts navigating the tree paths above came by less frequently. After all, it wasn't as though no one could leave the city if they wanted to. But the fact that I was, you know, still known as a *kid* might give them reason to stop me to figure out where I was going at this hour.

I moved hastily down the stone paved streets to the edge of the city, slipping from shadow to shadow until I got to the boundary. There, the jungle rose before me like a swelling tidal wave, ready to drag me under. Dense, dark, deep, and dangerous, you had to be a special kind of stupid to go out there alone at night.

No one had ever accused me of being all that smart.

I waited, hiding behind a cluster of ferns, until I saw a scout pass by, riding in the saddle of a large faundra doe. As soon as she was gone, I raced for the nearest trunk and started to climb, scaling the side of the giant tree and clambering onto the first low limb almost twenty feet off the jungle floor. My pulse raced and my senses were honed, listening for the faint footsteps of man or beast.

There was nothing—just the eerie, humming songs of the frogs and insects. I took a deep breath, my insides buzzing with a panicked sort of excitement as I got moving again. My breathing hitched as I crossed the border into the wild, leaving the city behind me. There were no scouts anywhere in sight. I was free. Wherever I wanted to go, whatever I wanted to do—

no one could stop me now. I was my own man.

I ran for the trees and struck out toward Maldobar. That's where I had to go. I wanted to see it for myself, the land where I was born. A kingdom filled with people with round ears like mine, and where dragons ruled the wide, open skies. It would take days to get to the boundary line, and that was if I didn't stop or get eaten by something first.

It sounded good at the time.

I kept up a fierce pace, sprinting along the tree-paths until my lungs burned and there were miles between Mau Kakuri and me. The rising sun was just beginning to break through the cracks in the canopy overhead, casting long beams of ethereal golden light all the way to the ground below. Fresh dew dripped off every petal and leaf. Colorful little birds squabbled and chased one another through the limbs.

And right about now, Kiran would be figuring out that I was gone.

Clenching my teeth, I pushed those thoughts from my mind and listened to the jungle instead. I couldn't hear the rumble of the falls or smell their moisture in the air anymore. Instead, I heard the ambient sounds of life all around me—the dripping of dewdrops pattering from the leaves, the rustle of bird wings, the chattering of insects, and the distant calls of sarbien monkeys. I spooked a young shrike that was napping in a sunny spot out on an open branch, warming his translucent wings. He hissed at me as I darted by, but didn't give chase.

Finally, I stopped to catch my breath and check my bearings. The jungle was a tangled mass of dense greenery and entwined tree branches. Getting lost would have been easy, but the first thing Kiran had ever taught me was how to navigate. It's the first thing all gray elves learned because if you couldn't find your way back home, you were guaranteed to get eaten by something.

The elves had their own system of roadways along the broad limbs of the trees, far above the jungle floor. They marked them with symbols engraved into certain places on the trees. A circle meant a road leading north. A circle with a horizontal line through it meant east, one with a vertical line meant west, and one with a single dot in the center meant south. Easy, right?

But those were just the main pathways that led between major cities. There were plenty of other destinations in the jungle like temples, mineral springs, hunting grounds, burial sites, and things like that. There were also warnings of things to avoid—like a grove of Greevwood trees that had sprung up too close to a city or village.

Novice warriors and scouts weren't supposed to leave those marked paths. But if you ever found yourself lost in an unknown part of the jungle, far from a city where someone might not hear you calling for help, there was always *the* tree.

Kiran told me that the humans navigated using the stars. Because of the dense jungle canopy, we didn't get to see the stars often. Or the moon, either, for that matter. However, if you climbed high enough to peek out of the canopy, you could see the tree from almost anywhere. Day or night, winter or summer, the tree was there. It never changed—never dropped its leaves in fall or grew an inch in springtime.

Paligno had planted that tree when the lapiloque had died—

or at least, that's what everyone believed. They said it had just sprung up, willed to being by the ancient god of life to cover the lapiloque's burial place and guard the entrance to his tomb. That was the reason the gray elves had adopted the custom of planting trees over the gravesites of their own loved ones. Regardless of how it had gotten there, the lapiloque's tree had grown to a size that towered over all the others in Luntharda. It loomed over the canopy, and could be seen for miles and miles. It was a fixed point, which is all you needed to navigate.

I'd only seen the tree once. When I was ten, Kiran had taught me how to climb up to the very top of the canopy and hoist myself through the barrier of leaves and brambles. Up there, the air blew freely, the sky was endless, and the sun was like a warm caress on my skin. I could see the tree from Mau Kakuri. It wasn't that far away, though it was closer to the boundary line with Maldobar than the city. Kiran said few people went to see it now. It was out of great respect for lapiloque that they let him sleep in peace, leaving the temple grounds untouched and the area around it free of civilization. They believed sincerely that one day he would rise again.

A load of crap, really. If there was one thing I knew for certain, it's that dead people stayed dead.

FIVE

After two days, I was exhausted.

I ran until my feet were so sore and blistered from my shoes I could barely stand to take them off. I didn't dare stop for more than a few minutes; just long enough to eat, drink, and catch my breath. I knew every second that passed meant Kiran was gaining on me.

I wasn't going to make it easy on him. I doubled back on my own steps occasionally, avoided leaving as much trace evidence as possible, but I knew Kiran was a keen hunter—arguably one of the best in Mau Kakuri. He would find my trail and he would be relentless in following it. My only chance was to get to the boundary first.

I stood out in Luntharda. My red hair, thicker human build, height, even my voice was a dead giveaway that I wasn't one of them. But if I could cross over into Maldobar, I could vanish into the tapestry of other humans without a trace. He'd never be able to find me.

At least, that's what I was hoping.

I limped along a narrow branch, surveying the ground, searching for a good, secluded place to hide and rest. The rushing roar of water drowned out the other jungle sounds. I could smell it close by like a crisp sweetness in the air.

Generally, this wouldn't be a good place to stop and make camp. Water meant lots of foot traffic—both from elves and from prey animals. Prey meant predators, which was something I didn't particularly want to contend with when I didn't have a bow.

But my water skin was empty. I was parched, my feet were aching, and I was far enough from any village or city that I felt confident I wouldn't see anyone else who might be able to tell my very angry parental guardian which direction I'd gone.

I began the steep climb down out of the trees. Either I was going to die or get something to drink, it was as simple as that. Slowly, step-by-step, I made my way across the damp soil to the edge of the water. I gave one last long look around and then cupped my hands into the water.

I drank until I could feel my stomach sloshing, and then I slung my bag off my shoulders. I refilled my water skin and slipped it back into my bag before I started taking off my shoes. I had angry blisters between my toes and my heels were bruised. Soaking them made it a little better, though.

After catching a few small fish by hand, I packed up my

things and retreated to the safety of the trees. I chose a dark place on a smaller, narrower limb to curl up and eat my dinner—raw. Gross, but I couldn't risk lighting a fire. Fire drew curious creatures from the depth of the jungle and that was exactly the kind of attention I was trying to avoid.

With my back against the trunk and my knees pulled to my chest, I gazed up at the interwoven branches of the trees overhead. It wasn't exactly comfortable. I was cold and sore. Sitting that way made my neck cramp. I couldn't help but think about how, miles from here, there was a soft, warm bed in a safe house where I could have been sleeping. Kiran wasn't a great cook, but at least whatever he made for us wasn't raw. I wondered where he was. For all I knew, he could be just a few feet away, watching me right this second, waiting to see if I would give up and go back home.

I sort of hoped he was.

I thought about Enyo, too. I hadn't even said goodbye. Our last words hadn't been nice ones. I'd said horrible things just so she would stay away from me. Kiran was right; she was just a child, too naïve to see that nothing good would ever come from being close to me.

Sure, I had gotten her into trouble plenty of times over the years. But this situation wasn't anything like those. This wasn't some prank, and I'd never set out to intentionally hurt her. If I let her get close to me now, knowing what Noh might do, I was intentionally putting her life at risk. And that wasn't so different from murder. Not in my mind, anyway.

For her sake, I hoped she would just forget about me.

I started nodding off as I listened to the sound of the water and imagined myself being carried away on it, weightless in the cool current.

I wondered if that's what it felt like to fly.

There were voices in the dark.

Someone was shouting.

I bolted to my feet out of a sound sleep, my mind hazy and my hands immediately going to my weapons. I looked around in a daze. But I was alone—nothing but the sound of the rushing water below.

At first, I thought it had been a dream. Or maybe Noh was playing tricks on me. He did that sometimes, the jerk.

Then I heard it again—the voices of men shouting echoed through the trees. My pulse raced. I squeezed my blades tighter.

Kiran? No. I knew he wouldn't be that stupid. Making that kind of noise in the wild at night was essentially a death wish.

Besides the voices sounded foreign. I couldn't understand them, at first, but then I recognized their language.

They were speaking the human tongue.

The noise carried through the darkness, making it hard to pinpoint where it was coming from. Then, out of the corner of my eye, I saw a flicker of light. Fire winked in the gloom.

Fire *and* noise? Seriously, how stupid could they be?

I crept closer, stalking carefully through the shadows along the overhanging limbs. A high-pitched yipping and guttural snarling made me freeze in place.

There they were—a company of men crowded together with torches and swords raised, pinned at the edge of the river by a snarling pack of snagwolves. The men wore thick armor made of metal and long cloaks of red and blue. Their hair was cut short and their ears were rounded. They were human—just like me.

Two of them were badly wounded and bound to makeshift stretchers made from limbs and vines. Their comrades gathered around them to stand guard against their attackers. Meanwhile, the snagwolves circled, their noses twitching at the smell of blood and fresh meat.

Suddenly, two of the men stepped off into the water. They tried to swim for the opposite bank, but the current was swift and their heavy metal armor weighed them down. They sank like stones, disappearing beneath the depths. There was nothing anyone could do.

The snagwolves closed in, their bright green eyes shining wickedly under the orange glow of the torches. They were spooked by the fire, although not enough to be discouraged. They hunted as a unit, and were as cautious as they were cunning. Their gnarled, green-tinted pelts mimicked the texture of roots and plants so they blended in perfectly with the jungle. They could hide in plain sight, and their powerful jaws could crush your bones to splinters. Once one got his teeth into you, there was little chance you'd ever be able to pry him off.

It was bad news for the soldiers.

The men tried to muster. One of them kept shouting over all the noise, calling to the others. He wore a different cloak than the rest, more intricate with a golden eagle embroidered onto the back.

The sight of that emblem struck a chord in my brain. That was the mark of Maldobar's king—so these had to be the men Kiran had been asked to find.

It was a miracle they'd made it this far. But at the rate things were going, they were all going to die long before Kiran or anyone else found them.

That is, unless *someone* was willing to get their hands dirty.

A snagwolf lunged at the leader of the soldiers, locking its powerful jaws around his calf. The man shouted and raised his sword to strike. Suddenly, a second snagwolf got a mouthful of his cloak and dragged him to the ground. His comrades stepped in to help, and were immediately attacked by the rest of the pack.

It was total chaos.

I clenched my teeth and coiled my legs beneath me; gripping my blades so tightly my fingers went numb. I took a breath and leapt out of the tree, hurling myself into the air with my arms spread wide. As soon as I felt my feet touch the ground, I kicked into a roll to ease the impact. It still knocked the wind out of me, and I was seeing stars when I sprang to my feet again.

But there was no time to recover. The fight was on.

I plunged both of my blades into the side of the nearest snagwolf. The creature shrieked in pain, drawing the attention of the rest of the pack. Their wicked green eyes turned to me, recognizing me as the greatest threat to their dinner plans.

Ripping my kafki free of the dead snagwolf, I sank into a crouch as the pack converged, attacking me in waves of snapping vice grip jaws and razor-sharp teeth. I whirled my weapons, spinning through maneuvers and slicing through the monsters one after another. I could hear Kiran's voice in my head, chiseling his training methods into my brain. *Don't think. Feel the rhythm of your enemy. Good. Now, react. Counter. Faster. Move with him. Never drop your arms. Watch your footing. Keep your breathing steady. Good.*

I kicked one snagwolf square across the snout, sending it rolling while I rammed my weapon through another's chest. My white blades were stained pink with blood. I was more focused than I'd ever been. My blood ran hot through my veins. I ducked as a snagwolf leapt at me, kicking into a roll and thrusting both kafki upwards into the belly of the animal as it sailed past me.

Out of nowhere, my shoulder exploded with pain. I yelled. One of the snagwolves had jumped me from behind. Now I was in its grip. Its jaws clamped down on my collarbone with crushing force, threating to snap it in half.

I flailed, tried to writhe free, but the more I fought, the harder the animal squeezed. My arm started to go numb. I felt my weapon slip out of my hand. Not good.

Suddenly, the snagwolf let me go.

I dropped to the earth, reeling from the pain and the sensation of my own hot blood soaking through my clothes. When I looked back, I saw the leader of the human soldiers standing over me. He had rammed his sword up to the hilt through the snagwolf's neck. One wrenching flip of his wrist twisted the blade and cut the monster's head clean off.

He looked down at me, breathless and pasty with terror. He asked me something in the human language, but I was too delirious to understand.

Then I saw it. Another one of the creatures stalking him from behind, green eyes winking in the dark, shoulders pumping in preparation for the attack.

I didn't think. There wasn't time. I still had one blade in my hand when I sprang up, shoved the human leader out of the way, and met the snagwolf in mid-air. I howled like a maniac and swung, jamming my kafki into the open mouth of the beast.

We fell together. The snagwolf landed on top of me, my blade still lodged in its open mouth—rammed straight through to the back of its head. The full weight of the beast bore down on me, crushing my lungs so I couldn't get a good breath until I managed to wrench myself out from under it.

I didn't have either of my weapons anymore when I staggered to my feet. My head was swimming with pain. Blood ran down my back. My vision started to spot and tunnel and I had to clench my teeth and flex my legs to force blood back up into my head.

Then I saw them—four angry snagwolves prowling toward me from all sides.

I was going to die.

I bent down to snatch up the nearest object I could use for a weapon: a big rock.

I raised the rock and shouted at the snagwolves, daring them to come at me.

The monsters recoiled, hesitating. They winced, tucked their tails, and bolted away from me. I stood in stunned silence, watching as the rest of the snagwolves retreated into the jungle, yelping and shrieking in panic like they couldn't get away fast enough.

A cold blast of breath tickled the back of my neck. I dropped the rock and slowly turned around.

Noh was lurking behind me, his form boiling like a menacing black cloud. He looked like a large, shadowy wolf again, which was kind of a relief. But that didn't mean I was happy to see him—even if he had saved my life.

His red eyes glowed in the dark and his mouth was twisted into a smug, wolfish grin. *"Death. Blood. Carnage. Slaughter. Such a glorious smell!"*

I frowned. "I won't thank you."

"You don't need to. I am eager to serve you, my master."

My gaze followed the trail the snagwolves had taken back into the jungle. "Go, then," I said at last. "Make sure they don't return."

"Yes, as you command." Noh's outline shivered with enthusiasm and he vanished without a sound or trace.

When I turned around again, I was met with a crowd of bloodied, wide-eyed human soldiers. They were gathering around me cautiously, and I could sense the tension in the air as they looked me over. I was a strange sight for them, a human dressed like a gray elf accompanied by a weird-black-misty-demon-thing. Not something you come across every day, even in Luntharda. They were eyeing me up as though they weren't sure whose side I was on.

Unfortunately, I didn't get a chance to argue my case. I smiled, managed a small wave of greeting ... and passed out cold.

SIX

My body refused to respond. My lungs wouldn't work. I couldn't even get my eyes to open. Everything spun, like I was being whipped around in a churning whirlpool. I couldn't tell up from down. There was nothing—nothing but darkness, confusion, and that aching, squeezing sensation in my chest as I ran out of air.

Was this what dying felt like?

"*There you are.*" A woman's whispering voice echoed through the dark, chilling me to the marrow. "*I was wondering when you would find your way.*"

W-what? I couldn't even take in enough air to reply.

"*It's time. You must awaken he who sleeps. You need his blood—pure blood—to complete the ritual.*"

Ritual? He who sleeps? Nothing about that made sense. I

didn't recognize that voice; I couldn't even concentrate on it because I was spinning faster and faster. Air—I needed air!

Something or someone smacked me across the face. Instantly, the spinning stopped. There was cold, moist earth underneath me. Strange voices muttered in the human language, seeming to come from all around. At first, it was just garbled and confusing. But as my head started to clear, I understood what they were saying.

"Wake up, boy!"

"Maybe he's dead?"

"He's not dead. Look there, he's breathing."

I was? Then why did it feel like I was still drowning? If I could just move a little, maybe I could break this trance before it crushed the life out of me.

"I think I saw his eye twitch!"

"Shh! Stand back! You're too close."

"He's not moving."

"Maybe if we poured a bit of water over his head? I've seen that work before."

Someone smacked my face a little harder. "Come on, boy! You're not dead. A reckless fool, maybe, but not a dead one."

Suddenly, my eyes popped open and I gulped in a deep, frantic breath of the cool night air. I wheezed and wheezed as my vision slowly cleared. Lying on my back, I stared up into the glare of torchlight. The human soldiers were crowded around me, peering down at where I was sprawled out on the ground. Their expressions were mixture of fear and bewilderment. When I stirred, a few of them jumped back.

I recognized their leader. He was kneeling next to me, and was apparently the one who'd been smacking me into consciousness. When he saw me moving, he let out a heavy sigh of relief. "Welcome back to the realm of the living."

"L-lumori," I rasped in elven.

"What?"

I struggled to remember the human word. I hadn't spoken that language to anyone but Kiran before, and even then, only on special occasions—like when I was being lectured. "L-lights. Douse the lights."

The soldiers exchanged confused glances.

"The lights will bring them," I said. "More ... from the darkness."

They didn't stop to ask who, what, or why. Immediately, all the soldiers began extinguishing their torches, either by stamping out the flames or running over to dip them in the water. Darkness swallowed us, and the soldiers gathered in close again. I guess they were warier of what might be hiding in the dark than me. Maybe that was because they'd also seen Noh.

The human leader helped me sit up. The pain in my shoulder from the snagwolf's bite made my vision spot and blur again. I clenched my teeth, unable to stop myself from shaking. The wound had been crudely bandaged, but I was going to need some real medical attention soon.

The air was tense. Everyone was looking at me, like they were expecting me to suddenly attack them, too. Really, though, I was in shock. I stared wordlessly at all the human men. I'd never seen so many.

"We'd all be dead if you hadn't showed up," the leader said. He gave me a broad, friendly smile and patted my back reassuringly. "You're quite a fighter for such a young man. What's your name?"

I hesitated. I didn't have a reason not to trust this guy—after all, he'd prevented that snagwolf from tearing my arm off. But it was kind of intense to answer questions with everyone gawking at me like that. I glanced around at my captive audience and lowered my head in embarrassment.

The leader seemed to get it. His expression softened and he gave me a sympathetic smile before commanding his men to prepare to move out. No one questioned him. They all scurried around, gathering their belongings and tending to their injuries, leaving us alone for the time being. There were considerably fewer of them now. The snagwolves had dragged more than a couple of them off into the jungle. Judging by the two smashed wooden stretchers, they'd taken the easiest prey first.

I shuddered to think I'd almost joined them in that fate.

"Just when I thought I'd seen everything this jungle could possibly surprise me with, a human teenager pops out of the trees and saves my life by fighting like a gray elf."

The leader chuckled as he sat down next to me. He wasn't very old, but he wasn't anywhere close to my age, either. It was hard for me to tell with humans. They wore their age more harshly than elves did. But the shaggy golden hair that fell around his neck didn't have any traces of white in it, and his tanned, sun-bronzed skin wasn't all that wrinkled. He did have a few tired-looking lines in the corners of his dark blue eyes, but the squared cut to his jaw still made him seem fiercely capable.

"Reigh," I answered at last. "My name is Reigh."

"Well met, Reigh. You can call me Aubren." He offered to shake my hand. Kiran had told me about that human gesture—it was a sign of friendship and trust.

I awkwardly shook it. Learning to be human was going to be harder and stranger than I'd anticipated.

"We need to move soon," I said. "We can't stay here. The smell of blood will bring other predators."

He looked worried. "Are you willing to go with us?"

It wasn't like I had a choice. They weren't going to last long otherwise.

"We need to make our way to the royal city of the gray elves as soon as possible. I am seeking an audience with Queen Araxie. Can you take us there?" His expression became earnest, almost desperate.

I couldn't hold eye contact for long. Talking to him, sitting next to him—it was bizarre to suddenly be this close to another human.

"What's the matter?" Aubren looked worried, like he was afraid I might refuse. "You don't know where it is?"

I scratched nervously at the back of my neck with my good arm. "N-no, I mean, it's just … I've never met another human before."

He raised his eyebrows in surprise. "Never?"

"Well, I've seen King Jace before. He's human, too. But I've never actually met or talked to him before."

"I see." I could tell by his tone he thought that was strange.

Poor guy. He had no clue just how strange I actually was.

"You're a long way from Mau Kakuri. But the Queen knows you're here. She's already dispatched a scouting party to find you and help bring you back safely."

Aubren's broad shoulders went slack. He slowly closed his eyes and bowed his head. For a moment, I thought he was upset. But then I heard him chuckle. "That's the first good news I've heard in months."

I started to get up, wincing and cursing under my breath at the pain in my shoulder. I was going to have to do something more permanent to fix the wound. Or rather, I was going to have to get someone to *help* me do it. But first, we had to get away from here—away from the water and the smell of fresh blood.

"I know a place we can take refuge for the night." I nodded for him to follow. "But we need to leave. Now. It's not safe on the jungle floor. Too many big hungry bad things are looking for food, and I can't fight them like this."

"Of course. Lead on, Reigh." Aubren shakily got to his feet, giving me an earnest, hopeful smile.

I took one look at his leg, which was still bleeding through the sloppy bandage he had wrapped around it, and realized this wasn't going to be easy. He wouldn't be walking very far. At least, not without leaving a rather obvious trail of blood for any hungry predator to follow.

We were going to have to find somewhere close to hide, tend our wounds, and wait for help.

While Aubren limped around, checking on his men and

getting them ready to move out, I searched around for one of their discarded torches. I broke off a piece of the charred end and found a smooth, flat stone. If Kiran was out here somewhere, looking for these guys or me, odds were, he'd be able to track us this far. So, I left him a message etched into the stone and positioned it carefully on top of a stack of more rocks, right in the middle of the clearing. It would be obvious, especially to a seasoned warrior and scout.

"Leaving breadcrumbs?" Aubren was standing over me, watching with a bemused grin.

"They might be a few hours away, or a few days. Either way, eventually they will find this. Then they'll know where to find us."

"Smart boy." He had a strange, almost impish smirk on his face when I turned to face him. He held something out to me— my two kafki.

I took the blades and slipped them back into my belt. "Not really. But if we are going to survive, I need you and your men to do as I say. No noise. No talking. And no fire or light. Follow in a straight line, right behind me. No one goes anywhere alone. And if you see any pink fruit lying on the ground, *do not* touch it."

Aubren didn't say anything else as we finished gathering the group and finally struck out into the jungle. I took the lead and immediately began looking for a good place to ascend into the safety of the trees. After all, the place I had in mind for us was a few miles away and the less time we spent on the ground, the better.

We crossed the river at a shallow place and kept going, making a zigzag trail through the towering undergrowth. The men clumped together. They were afraid, not that I blamed them, they'd been through a lot, and they kept looking at everything with tense apprehension. The jungle hadn't been gentle—not that it ever was.

At last, I found a tree covered in a network of thick vines that made something like a living lattice all the way to the lowest branch. It would be easy for novice climbers to handle. One by one, I sent the men upward and told them to wait for me.

Aubren's leg was getting weaker and he was losing blood because of the poor bandaging, so I waited to send him up last and climbed along beside him. I could see his hands shaking as he reached for every handhold. His jaw was rigid and the veins in his neck stood out against his darkly tanned skin. His forehead beaded with sweat, making his shaggy hair stick to his face.

At the very top, his wounded leg suddenly gave out. He slipped, losing his grip and began to fall backwards.

Without thinking, I lunged out, grabbed his arm, and roughly dragged him back against the side of the tree. For a few seconds, we just hung there together, panting as bits of bark fell the long distance to the jungle floor below. That was too close for comfort.

"H-heights don't agree with me," Aubren stammered weakly.

"Just a little further. We're almost there."

He looked at me, his brow drawn up in frantic distress. "If I don't make it, please take the rest of my men on to see the Queen. They must reach her. W-we need her help."

"That's not going to—"

"No! You have to promise me, Reigh. I have a duty to my people. I cannot fail them."

We stared at one another in silence. I got this weird feeling, like maybe I'd seen him before. Only, that was impossible.

Slowly, I nodded in agreement.

With his jaw set in determination, Aubren started climbing again. I watched him go, shakily scaling the distance to the first limb where the rest of his men were waiting. They helped haul him over the edge and made a path for me when I made my way to join them.

It took a lot of patience, coaxing, and time to get the soldiers used to using the tree paths. They didn't like the idea of hopping from one branch to another, even if there was more than enough room. I guess humans in Maldobar didn't do a lot of that kind of thing. They weren't very good at staying quiet, either. Progress was slow, very slow, and it was nearly dawn by the time we finally arrived at the spot I had in mind for us to stop.

A steep cliff jutted upwards, right against a group of trees whose limbs butted up and curved around the mossy rock face. The cliff was riddled with big ferns and flowering plants, but there were also lots of flat open spaces to perch and watch the jungle floor as it sloped downwards into a deep gorge.

But I was looking for the cave.

Kiran had brought me here once, a long time ago. He showed me where the cave was and how to secure it. He told me that if I ever got lost, I needed to try my very best to follow the river and find my way to this spot. This was a safe place, a hideout, where I could wait to be found and I wouldn't have to worry about anything bad finding me.

I'd avoided the cave before for that exact reason. I figured it was probably the first place Kiran would come looking for me. Now it was our best shot at surviving long enough to see Mau Kakuri.

The cave had a narrow entrance that was hidden from plain view. You had to know exactly where to look. Brushing back two big fern fronds, I saw it. My body went slack, and I let out a deep sigh. So far, so good.

There was a big, mossy stone rolled in front of the entryway to keep other animals from taking up residence in it. Normally, I could have handled that on my own. My injured shoulder was slowing me down, though, so I had to get a few soldiers to help me roll it out of the way.

"Okay," I told them. "You can light a torch inside. It will be safe."

Aubren eyed me skeptically. Maybe he didn't like the idea of squeezing through that narrow passage into a dark, unknown place. "You're certain?"

I nodded. "I'm going to collect plants."

"Plants?"

"Yes, you know … " I struggled to think of the right words. "For medicines. Herbs?"

Aubren seemed to understand as he smiled and patted my good shoulder. "Smart boy," he said again.

I was starting to like that kind of praise. Kiran never praised me for anything. Enyo said it was tough love because he didn't want me to get too cocky. Maybe it was, although it still would have been nice to get a little approval every now and then.

When I returned to the cave, my arms were full of firewood and a bundle of fresh herbs I knew I could use to make poultices and quick medicines to fight infection. The soldiers were pleased to see me, and gathered around as I began to make a fire in the middle of the cave.

The chamber was large—a lot bigger than the entryway suggested. There was plenty of room to stand and move around, and there were a few old bedrolls and animal hide blankets stored at the back that had been left behind by other travelers.

Once the fire was lit and the stone was rolled back over the doorway, the soldiers seemed to relax. They began peeling off their layers of armor and unfurling the bedrolls for the more severely injured members of their party. I watched silently as I sat, stoking the small fire. It was still surreal to see them, so many humans, just going about their business. They were completely different from elves—more so than Kiran had told me. They were much bigger in build, brawnier, and many of them had short beards. It made me rub my own chin, which had a few days' worth of short, rough stubble on it now.

Elves couldn't grow facial hair, and I'd felt like a huge freak when I'd first started growing some. Enyo had even teased me about it once, saying I might start growing hair all over until I looked like a big walking hairball. After that, I'd asked Kiran to teach me how to shave it off.

"So tell me, how does a human boy with hair as red as a ripe tomato wind up living in Luntharda, dressed like a gray elf? Do your parents live with the gray elves, as well?" Aubren asked as he sat down next to me. He wasn't looking so good. His face was a little ashen and he was still breathing hard.

"No, not exactly," I replied as I pulled out my medical kit and got to work preparing medicines. "You're going to have to roll up your pant leg so I can see the wound."

Aubren made painful grunting sounds as he obeyed. The wound itself looked gruesome. There was a deep, jagged bite mark right in the muscle of his calf. He was lucky, though, even if he didn't feel that way. The bite hadn't severed any major arteries and it was clotting well on its own. All I had to do was clean it, apply a good herbal poultice, and wrap it securely. Kiran would be able to do more when we got back to Mau Kakuri, but at least he wouldn't die of infection before then.

"I might have spared myself this if I hadn't given up my greaves," he muttered. "We had to shed a lot of our gear early on so we could move more quickly."

A wise decision on their part. According to Kiran, human armor wasn't practical for anything in Luntharda except making you harder for a Greevwood tree to digest.

"So where are your parents, then?" Aubren asked again. I

guess talking helped take his focus off me poking around the gaping holes in his leg while I assessed the full extent of the damage.

"I don't know. Somewhere in Maldobar, I guess. I was abandoned as a baby. The gray elves took me in."

"I see." He winced as I began pouring water from my water skin over it and cleaning out the dirt and grime. "Then why were you out here on your own? I didn't think gray elves traveled alone."

I avoided his eyes and pretended not to hear him. Taking some of the herbs I had gathered, I used the sharp end of one of my blades to cut and mash them into a slimy green paste. I smeared it over his wound, even when he flinched and hissed in pain.

"It might sting at first, but it will help with the pain and will keep it from getting infected," I told him. I took a glob of it on my finger and held it out to him. "Here, you should eat some, too. It will give you back your strength."

Aubren eyed the green goo doubtfully. Okay, so it looked gross—like a big slimy green plant-booger. Not to mention it tasted really, *really,* bad. But it would help, I was sure about that.

He shuddered and gagged as he let me swipe the goo onto his tongue. I let him have a few sips of water to wash it down. After that, he lay back on the stone floor, seeming to relax as the remedy took effect.

I finished my work by cutting up one of the animal hide blankets into a long, thin strip that I used to tightly bandage his calf. Kiran might insist on some stitches on the larger gashes later. I wasn't sure how much more pain Aubren could withstand right now, though. Humans weren't as strong as elves, even if they were bigger, and I didn't want to push him too far. I'd give it some time, see how the wound reacted to my remedy, and then decide if he needed more intensive treatment.

I went around to the other wounded soldiers, doling out the green herbal goo to any who needed it. I cut more bandaging strips out of the blankets, wrapped wounds, and even had to apply a few stitches to more serious gashes. It was hard work and all the while, the blood loss from my own injury was beginning to make my head fuzzy. I had no adrenaline left to keep me going, and I barely made it back to Aubren's side before I collapsed onto my rear. The shaking in my body had gotten worse and my face was dripping with sweat.

"Here," Aubren said as he sat up and moved closer. "Let me see. I'm no medic, but maybe you can talk me through it."

I hesitantly slipped off my black leather jerkin and tunic. I could feel the fabric sticking to my skin, soaked with my own blood. I didn't know how bad it was. I didn't want to look. Unfortunately, being the only person in the vicinity with any medical training meant I didn't have a choice.

My leather jerkin had protected me from the worst of it. There were a few deep punctures where the snagwolf's teeth had broken through to my skin, but for the most part, it had been the crushing force of his jaws that had left my shoulder badly bruised. As far as injuries went, mine were minor.

I shuddered and handed Aubren my water skin. "Just rinse it off and smear some of the herbal paste on it."

"You're sure?"

"Yeah. It'll be fine."

Aubren obliged. After he'd cleaned out my wound and dabbed some of the poultice on it, I talked him through how to properly apply a bandage to my shoulder. It was still looser than I would have liked. I guess he was worried about hurting me. I still gave him credit for trying.

"So, what made you want to run away from home?" he asked suddenly.

I froze and flashed him a panicked glance out of the corner of my eye. How had he known that?

"Relax. I was a teenager, once. I know it can be hard at times. You want to prove yourself as a man, even if your parents feel you aren't ready. And in your case, being raised by an entirely different race, I can only imagine you've had to deal with more than your fair share of challenges. It can't be easy."

"No," I agreed quietly. "It isn't."

"But I'm sure your family, gray elf or otherwise, is probably worried about you."

I ducked my head in shame. I knew he was right. Kiran was probably freaking out, driving everyone nuts trying to track me down. The only time I'd ever seen him lose his calm and collected demeanor was when something happened to me. There was one time in particular, when I was six or seven, and I'd fallen out of a tree while learning to climb. I'd broken my leg, and Kiran had been more upset about it than I was. It was one of the only times I could recall ever seeing him look scared.

I rubbed the back of my neck sheepishly. "I keep screwing

up. I thought it would be easier if I just left."

Aubren smiled warmly. "We all make mistakes, Reigh. Young, old, gray elf, or human—we all screw up every now and then. It doesn't mean our parents don't love us, though. I'm sure yours would agree with me; family sticks together. We always trust one another, and we never give up on each other. It's what makes family special."

I couldn't meet his gaze because, for the first time, I understood why it bothered me so much that Kiran wouldn't let me call him dad. It was like he didn't want me to be his family. And if he wasn't my family ... then I had no one.

SEVEN

The men settled in to wait, resting and going through what was left of my meager food rations. It wasn't much, although apparently, they hadn't had much to eat since they'd gotten lost. Many of them fell asleep on the cold stone floor, snoring loudly as though this was the first time they'd been able to rest. The cave became quiet then, except for the snoring and the occasional whispered conversation.

I sat by Aubren and kept the fire going, occasionally sprinkling wood splinters and twigs onto it. The light seemed to comfort them and the smell of the wood was fragrant. I'd chosen it on purpose. It wouldn't smoke much, and Kiran had told me that the smell of it was soothing. So far, that was proving to be true.

"What was that thing you were speaking to? That black …

smoke creature," Aubren whispered suddenly. He was stretched out on the ground next to me, his eyes closed, expression calm, and breathing steady.

My mouth twitched.

"I've heard stories since I was a boy about a young man, a dragonrider about your age, who could do things—strange, miraculous things."

"Lapiloque," I guessed.

Aubren didn't open his eyes as a smile slowly crept across his features. "We called him Jaevid."

"I'm not a dragonrider," I reminded him. Technically, I wasn't even a real scout. I was a kid. Just a dumb, useless, disobedient, ungrateful kid.

"Neither was Jaevid, when it all began. At least, that's how the story goes."

"The gray elves don't say his name. They believe it's disrespectful," I muttered.

He shrugged slightly. "My people once shouted his name in the streets, now they whisper it. It's not out of disrespect, though. I think they are waiting to see if he will keep his word or not."

That was surprising—to hear that the humans also believed he would return. "And what do you think? Do you think he'll come back?"

Aubren's eyes opened slowly. The corners of his eyes crinkled as he studied the ceiling of the cave. "Before all of this? No. I suppose I didn't believe it. I thought it was just a story, even if my father swore every inch of it was true. But there was never any proof that I could see, and it's our nature to want an explanation for things and to want to believe in a supernatural force that is moving events in our favor. We want to cleave to those ideas to give us hope in hopeless times."

He lifted his head slightly, leveling a puzzled stare in my direction. "But things change. That is, ironically, the only thing constant about our world. And when you came flying out of the trees, and I saw what you could do. I saw that creature appear … "

I looked away and studied the fire.

"Jaevid promised he would come back. He didn't say how. Are you him? Are you Jaevid reborn?"

I scowled. Okay, so maybe it wasn't *that* crazy of a question to ask. After all, I didn't know anything about the lapiloque's origins beyond stories, either. But I seriously doubted the chosen one of Paligno had done or seen any of the stuff I had.

"No," I muttered. "Definitely not."

"How can you be sure?" he pressed.

I cracked another stick in half and tossed it onto the fire, watching the sparks dance in the darkness of the cave. "Because, in the stories, lapiloque never murdered anyone by devouring their soul. He healed people. He brought hope and life, not fear and death."

Aubren didn't answer, and I was too afraid of what kind of expression I'd find on his face to look at him right then.

"What you saw wasn't some helpful forest spirit. His name is Noh, and I don't know what he is. I do know he isn't good, though. And neither am I. That's why I ran away."

It really sucked to say it out loud—the things I'd been feeling for so long. It made my eyes tear up and my teeth clench. I took a shaking breath and tried to recollect my nerve.

Then I felt a heavy hand on my head.

Aubren was sitting up, turning my head around to look him in the eye. "You saved us not once but twice. You rescued us from those creatures. Then you brought us here and treated our wounds. You could have just left us to die."

I swallowed hard.

"You seem to be a lot of things, Reigh. Whatever you are, however, I don't believe evil is one of them," he said as he patted my head like he was comforting a child.

I was afraid to say anything. My throat was tight and I couldn't get my eyes to quit watering up.

"You want to be taken seriously, like an adult? I think you should go back home and talk to your parents. Explain to them why you left. If it makes you feel any better, I'll go along to make sure they hear you out. Part of being an adult is having the courage to admit when you're wrong."

Aubren ruffled my hair and gave my head a playful shove as he let me go. "Who knows, they might even let you come back to Maldobar with me. I could certainly use a fighter with your skill."

My heart soared at that possibility. "You mean be a dragonrider?"

He chuckled. "I can't make any promises about that. I'm not even a dragonrider, myself. I couldn't get through the basic training. Heights, you know—I get sick every time. But maybe I can put you on a different path than one that leaves you wandering the wilderness alone."

I smiled and looked back at the flames, watching them smolder and hiss as they licked at the new bits of wood. "That sounds good to me."

It was dawn the next morning when I heard voices outside the cave. I recognized the muffled gray elven words and instantly got to my feet, nudging Aubren with my toe to wake him. He sputtered and finally seemed to realize what was going on.

The cavalry had arrived.

By the time I got to the entrance of the cave, gray elf scouts were rolling the stone back and letting the morning light pour in. It was so bright, I tried to shade my eyes with my hand. Through my fingers, I barely made out the shape of a man standing in the entryway, his outline silhouetted against the jungle.

Suddenly, he rushed at me.

I instinctively drew back into a defensive stance. I'd assumed these guys were friendly. Stupid, stupid, *stupid*!

I reached for my blades—which weren't there. Crap. I'd left them lying on the floor near the fire.

When I turned to look back, it was too late.

Kiran threw his arms around me and hugged me so tight I couldn't breathe.

Neither of us spoke, even after he let me go. I didn't know what to say. He'd never hugged me like that before. His brows were knitted and his mouth was mashed together in a hard line that made his chin wrinkle. He studied me wordlessly for what seemed like a long time. Then he muttered under his breath in the elven language. "We will talk later."

Right. We had bigger problems to deal with right now than my latest screw-up. I stepped out of his way and let him see what remained of the human soldiers, who were gathering around to marvel at Kiran and the other scouts curiously.

"The Queen sends her blessings and warm welcome," Kiran spoke to them in the human tongue. He was better at it than I was, and could speak it without an accent. "We were sent by her to take you to Mau Kakuri safely—"

"Kiran!" Aubren shouted, interrupting his speech. He broke through the company of his soldiers with his eyes wide, an excited smile on his lips. He rushed forward and clasped Kiran's hand, pulling him into a gruff hug.

Kiran smiled as he hugged him back. It was weird. I couldn't remember the last time I'd ever seen him smile like that at anyone. He actually looked happy.

I pinched myself to make sure I wasn't hallucinating.

They started talking, laughing, and acting like they'd known each other for years. I guess I shouldn't have been so surprised. After all, Kiran had lived in Maldobar for a long time. He probably knew lots of humans. But something about it was just … weird.

"And this boy? He's yours?" Aubren asked suddenly, turning the focus back to me.

My face grew hot with embarrassment.

Kiran gave a noncommittal shrug. "I came across him as an infant, not long after I dismissed myself from the court."

Aubren's gaze sharpened as he eyed Kiran a bit more suspiciously. "Is he Holly's?"

The question made Kiran's expression harden, his eyes becoming dark as he looked away. "When I found him, he was no one's."

Holly? Who the heck was Holly? The idea that Kiran might have *known* my parents had never dawned on me before. He'd never suggested he might have known them. But in a matter of seconds, my brain was swirling with a frenzy of questions.

"We should get going," Kiran changed the subject. "We brought shrikes to ensure a speedy return. I hope you can manage that far in flight."

Aubren laughed dryly, like that was a bad inside joke.

I wasn't laughing, though. I was trying to decide if I was upset, shocked, hurt, or just plain furious.

I didn't say anything to either of them as we helped the soldiers onto the backs of the shrikes. The scouts had brought more than enough, anticipating a much larger group of survivors.

The beasts were uneasy. The presence of the human smell made them stir and hiss, their six muscular legs flexing, talons digging into the meat of the tree limbs. Their long tails swished cautiously, while their hides of shimmering scales reflected the jungle like a mirage. They were a gray elf scout's mount of choice, as fast as lightning, as vicious as a viper.

I'd never ridden on one by myself. And today wasn't going

to be the first time, unfortunately. Kiran climbed on to the back of one and beckoned me to mount up in front of him—like a little kid. Great. How embarrassing.

We took off into the jungle, zipping through the trees at a speed that apparently humans didn't have much experience with. They screamed until they either went horse or got used to the abrupt, darting way the shrikes flew through the tree limbs.

We cut a three-day journey down to around sixteen hours. By dusk, we were at the outskirts of Mau Kakuri and seeing landmarks I recognized. Kiran and I were leading the group, and he chose the straightest course without stopping.

I thought we were going to the clinic. After all, more than a few of these soldiers needed medical attention—not to mention myself. But we blitzed over the rooftops, passing our home and heading straight for the royal palace. The closer we got, the further down I sank into the saddle. I was kind of hoping I might just disappear, maybe vaporize into the air like Noh. I mean, sure, I'd run away. But I hadn't done anything *illegal* or punishable by the royal court, had I?

Unless … they had found out about Enyo and I trespassing in their courtyard.

"Kiran," I whispered when we landed in the grand courtyard in front of the palace's sweeping front entrance.

He sent me a silencing glare.

Right. We were going to talk later.

It was after sunset, so the palace was draped in veils of darkness. The alabaster halls were cavernous and cool, and elegant gold braziers stood along the hallways and smoldered with fragrant incenses. The soldiers walked together in a clump like scared goats, staring around at the staggering beauty of the place as though mystified. The gray elven scouts followed us wordlessly, but as soon as we came to the antechamber that led into the throne room, they stopped, saluted Kiran, and left.

I started to leave, too.

Kiran planted a firm hand on my injured shoulder.

I winced.

I guess he hadn't noticed I was hurt. Aubren's bandaging attempt was covered by my shirt and jerkin. When he saw me flinch, Kiran immediately pulled both to the side long enough to see that I was, in fact, hurt.

His already frigid glare cooled even more. "How bad is it?"

I shook my head. "Not bad."

He snorted and nodded toward the throne room, indicating that I should follow them inside.

"Why?" I dared to ask.

He didn't answer.

As we entered, royal guards dressed in elaborate silks and wearing jewel encrusted scimitars pushed open the two huge wooden doors. Each door was engraved with infinitely complex floral patterns and closed behind us with a thunderous *boom*. My stomach started swimming, and my teeth were rattling. Before us, down a sloped walkway lined with more of those fancy braziers, was a raised stone platform adorned with plush animal skin rugs, low lounge sofas, and intricate silk cushions stitched with gold threads and glittering beads. There, seated amidst the cushions, were King Jace and Queen Araxie.

They stood as we entered, the lengths of their matching navy-blue robes spilling all the way to the floor and pooling at their feet. The Queen wore a headdress of blue and green feathers fitted into a golden crown, and the King had one of a similar style, minus the feathers. They looked at Kiran, the soldiers, Aubren, and me with similar expressions of relief and apprehension.

The Queen was the first to speak. "You are most welcome here, warriors of Maldobar." She spread her arms wide and offered a faint smile. "We understand your journey has been most treacherous. Many were lost. We grieve with you at such a loss."

King Jace nodded in agreement.

Her gaze fixed on Aubren. Her aged smile grew as bright and warm as a sunrise, crinkling her eyes and the corners of her mouth. "How you have grown! I hardly recognize you."

Apparently, I was the only one in Luntharda who didn't already know who this guy was.

Aubren grinned back and offered a deep, respectful bow. "My Lady, you are as beautiful as ever."

"I am an old woman now, my dear," she sighed resignedly.

"And yet I'm certain you could still best me in a duel."

Queen Araxie laughed and glanced back at her husband, who was smirking rather confidently. I guess he agreed.

"I know there is much to discuss, but let's first attend to your injuries. I would see you all fed, bathed, and given any manner of comfort you desire. Then we can speak frankly about the matter at hand." She waved her hand, calling in servants who began helping the more seriously wounded away into the palace.

At last, her gaze fell on me.

I was too scared to move.

"You are the boy who found them?" she asked bluntly.

"Found us?" Aubren chuckled. "We'd all be fodder if it weren't for him. He saved our lives."

The Queen's brows rose. "Is that so? So much bravery from so young a boy ..."

Something strange shimmered in her eyes. I saw her exchange a meaningful glance with the King, who was studying me harder now. He wasn't nearly as friendly looking as she was. His gaze was cold and piercing, and it made me feel about two inches tall.

"Well, I believe honors are in order then," she said and pulled a long feather from her headdress. She walked down the steps to stand before me, her multicolored eyes glittering with interest. She took the feather and lightly brushed it across my forehead before tucking it into my hair. "Let it be known the Queen of Luntharda has named you worthy of praise. You are now a scout, and one most favored in my service."

I could see Kiran's jaw tense out of the corner of my eye. He was gritting his teeth, like he was trying to restrain himself from objecting.

I bowed my head and managed a nervous smile. "T-thank you."

"Where is your bow?" she asked.

"I gave it away. It's a long story, Your Majesty."

The Queen's mouth quirked upward. "Well that will never do. A scout must have a good bow." She looked at Kiran for a moment, studying him silently with her eyes twinkling thoughtfully. She stretched out her hand, beckoning to one of the servants standing against the sides of the room carrying a beautiful bow and quiver. Both looked much finer than anything I'd ever owned and were engraved with the design of the royal seal—the head of a stag leafed in pure silver.

"Then you will have mine. Aubren means well, but I'm afraid he's mistaken. My hands are not as steady as they once were. They've forgotten much of their former strength. This bow served me well even in times of great trouble. I hope it will do the same for you."

I took the bow and quiver carefully, marveling at them before slipping them over my shoulder. I bowed again and thanked her.

"I welcome you both to stay here, as well. Kiran, I'm sure the soldiers would appreciate your expertise to help treat their wounds. My own medics might learn a thing or two from you."

She smiled like she was trying to console him, but Kiran's expression remained grim. Even so, he nodded stiffly. "As you wish."

EIGHT

The palace had a much nicer setup for medical care than our clinic. It was bigger, cleaner, and there were plenty of trained assistants to help with changing bandages, cleaning wounds, and helping administer different medicines and treatments. Even so, the royal medics watched intently as Kiran appraised each and every soldier, examining their injuries, doling out instructions and advice. The medics never questioned him, even the older ones. He had the most experience—especially when it came to battle wounds.

Kiran didn't want me to help him, though. He made me sit down on one of the patient bedrolls and commanded me to take off my jerkin and tunic. He didn't say much while he cleaned out the punctures left by the snagwolf's jaws in my shoulder. He did growl at me to be still when I flinched and cringed as he stitched some of the deeper wounds closed, though.

Okay, it was my fault he was angry, I'd defied him by running away in the middle of the night into the jungle and almost getting killed. Saving a few human soldiers didn't absolve me of any of that. Fair enough.

But I was angry, too. The idea that he might be hiding secrets about my birth parents was infuriating. I deserved to know. I *needed* to know.

Kiran didn't give me much of an opportunity to ask him questions. He bandaged my shoulder tightly, pushed a cup of tea into my hands laced with a bitter-tasting remedy, and went back to treating the soldiers.

It was the beginning of a very long night. Despite all our efforts, one of the soldiers had blood poisoning. I overheard Kiran talking to the medics. They couldn't get his fever to come down. He was in a lot of pain, but the only way to save his life was to … well, cut off the source of the infection.

I won't even try to describe what that sounded like.

Finally, at some point in the early hours of the morning, things got quiet. All the medics had retired, leaving behind their trained, hired servants to keep watch over the sleeping soldiers. The soft sounds of snoring echoed in the cavernous room, and only a few flickering candles gave off warm, gentle light.

Kiran didn't leave with the other medics. He sat down on the bedroll next to mine and started washing the blood from his face, arms, and hands with a wet rag. There was more crimson spatter speckling his silver hair, and his whole body sagged with exhaustion. I wondered if he'd slept at all since he discovered I was gone. Had he even stopped to catch his breath? Or had he been forging on for days on end, relentlessly until he found me?

"You should be asleep," he murmured when he noticed I was watching him.

"Who is Holly? Was she my mother?" The questions burst out of me before I could think about it.

Kiran's eyes darted up to meet mine, his forehead creased with surprise. "No. She wasn't."

My heart sank. "Would you even tell me if she was?"

"Of course, I would." All the stiff, stern lines on his face smoothed, and he bowed his head slightly with a sigh. Kiran scooted over and sat cross-legged next to me, his elbows resting on his knees. "Can you tell me why you left?"

I didn't want to. And as soon as I tried to explain, the words seemed to stick in my throat. I rolled over onto my side so I didn't have to look at him.

"Because I wouldn't let you become a scout?" he asked quietly.

"No."

"Because you wanted to prove yourself to me? Or to Enyo?"

"No."

"Reigh." He put a hand on my arm. His tone was surprisingly gentle. "Talk to me."

I did. I told him why I left—that I didn't think I could stop Noh from growing stronger, and that I knew my presence here in Mau Kakuri was putting everyone at risk. I was better off alone. And a very small, very childish and naïve part of me, had hoped I might find my parents somewhere in Maldobar.

When it came to telling him about seeing Noh again while fighting the snagwolves and the mysterious woman's voice I'd heard in the dark—I hesitated. In the past, I'd always been perfectly honest with him about everything that happened, especially when it came to stuff like that. After all, I assumed he could help me or protect me somehow. Now … I knew that wasn't the case. Whatever was happening to me, Kiran couldn't stop it any more than I could.

When I finished, he looked at me squarely, the dim candlelight catching over his multihued eyes. "Reigh, where you came from doesn't matter. Those events are set, and no one can change them. It's where you are right now, and what you plan to do next, that matters. The past belongs to time, the future is still yours."

"But it matters to me! I want to know why I am the way I am. I want to know what Noh is, and why he's bound to me. Maybe my parents know somethi—"

"No," he interrupted with a growl. "Leave it alone. I mean it."

I was stunned. I rolled over to find his expression closed and dark again. We sat in silence, me gaping at him while he glowered down at the floor.

At last, he looked up with a grim scowl. "You must not look for your parents, Reigh. Not yet."

"Why not?"

He shook his head. "The time will come for that soon enough. For now, try to enjoy things as they are."

As they were …? I didn't know what that meant. How could

I enjoy not knowing who or what I really was? It sounded stupid, like he was telling me I was too young or naïve to understand. I frowned and rolled over onto my side again.

"Aubren thinks I'm some sort of reborn lapiloque," I muttered angrily.

He snorted. "Is that so?"

I didn't answer. The fact that he dismissed it so lightly made me even more frustrated. Something was wrong with me. Something big—something dangerous. And whatever it was, Kiran knew and had no intention of telling me.

I overslept. That—or Kiran had slipped a little something extra into my medication to make sure I didn't go sneaking off in the night again. If that was the case, it worked. I slept like a corpse, and by the time I finally cracked an eye, it was nearly noon. My stomach was rolling with hunger, and the pain in my shoulder was nothing more than a dull ache.

I sat up, rubbing the grogginess from my eyes. Around me, the clinic bustled with activity. The medics and their helpers were going around administering meals, clean bandages, and more medications. The man with blood poisoning had improved greatly, despite having his arm amputated. He even seemed to be in good spirits. Not dying tends to make the whole world seem brighter, I suppose.

I peeled off the bandaging from my shoulder to get a look at my own injuries. Kiran's stitching job was as efficient as ever, and the wound was no longer angry or inflamed. Thanks to his care, and whatever mixture of herbs he'd used, it seemed to be healing already.

Kiran, however, was nowhere to be seen. The more I looked around, the more I realized another face was missing, too—Aubren.

I bent down to grab my jerkin and tunic so I could get dressed. Instead of finding my old scout's clothes, tattered and caked with dried blood, I found a brand-new tunic and black leather jerkin neatly folded beside my bedroll. Both were nicer than my old ones. The tunic was midnight blue, almost black, and made of fresh silk with intricate, silver, star designs stitched onto the sleeves and collar. The jerkin was black, to match my other gear, but it was made of many layers of tanned faundra hide. The outermost layer had details crafted from shrike scales in the shape of the royal stag's head, with elegant antlers sweeping up each side.

Somehow, I doubted these had come from Kiran. The scales shimmered like mirrors in the light when I put it on. It brought a wicked grin to my face; I'd never worn anything this awesome before.

With my kafki on my belt and my new bow and quiver strung over my back, I strutted out of the infirmary hall and started looking for Kiran. The palace was huge, and I got lost more than twice in the airy marble halls. The whole place smelled faintly of incense, and there were numerous hallways that were open to the cool, moist air that flowed in from the falls. Elegantly crafted covered bridges arched over some of the rocks, revealing curtains of water and swirling mist.

I rounded a corner, trying to find my way back to the throne room. I had a feeling that was where I'd find Kiran and Aubren, probably talking business with the King and Queen. Not that I had any expectations of being included in that discussion, but I wanted to hear about what was going on in Maldobar. What were Aubren and his men doing risking their lives in the jungle? Whatever was happening in the human kingdom, it must have been bad.

The sight of her, standing in a small courtyard beneath a willow tree, stopped me dead in my tracks. I wouldn't have seen her if not for the dress she was wearing—a beautiful billowing gown with long bell sleeves. The dress was pastel colors in every hue of the rainbow, and looked so light that the breeze from the falls made it ripple and swirl around her. Her hair was a polar shade of silver and hung down her back in smooth lengths like bolts of satin.

I couldn't see her face—not at first. She stood with her back against the trunk of a willow tree, looking up into its limbs as though deep in thought.

Then she looked right at me.

I froze. My face started to get warm. Busted.

Her eyes were creepy. One was a bright, crystalline shade of blue. The other was green. It made it hard to decide which one I should look at. The rest of her, however, was really pretty. She had a small, round face and ears that were only slightly pointed. Whoever she was, she was a halfbreed—half human, half gray elf.

"I can hear you there," she said suddenly. "I don't know your sound. Who are you?"

"My what?"

"Your sound. Everyone has one. A way they breathe, a rhythm to their movements. It's like music, and everyone's is different. But I don't recognize yours." She smiled slightly and her strange eyes panned away, staring at the ground right in front of me.

"You mean you can't see me?" I asked, like a complete moron.

Her tiny smile grew wider. "Of course not. I suppose that means you aren't an assassin or another one of those pompous suitors, then. They always know I'm blind and tend to be ridiculous in making sure I know they are okay with it."

"Oh."

"So, who are you?"

I blushed harder and scratched at the back of my neck. "My name is Reigh. I'm Kiran's so—er I'm his … "

She canted her head to the side with a confused wrinkle in her brow. "His what?"

I sighed. "I'm not even sure anymore. Pet, maybe?"

That made her giggle, which in turn made my head spin and my face flush even more. She looked young, maybe even close to my age. "You're funny, Reigh."

I dared to take a few steps closer, brushing back some of the willow fronds as I joined her under the tree. "Funny-looking, maybe. Not that you'd know."

She laughed again and her strange, mismatched eyes twinkled with enthusiasm. "My name is Hecate."

I stuck out a hand to shake, mimicking the human greeting. Then I remembered she couldn't see it and awkwardly drew it back. Thank the gods she couldn't see that. "So, other than young and funny, what else do I sound like?"

She pursed her lips. "Hmm. You have a certain warmth and kindness in your voice. It makes me think you would make friends easily, but you are a little cocky. So maybe you've got a short temper. Your heartbeat gets faster whenever you come closer, so you must think I'm pretty or maybe scary."

"Definitely scary. Terrifying, really."

She giggled and pointed her gaze directly at my chest, which was about eye level for her. Now that I was close to her, she probably wasn't an inch over five feet.

Suddenly, her expression twisted. Her eyes widened and she drew back slightly. "T-there's something else. A whisper. A voice like … "

She didn't get a chance to finish. Someone shouted behind me, startling both of us. To my surprise, Hecate lunged forward and awkwardly grabbed my sleeve as though she were afraid and using *me* as protection.

My chest swelled a little with pride.

Someone was coming down the hallway, calling her name over and over. Any second they were going to come around that corner and find us.

"It's my bodyguards. They'll make me go back to my room," she said weakly. "Please. I don't want to go back there. Not yet.

I never get to go outside anymore."

Like I said, no one has ever made the mistake of calling me a genius. I didn't even ask for an explanation. Grabbing Hecate's hand firmly, I dragged her away from the tree and down another hallway. We took off at a sprint, me leading the way.

She was much smaller, and so frail I was a little concerned she might faint. Her cheeks were rosy and she was out of breath when we came to a huge atrium where four halls intersected. The domed ceiling overhead was a giant stained-glass design of a flower, and off to the left I spotted the familiar set of giant double doors leading to the throne room.

I took us slowly down the hallway, looking for a side entrance, maybe something the servants used, so we could see inside. Down a narrow passageway, I found a small door that led up onto a platform. A big tapestry covered it, but we could hear conversations. I recognized Kiran and Aubren's voices right away.

When the Queen spoke, Hecate squeezed my hand tight. Sadness crept over her face as she whispered, "My grandmother is in there."

"Grandmother?" I choked. "You mean you're a princess?"

The sadness in her eyes intensified and she didn't answer.

Suddenly, the tapestry was snatched back, exposing us. Hecate gave a yelp of alarm before she hid behind me. My body went stiff, paralyzed with shock. I still had a firm grip on her hand as I looked up …

… directly into the scowling face of her grandfather, King Jace.

NINE

Behind the King, I caught a glimpse of Kiran. His pasty expression was one of pure mortification. I watched him bury his face in his palm and slowly shake his head. He was probably hoping this was just a nightmare and he'd wake up.

I was kind of hoping that, too.

No such luck, though.

"Eavesdropping, are we?" the King's sharp gaze seemed to pierce right through me. "And with my granddaughter, no less."

"We weren't, I promise." Hecate's voice was quiet as she stepped out from behind me. "We just got lost. I went out for a walk and got turned around. I asked this boy to help me find my way back to my room."

"The ignorant leading the blind," the King snorted. "I can't think of anything more disastrous. This boy is a guest here,

Hecate. He doesn't know where he's going, either. Where are your bodyguards?"

Her expression drooped and she shifted uncomfortably. As far as liars went, Hecate wasn't one of the best I'd ever seen. I guess we had that in common.

"It's all right, Jace. They can join us," the Queen called suddenly. She was sitting amidst the silk cushions, across from Aubren and Kiran.

"They're only children," he protested.

The Queen's smile was strangely cryptic. "So were we, once."

King Jace didn't push the issue. With a dissatisfied sigh, he pulled the tapestry back further and nodded for us to go ahead. I slunk past him and made a wide berth with Hecate trailing behind me. When he noticed she was holding tightly onto my hand, the King's eyes narrowed dangerously. Yikes.

Hecate released her hold on me when Queen Araxie insisted that she sit beside her, and I went across from them to settle down between Kiran and Aubren. Kiran was still gaping at me in disbelief, like he couldn't decide if he should smack me over the head or throttle me.

But hey, how was I supposed to know she was a princess?

One look at Aubren, and I realized his eyes were fixed on Hecate, wide and mystified. His lips parted and he cleared his throat, looking down as though he were embarrassed. His face was even a little flushed across the nose.

At first, they kept the conversation light. Servants brought in silver platters of freshly cut fruit, roasted nuts, and grilled fish rolled in delicious vegetable leaves. They were probably meant to be finger foods we could all snack on, but I went ahead and started stuffing my face. I couldn't remember ever eating anything that fancy or delicious.

Then the adults got down to the business at hand.

"You know why I'm here," Aubren said bleakly. "My father might be too proud to call for aid, but I can no longer turn a deaf ear to the cries of my people."

"What has Felix said?" King Jace's attention—finally—wasn't focused on me. He didn't look any happier though as he listened to Aubren explain.

"Our relationship was strained even before, but after the first wave of enemy forces struck our shores not six months ago, my father has closed himself off inside the castle at Halfax and is determined not to let the royal city fall. He's recalled most of the dragonriders there to hold it. Meanwhile, the rest of the kingdom is left to be ravaged as the enemy marches uncontested."

"Who are they?" Queen Araxie sounded worried.

"That's just it, we know very little about them. What we have learned has come at a great price. They call themselves Tibrans, and it seems most of their forces are comprised of slave soldiers captured from other kingdoms they've already overtaken. Their leader is a man who calls himself Argonox. He sent an emissary to my father's court mere days before the invasion, to announce that we would be given one opportunity to peacefully surrender and be added to their Empire."

King Jace sank back in his seat and rubbed his forehead. "I can imagine how Felix responded to that."

Aubren didn't answer right away, although his eyes blazed

with quiet anger as his hand clenched around his half-empty goblet of wine. "My sister urged him to fortify the Four Watches by calling out any able-bodied dragonrider, even those in retirement. My father refused and when she rebelled, he banished her from Halfax. She now fights as a rogue, leading a company of other riders who are loyal to her. They've all been branded outlaws, but they are the only reason we held Southwatch for as long as we did. I've been able to communicate with her in secret. She's made a makeshift base for her operations in the mountains near Blybrig Academy."

"Wait a minute," I interrupted and pointed a finger at Aubren. "You mean *your* father is the King of Maldobar? You're a prince?"

Everyone stared at me—even Hecate—like that should have been obvious.

Kiran swatted me over the back of the head.

Aubren, on the other hand, chuckled. "I suppose I should have mentioned that sooner. I am Aubren Farrow, oldest son to King Felix Farrow of Maldobar."

"Oh." I swallowed hard. That meant Kiran and I were the only non-royals in this gathering. Talk about a lot of pressure.

Aubren took a deep breath, and the mood darkened, as he slowly lifted his gaze to the King and Queen with a glint of desperation in his eyes. "The Tibrans have burned everything from Southwatch to Mithangol. We had concentrated our forces there, hoping to drive them back to their ships, but they struck our soil again from the east. Northwatch has been overtaken, along with Dayrise, Eastwatch, and the Farchase

Plains. The Tibrans come in numbers we cannot count. Their war machines are beyond anything even our best dragonriders can contest. In months, they have reduced our forces to nearly nothing. Without your help, I fear Halfax will fall and with it all of Maldobar."

The silence was heavy. I looked to Kiran, trying to gauge by his expression how bad this was. The answer I got wasn't what I was hoping for. His forehead was creased with deep, hard lines and his mouth was drawn tight into a frown. Though he hadn't said a word, his chest heaved slowly with deep, wrathful breaths that made his nostrils flare.

It was bad—*extremely* bad.

"Can the Tibrans be reasoned with? Can we call for a council with this Argonox?" King Jace asked.

Aubren looked back down at his cup. "I tried sending a messenger to him, asking for that very thing soon after my sister was banished. The messenger was immediately sent back to me … one piece at a time."

The King and Queen exchanged another look, this one more worried. Between them, it seemed like Hecate was growing smaller and smaller. She'd stopped eating and was sitting with her head bowed low, her expression twisted with a look of fear.

"Please." Aubren put down his goblet and got on his knees. He leaned forward, bowing his head nearly to the floor to show the deepest of respect and humility. "Please help us. I know you owe us nothing, and we've no right to ask such a thing of you, but I came to beg for your aid."

The silence was uncomfortable. I was human, sure, but I

knew what the gray elves thought about foreign wars. They did not like getting mixed up in other people's battles and problems. It just wasn't done—at least, not unless some personal offense had been committed.

You know, like stealing one of their sacred, divine artifacts and almost ending the world.

I knew what the answer was going to be even before Queen Araxie spoke. "Aubren, my dear, please understand me. I feel great sorrow for your people, but I can't go against the laws of my own. We abstain from war unless we have been provoked directly. That has been our way for centuries. I will send out a decree, inviting any of my warriors who are willing to go with you to fight, however I doubt the numbers will be significant enough to help you."

Aubren's shoulders drooped and his face blanched with despair. "Then I beg that you take me to the place where Jaevid rests. He promised my father he would return when we were in need. Now is that time. Let me ask him for help."

"Aubren," the Queen started to object.

"I know you don't think it will work," he interrupted, his voice cracking with emotion. "But I told my men I would not return until I had tried everything. And unless I do this, I haven't kept my word."

"It's not far from here. We could manage the journey in a day if we went by shrike," King Jace pointed out.

The Queen flashed him an exasperated glare. "We have tried many times to wake the lapiloque without any response. I seem to recall you reminding me of that fact."

"But we aren't Felix's heir," King Jace countered. "That promise wasn't made to us."

Aubren's jaw tensed.

They were at a stalemate. No one spoke as the Queen and King sat, staring each other down until, at last, a small voice interrupted.

"Let him try," Hecate murmured.

Aubren raised his head to stare at her, eyes wide.

"Is that what the gods have told you?" The Queen shifted uneasily.

Hecate shook her head, making her silver hair swish. "No. It's not that. But he came so far and has sacrificed so much to be here. Many have died for this chance. It would be cruel to turn him away now, and you are not cruel, grandmother."

Aubren's cheeks and nose had gone red again.

The Queen pursed her lips, considering Hecate for a moment before finally nodding in consent. "Very well. We will give it one day."

"Thank you, My Lady," Aubren lowered his head again.

"Thank your fiancée, Aubren." The Queen arched a brow, a coy smirk playing on her aged features.

Aubren sat back stiffly, still blushing as he stole quick glances in Hecate's direction. "Y-yes. I am … most grateful."

Wait—*fiancée*? I stared between them, Hecate and Aubren. Was this some kind of joke? Were they teasing him?

I didn't get a chance to figure it out.

"I should go with him," King Jace murmured. "If it does work and he awakens, there should be at least one person there he recognizes."

"I agree. And we will tell no one of this attempt to awaken Iapiloque," the Queen said firmly. "Only you and my most favored scout will accompany Aubren there."

The King arched an eyebrow suspiciously. "Your most favored scout?"

Queen Araxie smiled, panning her shimmering gaze directly to me.

My stomach hit the soles of my feet. I was really wishing, at that moment, that I didn't have a mouth full of food.

"Of course," she said with a satisfied smile. "Reigh will be your security escort."

I was hoping I would feel epic, saddling up my own shrike to ride out under the cover of darkness on a secret mission for the Queen to save Maldobar. But as I sat atop the squirming, snarling beast—I couldn't get my teeth to stop chattering. My throat was tight and my hands were so sweaty I could barely grip the saddle. Something in my gut told me this was a bad idea. I wasn't ready yet. It was one thing to go off by myself. Now I had other people—important *royal* people—counting on me to protect them.

Next to me, Kiran was talking me through how to maneuver

and communicate with the shrike, which was the fastest route to take, and what to do if we came under attack. I'd already been through scout training. I knew all of that already. And yet, now that I was sitting on a shrike, it was like someone had scrambled my brains so I couldn't remember a thing. *What was a shrike? Who was the lapiloque? What the heck was I doing?*

"Reigh?"

Kiran grabbed my arm tightly to get my attention, and I realized I had no idea what he'd even been saying.

"You need to calm down. It's going to be fine."

"A-are you just saying that because it's the Queen's orders so you can't do anything to stop it?"

He gave me a faint, resigned smile. "No. I'm saying it because it's true. You are ready for this. It's not far to the temple grounds, you know the way, and it's only one day. Just remember what I've taught you. Concentrate."

I nodded shakily.

"The Queen's declaration of you as a scout makes you a man now. That means you have to be able to handle yourself in situations like this. So, take a deep breath. You'll be all right." Kiran patted my arm and stood back, making room for our takeoff.

"And if Noh shows up?" I couldn't bear to look at him. "What if he hurts someone?"

"Reigh." His voice was quiet. "I know you. And I know you won't let that happen. You can do this."

I squeezed the saddle harder.

"Now go on. Make me proud."

Those words were buzzing in my head as we took off into the jungle, leaving the palace and Mau Kakuri far behind. Jace and Aubren were riding together, which slowed our pace somewhat since shrikes didn't like to carry more than one passenger. It was safer, though, especially since Aubren wasn't all that great with heights ... or speed, for that matter.

They followed behind me as we zipped through the trees, sticking to the highest paths that kept us far away from the jungle floor. Kiran was right. I knew the way. And even if I got lost, all I had to do was break above the canopy long enough to catch a glimpse of lapiloque's tree. That was our destination.

I leaned down, letting my body lie flush against my shrike's back while his translucently feathered wings flapped rapidly. Their motion was more like the wings of a hummingbird, giving off a low hum that sent us surging forward at incredible speed. They could corner and hover, even fly backwards somewhat, and their mirror-like scales hid them well against the dense backdrop of leaves, vines, flowers, and branches. In Luntharda, there was no other creature that could match the speed of their flight. We were relying on that to get us to the temple without issue.

So far, that was working out fantastically.

As dawn began to break, splintering the canopy with pale shafts of golden light, I knew we were getting close. I hadn't gone up to check—I could just feel it. There was a sort of energy in the air, so thick I could practically taste it, as though all the trees here were holding their breath. It was a silence so deep and complete, breaking it seemed like a crime worse than murder.

About a mile away from the temple grounds, our shrikes

started to get skittish. They landed, chirping and shivering with anxiety, and wouldn't go another step. I couldn't decide if that was good or bad. On the one hand, it meant other dangerous predators wouldn't go near this place. But then again, I couldn't shake the sense that we weren't supposed to be here.

"Let's make this quick," King Jace murmured as he climbed out of the saddle and held the shrike steady long enough for Aubren to do the same thing.

"What's the plan?" I looked to him, since of the three of us, he was the only one who'd actually been here before. After all, he'd known the lapiloque. I wanted to ask him about it. Of anyone I'd met, he seemed like he might take a more realistic stance on the whole thing. Although since he'd caught me holding hands and sneaking around with his granddaughter, I doubted he would want to share life stories with me—even if I hadn't meant anything by it.

"We go to the tree and see if there's a way down into the tomb. From there …" Jace cast Aubren a meaningful look. "I don't think it's up to us."

Aubren nodded, still holding onto the nearest tree trunk to steady himself. His face had gone pasty white and he clamped a hand over his mouth as he retched. I guess flying still made him nauseous.

"And if something goes wrong?" I asked.

"Then we fight." King Jace shrugged like that should have been obvious.

"And if something goes *really* wrong?"

He smirked. "Then we run away bravely."

Right. Well, at least that last part sounded easy.

I checked all my weaponry one last time before tying our shrikes off to a nearby branch so they didn't leave us behind while we were away violating sacred ground. Shrikes weren't terribly loyal by nature—and if things got bad, I seriously doubted they would come sweeping in to our rescue.

We were on our own.

TEN

The temple grounds had been all but swallowed by the plant life around it. Trees had snagged the crumbling stone structures in their roots, slowly crushing them to rubble. Tall ferns had muscled their way up through the paved walkways, and thick vines snaked their way up the statues. The structures were barely recognizable, hidden beneath forty years' worth of moss and other plant life.

But you couldn't miss the tree.

It was monstrous, an absolute behemoth even next to the other giant trees in Luntharda. The base must have been about two hundred feet in diameter, and the trunk thrust straight upwards, breaking the canopy and soaring far above it. Standing before it, gawking up at the staggering size, King Jace, Aubren, and I didn't say a word for several minutes.

Finally, Aubren whispered, "Incredible."

King Jace didn't comment. He started walking toward it, his expression locked into a determined scowl. He marched all the way around the base of the trunk with us tagging along behind him, scouring the area for some crack or crevice that would let us get inside the chamber that was supposed to be buried deep below. After several hours of searching, however, we couldn't find anything. The tree's base sealed off any possible way of getting into that chamber.

All the while, my head throbbed and pounded. I was sweating, and not from exertion or heat. The closer I got to the trunk, the more it seemed like my brain was pulsing against my eardrums. It felt like pressure—as though I'd sunk down to the bottom of the ocean, and it made my skin prickle with wave after wave of shivering chills. I couldn't wait to get out of here.

"Something wrong?" King Jace was eyeing me like he thought I was up to no good.

I swallowed hard, trying to shake off the creepiness of this place. "No. I'm fine. So what now?"

He nodded at Aubren. "He makes his request. Then we see what happens."

Aubren was looking pretty pale, himself. He wobbled up to the tree's massive trunk, struggling to find solid footing amidst all the rocks and roots. King Jace and I stood back and watched as he finally reached out and laid a hand against the trunk.

"It's warm," he said with surprise. "I-it's almost as though it's vibrating. No—pulsing. Like a heartbeat!"

I took a careful step backwards. A tree with a heartbeat, now that was weird even by Luntharda's standards.

"Do you think he can really hear us?" Aubren was gazing up into the tree's outstretched limbs again.

King Jace's expression went tense. His mouth scrunched, and he looked away as though a bad memory had suddenly resurfaced. "Just go on and be done with it."

Aubren squared his shoulders, took a deep breath, and pressed both his hands against the tree. "Jaevid, if you're there ... please, hear me. My name is Aubren, and you knew my father, Felix. You were his most trusted friend. And even if he's not here to ask for it himself, he needs your help. We all do." He bowed his head slightly, his voice holding a tremor of desperation. "Maldobar will fall unless something is done to stop Argonox and the Tibrans. We cannot win against this enemy. I've seen with my own eyes what they are capable of. I know the depth of their treachery and malice. Please, Jaevid. Please keep the promise you made to my father. Help us in this fight."

I wasn't sure what was supposed to happen. We all stood in uncomfortable silence, watching and listening for anything to happen. Nothing did.

The tree didn't move. The temple around us remained quiet and completely indifferent to our presence.

At last, Aubren pulled his hands away from the tree. "Will you do nothing?"

A few more minutes passed, and he turned away. As he walked back toward us, I could see his mouth twitching and his brow furrowing, as though he were steeling himself to keep his emotions in check.

There was nothing more any of us could say. The answer seemed clear. If Jaevid was somehow in that tree, he had no intention of coming out.

"We should go back," King Jace decided aloud.

"Isn't there anything else we can try?" Aubren pleaded. "I came all this way. So many of my men died to get us here."

The King grasped his shoulder. There was a sympathetic sorrow in his gaze. "I knew Jaevid, just as I knew your father during the Gray War. Believe me when I say, it was not in his heart to stand idly by while people suffered. Helping others, healing them, was as important to him as his own life. If there was a way for Jaevid to come back, if he had any control over it at all, I believe he would have already done it by now."

Aubren let out a shaking sigh. His face screwed up as he clenched his teeth. "It's not right. Why would he make that promise?"

"I don't know," King Jace admitted.

We left the temple grounds tired and even more frustrated than before. I had to admit, the further away from the tree I got, the better I felt. My head stopped pounding and all my muscles relaxed.

When we arrived back to where our shrikes were waiting, napping in a patch of sunlight, we settled down to let them rest while we ate and drank from the rations of food we'd brought along. Sitting in a circle, none of us seemed to feel much like talking. It was weird, though, to just sit there and not say anything. So, as long as King Jace wasn't leering at me, I decided I'd ask a few of those questions that had been nagging at my brain.

"So, you really did know the lapiloque? Like, he was an actual person and not just a story?"

The King glanced over at me briefly. "Yes. And you can call him Jaevid, if you wish. I'm sure he'd prefer that, regardless of what gray elf custom demands. I was his instructor, one of the ones who trained him to be a dragonrider."

"You were a dragonrider, too?"

He gave a half-smirk. "A long time ago, yes."

This was getting interesting. "So? What was he like?"

"When I first laid eyes on him, I thought he was one of my former comrade's attempt at a very bad joke. He was a halfbreed, and probably less than half your size. He'd never lived here, in Luntharda. In fact, you probably know more about gray elf life and customs than he did."

I couldn't stop grinning. "No way."

"Absolutely. I felt a little less sorry for him after gray elf puberty finally put more meat on his bones. But it didn't do anything to make him meaner, which probably would have served him better at the academy. Blybrig Academy is no place for the small and timid, neither is the battlefront." King Jace rubbed his wrinkled mouth thoughtfully. "He was about your age, maybe a year or two older, when we first came here to the jungle. I'd see him do strange things even before that, though."

I leaned in closer. "What kinds of things?"

"He could heal people with his bare hands. He saved my life that way more than once. But he could do much more than that. By the time it was all said and done, I think everyone here and in Maldobar had much more respect for what being the lapiloque really meant—and for the ancient gods we all assumed had faded from this world eons ago."

"Did he know he was the lapiloque? I mean, like when he first started having those powers. Did he know what he was supposed to be?" I shifted uncomfortably.

King Jace cast me another brief, appraising look. "No, I don't believe he did. And sometimes it seemed to scare him. It was a definite shock for the rest of us. We don't see much in the way of miracles in Maldobar, usually—not that we don't need them. Now more than ever, it seems."

"Oh."

"Jaevid tried keeping his abilities from everyone, even from the people who loved him—the people he should have been able to trust. I think that caused him a great deal more suffering. It seemed to haunt him." His eyes flickered away, back in the direction of the tree. "He didn't have a choice about what he went through, but he did have a choice about whether to go through it alone. He *chose* to be alone for most of it. And I doubt he would recommend that path to anyone else."

Somehow, I had a feeling King Jace and I weren't talking about Jaevid anymore. I looked down at the piece of stale bread in my hand and thought about that. Kiran knew about me—the things I could do that no one else did. He'd warned me ever since I was little *never* to tell anyone or show them what I could do. Now, things had begun to happen that I didn't even want to share with him because I was afraid. I was bottling it up, hiding it, just like Jaevid had. Maybe … that wasn't the right thing to do, after all.

What if someone needed me the way Maldobar needed Jaevid?

Aubren stayed silent as we journeyed back to Mau Kakuri. Not that I blamed him, really. I could only imagine what he was feeling. His features sagged in a somber, listless frown. His dark blue eyes panned aimlessly around us, as though he were still searching for a miracle.

It seemed the jungle was fresh out of miracles for now.

For some reason, the whole situation put a fire in my blood that refused to calm. It shouldn't have mattered. It didn't involve me, right? Why should I care what happened in Maldobar? Life in Luntharda was going on as usual.

And yet …

Fury blazed through my body and my jaw ached from grinding my teeth. To think that this Jaevid guy had made a promise like that—one he couldn't even keep. Seriously, why would he do that? He was the lapiloque, the spokesperson for the god of all wild things. People trusted what he said, probably more than anyone else. Why get their hopes up? Especially now, when things were so dire for Maldobar. It wasn't right.

Under the cover of night, we swooped low over the rooftops of the royal city on the backs of our shrikes. I'd never seen it from the air like this. The misty breeze was cool against my face. All the streams and little rivers that ran from the base of the falls all through the city shimmered in the moonlight. Colorful glass lanterns hung like globes of warm light in the dark, marking sloped bridges and city squares.

It was breathtaking, and yet my head still swam with anger as we landed on one of the palace's raised courtyards. There was a small party waiting to welcome us back. Among them, I saw the Queen dressed in billowing green robes. Her hopeful expression shattered into sympathy and sadness when she realized Jaevid wasn't with us.

Kiran was there, too. He was the only one smiling faintly as we touched down. I guess he was glad to see I hadn't been maimed, eaten, or chopped into a million pieces.

I climbed down off my shrike and started unfastening my gear from the saddle. I wasn't used to riding for so long, and my back was aching. Two long rides in a day was a lot even for a seasoned scout.

"I take it things didn't go well?" Kiran asked quietly as he stepped in to help me with my bag.

I shook my head. Out of the corner of my eye, I saw the King and Queen embrace and begin speaking quietly to one another. I suspected they were probably having a similar conversation.

"Well, I am glad to have you back home." Kiran patted my shoulder reassuringly. "I bet you're hungry."

"Gods, yes." I sighed.

Our group moved inside, and Aubren left with the King and Queen while Kiran and I were left to our own devices. We'd been given a big suite to use for the night that was prepared especially for us. There were two bedrooms, a bathroom, and sitting room all adorned with the finest things you could imagine—animal pelt rugs, polished white marble, silk sheets, feather pillows, and even a new change of clothes for both of us spread out on a table. I took my time soaking in a tub of warm water to wash the sweat and jungle grime off my skin. I'd been hoping it would help ease my temper, and yet that anger still simmered in my soul.

Afterwards, I changed into clean clothes and let Kiran twist my hair into a soggy red braid down my back. I couldn't braid it very well myself. My hair wasn't like a gray elf's—it was thicker, heavier, and coarse. Having it braided just made things easier and kept it from getting in my way.

"What did you think of the temple grounds?" he asked as he knotted off the end of my braid.

I shrugged and moved to put on my boots. "It felt like I didn't belong there."

"It feels that way to most everyone. That's why we have left it untouched. I suspect the lapiloque prefers that it isn't interfered with."

I clenched my hands. "Jaevid doesn't prefer anything. He's dead. And he's not coming back."

I caught a glimpse of his disapproving scowl.

"It's time to be realistic. Maldobar is in actual danger right now. We can't rely on someone's dying promise from forty years ago to do anything about it." I growled as I snatched up my kafki and belted them to my hips.

"Reigh, I would take the lapiloque's word over an army of a million men."

"Then you're an even bigger idiot than Aubren," I snapped.

"The way I see it, either he's a liar or a jerk— 'cause either he can't come back or he can but he's choosing not to. Either way, I'm not going to get sucked into believing something that obviously isn't true."

Kiran opened his mouth to argue, but I didn't give him the chance. I stormed out of the room and slammed the door behind me. My stomping footsteps echoed over the cavernous palace halls as I started looking for the dining hall. I was seeing red, not paying attention to where I was going.

"*We could help them*," a familiar voice hissed from the dark.

I felt the familiar chill of Noh's presence creep up my spine.

"*Death is our business. We are very good at death.*" He snickered.

I glanced sideways to where I could see his red, bog fire eyes flickering in the shadows. He prowled out of the gloom, materializing in his usual shape of a big black wolf with a grinning, toothy mouth.

"What are you saying? That I should go to Maldobar and let you kill Tibrans?" I narrowed my eyes at him.

Noh stalked around me in a circle. Every time his misty body brushed against me, I got another terrible chill. "*War is a game, my master. Victory goes to the best killer. And in that game, we are king.*"

I tried to think of a good reason to say no. I knew he wasn't saying this because he wanted to help Aubren or Maldobar. Noh wanted to kill. It's all he ever wanted. But it wasn't a bad idea.

"I have to know you'll obey me," I said. "Without question. Without hesitation."

Noh's smile widened. His smoky black form rippled with delight. "*Always, my master.*"

ELEVEN

Sitting in the royal dining hall, I looked down at the fancy arrangement of food on my plate and wished I felt like eating. It smelled wonderful, and I was starving. But I was so nervous I couldn't even think about it.

All around the long dining table, guests of the King and Queen sat on the floor with intricately stitched silk cushions as padding. Aubren and the rest of his men were wearing new gray elven clothes of colorful silk. They eyed the spread of food curiously, as though they weren't sure what most of it was or how they were supposed to eat it. They liked the sweet berry wine, though, and had no problem diving right into it.

Any other time, I would have been driving them nuts with questions about Maldobar. There was so much I wanted to know about it, the dragonriders, and what sorts of things they ate and drank there. But at the moment, I just wasn't in the mood.

Across the table, the mismatched gaze of Hecate was fixed on me like she was studying me—only, I knew she wasn't. She couldn't see me at all, so she must have been listening. I wondered if she could hear the way my heartbeat was racing or how my thoughts were running around in circles in my brain like a vortex.

Sitting beside her, Aubren was still staring vacantly down at the table. His brow was burrowed deeply and his entire demeanor was still somber. I guess he was probably trying to figure out what to do now that he'd run out of options to help his kingdom. He hadn't said a word yet, and was the only one of the humans at the table who wasn't on their third glass of wine.

Next to me, Kiran was still angry. I could tell because of the pulsing vein that was standing out in the side of his neck. I could practically taste his anger in the air. He wasn't finished with our argument, and I had a feeling he was already plotting out what he was going to say as soon as we were alone again.

The Queen's calm voice filled the tense silence. "As promised, I sent out a decree calling for any able scouts or warriors who were willing to go with you to Maldobar's defense to come right away."

Aubren looked hopeful for a second. "And?"

The Queen sighed. "As I feared, my people are reluctant to leave the jungle. It has been a long time since the end of the Gray War, and with your father's help we have rebuilt much, but our numbers are still miniscule. I can't go against the customs of my people. Our warriors, as you know, are all volunteers. It's their choice if they want to fight or not."

Aubren leaned forward, resting his elbows on the table and covering his face with his hands. "So not even one person volunteered?"

Queen Araxie placed a comforting hand on his arm. "Please don't despair. We will open our borders and have scouts waiting to help any refugees who wish to come here. And we will give you any weapons you might desire to take with you. Shrikes, too, if you wish."

Shrikes and weapons weren't going to help. Even I knew that. But Aubren forced an anguish-ridden smile and thanked her politely.

I took a deep breath. It was now or never. "I'd like to volunteer."

Everyone stopped eating and stared at me.

"W-with your blessing, of course, Your Majesty," I added quickly.

The King and Queen exchanged a glance. Beside me, Kiran's eyes looked like they might pop right out of their sockets. And Aubren, well, he just sat there with his mouth hanging open.

"We need to discuss this," Kiran began to object.

"There's nothing to discuss. I want to go. I want to help them fight the Tibrans."

"You're too young," he started to shout. "You've only been a scout for one day! And you've never fought in actual combat!"

"He's right," King Jace agreed. "Your bravery is admirable, Reigh, but you're just a boy."

I clenched my teeth against all the things I wanted to scream at them. Boy? I was a scout, wasn't I? Didn't that make me a man now? I had just as much right as anyone in Luntharda to volunteer.

"And it was just a boy who saved us from Hovrid and the wrath of Paligno's Curse," Queen Araxie spoke softly. Her color-changing eyes gleamed with memory as she studied me. "A boy ended the Gray War and saved the lives of millions around the world. Perhaps a boy can save Maldobar, too."

I sat back and blushed.

"I grant you my blessing," she said. "If it pleases Aubren, of course."

Aubren didn't answer right away. He was still gaping and glancing around at all the mixed expressions of approval and rage he was getting. Kiran gripped his dinner fork like a weapon, and King Jace glared at his wife like he'd just been betrayed.

"Very well, then." Aubren turned a grateful smile to me at last. "We'll leave in a few days, once my men can manage the journey. If you change your mind before then, it's all right. I would understand if you decided to stay here with your family."

That was just it, though, I wasn't leaving my family—I was setting out to find them.

Alone in our room, Kiran was eerily calm. It was really freaking me out. He took his time removing his boots, unfastening his formal leather jerkin and vambraces, and settling into a chair by the fireplace.

He took out his long bone pipe and began packing it with fragrant dried leaves. Having that long, slender pipe sticking out of the corner of his mouth made him seem even more the stoic old warrior. His stern, chiseled features were sharpened by the glow from the fire and the dancing of the flames reflected in his multihued eyes.

I didn't hang around until he was ready to give me the sever tongue-lashing I suspected was brewing. Retreating immediately to my own room, I hesitated in the doorway. Movement caught my attention.

There was a face looking in through my balcony window.

I clamped a hand over my mouth to keep from screaming like a scared little kid.

It was Enyo—curse her.

She put a finger over her mouth, gesturing for me to be quiet. Once I managed to collect my nerve, I shut my bedroom door and slipped quietly out onto the balcony to join her.

"You scared me to death. How did you find me? Geez, how did you even get up here?" I kept my voice down as I leaned over the edge of the balcony, sizing up the extreme climb she must have made. We were nine stories off the ground, at least.

With the soft, moist breezes from the falls billowing in her dark hair, Enyo suddenly threw her arms around me. "I'm so sorry, Reigh. I know you didn't want to see me anymore. But Kiran came to our house looking for you. He said you ran away. He was so upset; he thought I might know where you went. And then I heard about the human soldiers coming here, that you saved them somehow … "

I relaxed in her embrace. "It's okay, Enyo. I'm fine, really."

She squeezed me harder. "You're so stupid. I can't believe you ran away."

"I didn't think it was safe for me to stay here anymore. I don't want anyone else to get hurt. Especially you and Kiran."

She glared up at me. "You're my best friend. It doesn't matter what you can do—"

I covered her mouth with my hand. "Don't say that. You don't know what I can do."

Her eyes bored into mine. Slowly, I took my hand away from her mouth and found her frowning hard.

"You don't trust me?" she asked.

"It's not that."

"Then what? I thought we could tell each other anything."

"You don't understand; it's not that simple."

Enyo crossed her arms and cocked her chin up challengingly. "Just because I haven't gone through the change yet doesn't mean I'm dumb, you know. You don't have to treat me like some insignificant little child."

"I know."

"So, what is it then? What are you so afraid of?"

I shut my eyes tightly and turned away. "I'm not like you. I'm not like anyone else, okay? I can ... feel death."

"What?"

"I don't know how to describe it. If someone is about to die, or if someone has died, I just know. I can sense it. Sometimes, I can even see it, like their life is a bright spot that's wavering and going dark. It's been that way ever since I was little. That's why

Kiran wants me to work with him at the clinic all the time—you know, not just because he wants to keep an eye on me. It's also because I can tell which of the patients are going to make it and which ones won't. And sometimes, if I lose my temper, bad things happen."

"What kind of bad things?" Her voice was softer, as though she were afraid someone might hear us.

I didn't want to tell her. I didn't want anyone to know because, honestly, there were a few things that not even Kiran knew about. But before I could stop it, the truth came pouring out of me like a spewing geyser.

I sat down on the edge of the balcony with her, our legs threaded through the railing and watched the falls pouring endlessly over the rocks below as I told her as much as I dared about my dark friend who liked to lurk in the shadows.

"So that creature, the one that looked like you, he's some kind of bad spirit?" she guessed.

"I guess. It's hard to say. Noh calls me master and follows me everywhere. I've been seeing him since I was a toddler. Kiran suspects he's been with me since I was born, haunting me all the time. Until recently, no one else could see him. And he's never looked like me before. Usually, he just appears like a black wolf."

"Do you think he's the reason you can feel death?"

I shrugged. "I don't know."

"So that time in the jungle, when the stag was going to kill us, you set Noh loose?" Enyo's gaze caught mine. "He was the one who saved us?"

I nodded.

"And you can control him?"

"Most of the time, yes. But lately, I dunno, it's like he's getting stronger. He appears more often. He thinks we should go to Maldobar and fight the Tibrans."

Her brows snapped together instantly. "What?"

"I already volunteered. I'm going back to Maldobar with Prince Aubren."

"You can't. You'll be killed!"

"Enyo—"

"No! Reigh, do you even hear yourself? Is it even you that wants to go, or is it just Noh? How do you know he's not manipulating you?"

"Because if I don't, Maldobar is going to be destroyed. Prince Aubren said it himself. That's the whole reason he came here. They don't stand a chance against the Tibrans. They came here to beg for help because otherwise, their whole kingdom will fall. We even went to the old temple to ask Jaevid."

Her eyes grew wide. "You *what*?"

"Yeah. Aubren went to ask him to keep his promise to help Maldobar. And you know what happened? Nothing!"

Enyo shrank back, her face clouding over with anger. "T-that's not how it's supposed to work. He said when we needed him, he would return."

"Just give it up already. He lied! He isn't coming back. So, someone has to help Maldobar before it's too late." I growled as I started to get up. "And I guess it's going to be me."

Enyo grabbed onto my sleeve. "And if it goes wrong? If you can't control Noh anymore? What then?"

I lost my steam and stopped, scrunching up my mouth while I tried to think of a good comeback.

"I'm not saying you won't be able to help. Maybe you're right. Maybe you can destroy all the Tibrans," she whispered. "But what if you can't stop there? What if Noh destroys what's left of Maldobar in the process?"

I swallowed hard. When I looked back at her, Enyo's bright eyes were gazing up at me earnestly. I got a weird feeling, seeing her that way. The weird kind of feeling you shouldn't have about a girl who's only supposed to be your best friend.

"I'm sorry, Enyo. All those things I said before—that I couldn't stand you—they weren't true. I hate this. I hate being a monster."

Sadness clouded her face and she let my sleeve slip out of her grasp. "You're not a monster, Reigh."

I tried to smile. "Guess we'll find out, won't we?"

She looked at me bleakly, her chin trembling. I could tell she was trying to keep it in. Silly girl, she always tried putting up a courageous front. I took her chin and turned her a little so I could kiss her cheek.

When I leaned away, her face had turned bright pink.

"Better not try following me. I mean it," I warned.

She opened her mouth, but no sound came out.

I went back inside, locking the balcony door and closing the drapes. I knew she could find her way back down. She was crafty, and a much better climber than I was—obviously. There's no way I would have even tried scaling the side of the palace like that.

Dang. I was going to miss her.

TWELVE

There are a lot of scary things in Luntharda—but nothing ever frightened me as much as Kiran did when he was angry.

He hadn't spoken to me for two whole days. Not a word. Not a cough. Not a sneeze. Not even a whistle. It was like I might as well have been invisible. And while before I would have been okay with having some space, the fact that I was about to leave my whole world behind to go to Maldobar and fight in a war made his silence beyond terrifying.

We left the palace long enough to go home so I could pack my things and say my goodbyes. The Queen had given me a new full set of scouts' robes all made from the finest materials in varying shades of black, royal blue, and emerald green.

The morning we were supposed to leave for Maldobar, I put them on piece by piece, taking the time to admire myself in the mirror before I strutted out into our living room. I was hoping Kiran would say something—I would have even been glad for an insult at that point. Just something so I'd know he was aware I was still alive.

But he didn't even look up as I walked past.

I pretended to rummage around in our pantry for something to eat, and then peeked back around the corner to watch him. He was just sitting there, on his favorite cushion, puffing away at his pipe and flipping through one of the thick medical journals he'd brought with him from Maldobar years ago. The pages were as yellow as dying leaves and crinkled whenever he turned them.

I cleared my throat, then quickly ducked away to see if he would look.

He didn't.

I tried it again.

No response.

My frustration mounting, I narrowed my eyes and briefly entertained the idea of hurling a loaf of bread at him. Then I noticed what he was wearing.

Kiran was dressed in his scout's clothes.

"Father?" I used the forbidden word as I emerged from the pantry.

At last, his gaze raised and met mine.

"Can we talk?" I tried my best not to sound like a scared little kid.

The resigned way Kiran took his pipe out of his mouth and

let out a heavy sigh told me I'd failed in that. He gestured to the seat next to him. "Come on, then."

I crept across the room and quickly sat down.

"Reigh," he began, "I need to apologize to you."

Okay, now I was *really* scared.

"I shouldn't have been so quick to argue against your desire to go to Maldobar. I suppose it's natural you would want to help your kinsmen or to find your parents. And while I do fear for your safety, I'm not within my right to forbid you from going. As I said before, being a scout now makes you a man, and that means you are free to make your own choices."

I tried to swallow without choking.

"But you need to understand, that also means you will have to endure the consequences of those choices—which may very well be something I won't be able to save you from."

"I understand," I rasped. This wasn't at all the verbal smack down I'd been expecting.

"I've volunteered to go with you as far as the border, to help guide you and the rest of the soldiers there as safely as possible. But once we reach that boundary, we will have to say our goodbyes." Kiran looked at me squarely.

I chewed on the inside of my cheek, wondering why he was saying all this now and why he'd been so silent the past few days.

"What is it you wanted to talk to me about?"

I couldn't remember for a moment. Once again, I was wondering if Kiran knew who my parents were. If he did, then why wouldn't he tell me? What was he hiding?

My gaze wandered down to my boots. I sat, fiddling with the buckles, and tried to explain. "I'm sorry, too, for running away. And for volunteering for this without talking to you about it first. I keep disappointing you. I shouldn't have said those things about Jaevid. I know you knew him, and that he was your friend. I just got so frustrated."

"I've had my share of doubts over the years. Don't think for a moment I haven't. You're right; I did know Jaevid. Just because we think we need him so desperately now doesn't mean we genuinely do. Maybe he can see things we can't, opportunities for hope we don't yet know about. That's what I choose to believe, anyway." Kiran sighed again, more deeply this time. "As for running away, I'm only disappointed that you decided your only option was to leave rather than trying to talk to me about it. I had no idea you felt things were so bad."

I hung my head. "I just didn't know what else to do."

"Reigh, I don't expect you to be perfect. I'm certainly not. And even if you feel you can't talk to anyone, I hope you will always know you can talk to me about anything. I may not be your father, but I could not love you more if you were my son."

I had to change the subject. Kiran was being unusually open and it was beginning to terrify me worse than the silence.

"I feel bad for Aubren," I murmured. "He came here looking for a hero."

Kiran's mouth curled into a smirk. "I suppose he'll have to settle for you."

I smirked back. "Right. Never send a hero to do a monster's job."

The sun wasn't even up, but we were ready go.

The Queen had given Aubren and his men new gray elf styled weapons and armor, and even lent us some of her fastest shrikes—which none of the soldiers, including Aubren, were very thrilled about—to get us to the border faster. We also had enough food and water to get us through the journey. Kiran was in the lead, riding alone so that he could guide us on the safest path. I was next in line, Aubren clinging to my back like a scared kitten. He had a death grip on my shoulders even before we took off. According to Kiran, I was in charge of making sure he didn't die before we got him back to Maldobar. That included falling off the saddle, getting eaten by something, or wandering off and getting lost.

Human princes were turning out to be a lot of trouble.

The rest of our party rode behind us, doubling up with other scouts or attempting to ride on their own. We kept a close eye on them to make sure they could handle it. Riding a shrike isn't easy, even if you're lucky to get one of the more docile ones.

As the dawn began to break, Kiran gave me a nod and gestured skyward. It was time to take off. I sank down into the leather-crafted saddle and patted my shrike's scaly, shimmering neck. The creature snapped his jaws, hissing and fluttering his translucent wings with eagerness. All six of his muscular legs flexed, his long tail swished, and in a flurry, we took off into the jungle.

Aubren only screamed for a few minutes, which for him was progress. I tried to get him to focus on what was ahead instead of the deadly, thirty-story drop from the trees.

Kiran pushed us hard. We didn't stop until late in the afternoon to let the shrikes rest while we got a bite to eat and something to drink. The soldiers wobbled around like newborn fawns after riding for so long. Their legs weren't used to it. Mine weren't either, but I tried not to waddle even though my legs and calves were cramping like crazy. Rule number one of being a scout was you had to look cool. Okay, so maybe that wasn't an *official* rule. But it was certainly a given.

It hurt worse when we got underway again. I was sure I was going to have bruises where Aubren was gripping my shoulders the whole time. I guess he didn't remember that I had been gnawed on by a snagwolf a few days ago. Even with the herbal remedies helping my wound heal faster, my shoulder was still tender—especially with a grown man wrenching on it.

Needless to say, late that night when Kiran finally gave us the signal to stop, I was beyond ready for a break. I waited until Aubren had dismounted and was off helping his own men get settled onto the broad, lofty branch where we were going to make camp before I staggered down off my shrike's back. The animal grumbled and shook himself, flicking me an irritated flare with vivid, glowing green eyes.

"Tell me about it," I muttered back as I rubbed my sore

shoulder. "And we have to do it again tomorrow."

Dinner was meager. While we'd brought along enough rations for everyone, dried meat, roasted nuts, stale bread, and some sundried fruit wasn't the appetizing spread I wanted. Still, it filled the gnawing emptiness in my gut.

The limb we were camping on was about twenty feet wide and had a nice flat area for everyone to sit and get comfortable. It was plenty of room, even for a group our size, and far above the dangerous jungle floor. Kiran spread out his bedroll next to mine, and then drew straws for who would stay up for first watch. It was safest to do it in pairs, just to make sure no one accidentally nodded off on the job.

Aubren and I drew the short straws.

Everyone settled in for the night. Men curled up on their bedrolls, or propped themselves up on their bags, and passed around a wineskin filled with strong berry liqueur. Soon, the soft sawing of snores filled the cool night air. Even Kiran was wheezing quietly, stretched out on his side with his arms folded and his favorite curved dagger within reach.

Aubren and I sat down on the edge of the limb. It was so dark we couldn't see the jungle floor. I guess that's why the height didn't seem to bother him so much—that, or he was just too tired to care.

All around us, Luntharda was making a harmony of night sounds. Frogs and nocturnal birds made eerie calls through the network of vines and plants that clung to the sides of the trees. Fireflies lit up the gloom with spots of colored light in pink, green, and blue. In the distance, I heard snagwolves yipping to each other. They were on the hunt for an easy meal.

"This place is terrifying," Aubren said suddenly, keeping his voice down so as not to wake the others. "But it is undeniably beautiful."

"I guess Maldobar is different?"

"Very much so." He nodded in agreement, and then glanced at me with a curious arch in his brow. "You've really never seen it?"

I fiddled with the sheath of one of my kafki blades. "No. At least, not that I remember. Kiran said there aren't any trees like ours, that most of the land is open and flat, or with small rolling hills covered in grass. He said there are mountains like heaps of rock so tall they scrape the sky."

"Well, he's not wrong. It is beautiful, too, but in a much different way," he replied. There was a subtle, sad smile on his face. "I didn't thank you before, but I am grateful."

"For what?"

"For volunteering to come back to Maldobar with us. You have courage beyond your years," he said quietly.

"Don't thank me yet. I'm not sure if I can really help you or not."

His smile widened, although there was a hazed darkness in his eyes. "If you fight as well as you did against those wolf-creatures, I suspect you'll do just fine."

"Maybe. Kiran was right, though. I've never fought in a real battle before. I've never even fought against another person. Not for real, anyway. I've sparred plenty of times but it doesn't count when the other person isn't trying to kill you."

"No, I suppose it doesn't."

"Anyway, I don't know how useful I'll actually be. I'll try, though." I sat back, leaning my weight against my hands and watching the eerie stillness of the canopy overhead. No wind got through, so not a single leaf rustled. I cleared my throat. "So … you're engaged to Princess Hecate?"

He swallowed. "Yes. Well, actually, I was engaged to her three elder cousins, first. Not all at the same time, of course. My father negotiated a marriage for me with a princess from Luntharda. I suspect this was to further strengthen our alliance. But one by one they all met a premature death."

"I remember that—when the last one died, that is. No one ever said what happened, but there were rumors about an illness. The whole city was in mourning after. That must have been five years ago."

Through the gloom of the night, I could just make out the sorrow on his face. "I'd never met Hecate before this," he spoke quietly. "Maybe it's selfish, but I tried not to talk to her at all. I've never written to her or asked to visit."

"Why not? She's nice." I rubbed the back of my neck. "And just for the record, the whole hand-holding thing wasn't a big deal. We're not … you know."

"No, it's not that. I suppose I'm a coward. I met the last three princesses, her cousins that I was supposed to marry before. They were all kind, lovely women, too." He let out a slow, despairing breath. "Hearing that they had died was terrible. Knowing them before hand, even liking them a little, made it all the worse. I suppose I just don't want to go through that again. I don't want to get my hopes up."

I wasn't sure what to say to that.

"Besides, what must she think of me? I'm a hand-me-down fiancée, more than fifteen years older than her. We were never supposed to be together." He leaned forward and rubbed his brow. "Our father made it no mystery that while I am the older sibling, it will be Jenna who eventually wears the crown. She is his chosen heir, not me. Even my own father has found me lacking. And then I had to humiliate myself in front of Hecate's grandparents, begging for help to save my kingdom. Not exactly the best of first impressions."

"Don't worry too much about it." I patted him on the shoulder. "Besides, you don't look *that* old."

Aubren chuckled. "I was surprised to learn Kiran had adopted you."

"Really? Why?"

"He served my father as an ambassador and advisor for a long time when I was younger. But once I was old enough to stand and hold a blade, my father urged him to teach me to fight. Kiran tried, but insisted to my father I didn't have a fighting spirit." He rubbed the dark stubble on his chin thoughtfully. "I realize in the gray elf culture, that's not such a bad thing. Men can be other things besides warriors and scouts. It's not quite the same in Maldobar—not for princes, anyhow. I may not be destined to wear the crown, but I am expected to be able to fight to defend it."

"You're not that bad with a blade," I said. "You held your own against the snagwolves. That's not easy."

Aubren shrugged. "I can fight, and I did learn. But I think

what Kiran meant and what my father didn't understand, was that while I could wield a blade with competence, I have no taste for violence and no love for the glory of battle. I much prefer diplomatic solutions, which aren't always popular when your kingdom is known for being a source of great military brute strength. Most likely another reason I wasn't my father's first choice as heir."

"Yeah. I guess I can see that."

"Now my sister, on the other hand, she's a lot more like my father. You remind me a bit of her, too. She's fierce, driven, fearless, and as stubborn as an old mule. She soaked up Kiran's teachings like a sponge, and it wasn't surprising to any of us— except my father—that she wanted to be a dragonrider like he had been. He was appalled. To this day, I'm not sure he approves. But trying to stand against her is like trying to tame a hurricane."

"But you said she was one, right? A dragonrider?" I studied him. The idea of dragonriders had always intrigued me. I just assumed all human soldiers could ride them. After all, plenty of gray elf women were warriors, scouts, and could ride on shrikes if they wanted.

"After years of begging and tumultuous arguments, he finally agreed to let her go to Blybrig Academy to learn to be a dragonrider. She was the first female student to attend. And on her first day, she had broken three boys' noses and sent one to the infirmary with a broken jaw."

"Bravo." I laughed quietly.

Aubren was smiling. I could see his eyes glinting with

satisfaction. "Indeed. My father had warned her that the other students wouldn't like that she was there. I think maybe he was hoping she would be discouraged and would come home. But that stubbornness of hers knows no bounds."

"So, what about you? Where will you go now?"

He let out another unsteady breath. That spark of joy in his eyes snuffed out by worry. "I suppose I will try to find my sister. I don't know how many riders she still has fighting for her. Perhaps together we can work out some sort of a plan to collect what remains of our forces and make a final stand against Argonox before he can overrun another one of our cities. Apart from that … "

His voice faded before he finished. He didn't have to, though. I could read the defeat in every corner of his expression. Getting help from the Queen of Luntharda had been his Plan A. Plan B was trying to resurrect Jaevid. So now he was on Plan C with not much hope and a limited amount of alphabet left to work with.

"We'll figure something out." I tried to sound encouraging.

He forced another smile for my benefit. "Yes, one way or another."

"So why did it surprise you that Kiran took me in?" I asked.

"Oh, because when I was young he never seemed very comfortable around children, especially young ones. I remember when my sister was an infant, he held her like she might be explosive. She threw up right down the front of his shirt. It was funny to watch. I suppose those nurturing instincts didn't come naturally to him then. He must have changed a lot to go from being intimidated by merely holding an infant to charging headlong into single parenthood."

The idea of Kiran being covered in baby vomit made me smirk. I wondered if I'd ever done anything like that when I was a baby. "Yeah. I guess I broke him in pretty good."

"It's a shame he never married. I suppose losing Holly was more than he could bear."

"Holly? She's the one you thought was my mom, right?" I probed. "Kiran said she wasn't."

Aubren's mouth tensed, quirking downward as though maybe he wasn't so sure about that. "Well, her hair was red, like yours. She ran a medical clinic in the royal city, and was very talented with healing and tending wounds. Somehow their paths crossed during the war. He never said it around me, but I think he loved her quite a lot."

I could tell by his tone that this story wasn't going to have a happy ending. "What happened to her? Why didn't they just get married?"

"I don't know," he replied quietly. "She died young, or so I heard. I don't think she ever married, either."

I glanced over my shoulder to where Kiran was lying. Somehow, he was able to scowl even in his sleep. "I used to wonder why he never had a wife. I just assumed it was because of me."

"Love is a complicated and powerful force," Aubren said. "It can either sustain or destroy you. Sometimes both … even at the same time."

THIRTEEN

"*Wake up.*"

The sound of whispering woke me up suddenly. I squinted angrily through the dark at the bedroll next to mine where Kiran snored faintly.

Chills swept over my body, rattling me and instantly made my pulse race. It wasn't Kiran.

"*Something is coming.*"

I snapped to my feet, snatching up my kafki and startling a few of the soldiers awake. The two who were keeping watch turned around to stare at me with bewilderment.

"What's going on?" Kiran slurred drowsily as he sat up.

"Shh!" I commanded, freezing in place as I slowly surveyed the area around us. The jungle was dark, calm, and silent—nothing out of the ordinary.

"*It's close.*"

My body got another jolting chill. This was new. Noh was always there, hiding in the shadows and in the back of my mind, but he'd never given me a warning like this.

Just in case, I drew both of my kafki and sank into a fighting stance, my eyes still keen on the jungle around us.

When Kiran saw me get ready, he jumped to his feet, drew his bow, and nocked an arrow. "What is it, Reigh?"

"I'm not sure yet." Around me, the noise of soldiers getting up and rummaging around was making it hard to focus.

"*Close, very close.*"

I shut my eyes tightly.

Then I felt it—like a white-hot splinter in my mind. A source of hostility. A threat.

I opened my eyes and whirled around, just in time to see a monster burst out of the foliage and onto the branch. Our shrikes let out feral screeches of alarm and took off in a flurry.

The huge beast lumbered forward on four long, two-toed legs with wicked black talons the length of my forearm. Its green and black scaly body rippled with muscle, and its long whip-like tail lashed in the air with a deafening popping sound.

"It's a surtek!" Kiran shouted to the rest of the scouts. "Aim for the mouth!"

Arrows started to fly. Men shouted.

The monster reared up and let out a furious battle screech. Its eyes were tiny, and its mouth wasn't all that big either. Inside it were rows of tiny jagged teeth.

But it was the pincers you had to worry about.

On either side of its flat, scaly green jaws were huge pincers like horns. They had rows of points inside them like the teeth of a saw, and they snapped together angrily as arrows zipped past its head and bounced off its thick hide.

"Fall back! Form ranks!" Aubren shouted at his men.

Kiran grabbed the back of my tunic and started dragging me backwards away from the creature. He was screaming in elven, barking commands to the scouts who were still firing arrows as quickly as they could.

I looked back, just as the surtek snapped its tail again.

It wrapped around the leg of one of the men and dragged him in closer. Those deadly pincers got him, squeezing him in a death grip. Then came the shock—a burst of electricity stronger than a bolt of lightning. You could feel it in the air, a deadly surge of current meant to kill.

I didn't want to see. But I knew even if I shut my eyes and covered my ears, it wouldn't help. I felt the soldier's soul leave his body like a tearing sensation straight through my chest. It sent another cold wave of shivers through me.

We couldn't win. We couldn't outrun it. More people were going to die. Someone had to do something.

I had to do something.

I ripped away from Kiran's hold on my shirt.

"Reigh! No!" He reached for me again, missing by inches.

I charged straight for the surtek, my blades raised to strike.

The surtek screeched and lashed its tail in my direction. I could hear the crack of the whiplash and felt it close around my legs. Instantly, I skidded to a halt and took a swing—slicing off its end.

The monster roared in pain and fury. I kicked away the

dead end of its tail and dodged as it snapped those pincers mere inches from my face. I could practically taste the electrical current popping across my tongue.

It moved like a blur, lunging, snapping, while trying to flog me with the now bloody stump that was its tail.

I tried to keep up. I dodged and rolled, springing out of the way of every strike.

Suddenly one lucky swing from that tail-stump struck me right across the chest. I went flying end-over-end like a ragdoll over the edge of the branch. I lost my grip on my blades as the wind rushed past me. I was falling—plummeting. Leaves and vines scraped my face. I could have sworn I heard Kiran shouting my name.

Then, the wind was knocked out of me as I hit another branch. I coughed as spots swirled in my vision.

I was lying flat on my back, staring up at the branch overhead where I'd been just a few seconds before.

The surtek was coming straight for me. Using those long talons, the beast scaled down the tree and sprang, pincers open wide.

I clamored to my feet, glaring up at the monster with my teeth bared. No more games. I'd tried it Kiran's way. Time to try things *my* way.

"One blast," I whispered. "That's it. No one else dies. Got it?"

Noh's sinister laugh rang out, and I couldn't tell if it was real or just in my head.

The surtek gripped me in its pincers, ripping me right off my feet and into the air again. Its gaping maw was directly below me, ready to swallow me whole once I'd been shocked to death.

I squeezed my eyes shut. My hands curled into fists. I felt cold—horrible, hopeless cold overtake me. It surged through my veins, and made every muscle in my body go rigid.

I threw my head back and yelled. The surtek's pincers began to turn black. The animal screamed in panic as the blackness spread quickly, engulfing its body, and sticking like tar. There was no escaping it.

I snarled at the beast and grabbed the pincers, pouring every ounce of my will into a blast of my power.

With one last pitiful shriek, the surtek's body suddenly went stiff. It froze in place, still holding me aloft in its pincers. Then it began to shrivel up. Its body warped and shrank like a sun-dried grape, leaving nothing but bones and a big mummified corpse.

The fragile, skeletal body of the surtek couldn't support my weight. I hit the ground again and landed on my rear end. Looking up, I watched as the rest of the corpse began to crumble into a heap of black ash.

"You lose," I whispered.

It was the first time using my power hadn't rendered me unconscious. Every time before that, letting him off the chain was costly and something I didn't dare do except as a last resort. It left me drained and useless, usually unconscious for a few hours. But as I staggered away from the surtek's remains, I could tell something was different. My head swam, my vision spotted a little, but I didn't pass out.

This dark power within me—Noh's power—was getting stronger.

As I climbed back over the edge of the limb where Kiran, Aubren, and the rest of our companions were waiting, I could read the telltale signs of fear on every single one of their faces. Even Kiran was looking me over with a deep furrow in his brow. He was the first to speak up as I stumbled toward them, tripping over someone's abandoned bedroll.

"Are you all right?"

I stooped to pick up my weapons and slipped them one at a time back into their sheaths at my hips. "Fine."

Kiran grabbed my shoulder firmly, forcing me to stop and look at him. "I'm serious. Are you okay?"

That's when I realized he wasn't asking about my physical health; he wanted to know if Noh was still around.

I looked away, briefly catching a few apprehensive stares from the rest of our group. "I'm fine. So long as no one starts gathering pitchforks and lighting torches."

His jawline relaxed and he let go of my shoulder. "Try not to take it personally."

I stole a quick look at Aubren to see if he was as pasty looking and terrified as the rest of his men. Of them all, he was the only one studying me as though he were trying to figure me out. Good luck with that, buddy.

Under Kiran's stern instructions, everyone got busy packing

up our belongings so we could be on the move before the sun came up. I helped four of the scouts round up our shrikes, which had fled to other trees to watch us get eaten alive. Like I said, they aren't inherently loyal creatures. Sometimes I wondered if they had much of a brain at all.

By the time we got back, everyone had calmed down and was ready to go. Aubren didn't say much as I helped him climb onto our shrike's back, and part of me wondered if he was having second thoughts about letting me tag along with him to Maldobar. Then again, he might have just been upset about losing another one of his men. Either way, he must have been distracted because he didn't scream when we took off this time, although he was still gripping me hard enough I'd have more bruises to show for it.

We rode hard all day and the next, stopping overnight again to let the shrikes rest. This time, we put four people on night watch shifts instead of just two. Kiran was insistent we keep the noise down and not use any more torches than was necessary to get everyone settled in. The less noise and light we made the better.

I noticed that everyone except Kiran was making a wide berth around me now. The soldiers watched me from a distance, their eyes wide and haunted. The other scouts had never been very buddy-buddy with me before, and now they were even less willing to sit and talk to me. Even Aubren didn't have much to say, although I wasn't sure if it was because of what I'd done or because we were getting closer to his kingdom.

It was late on the fourth day when I noticed the light was changing. It was brighter somehow, and the air felt cooler and much less heavy with humidity. We were getting close to the border.

We passed markers carved into the trees, symbols that reminded us of the boundary line ahead. Some of the marks looked very old and warned about the dangers of dragonrider patrols. Those marks, Kiran told me, had been put there during the Gray War.

I don't know what I was expecting to see when we got to the boundary line. After all, I'd heard others talk about it before. Some of them made it sound horrifying. Others made it sound beautiful. To me it just seemed abrupt.

One minute we were in the thick of the jungle, surrounded by the familiarity of the giant trees and overwhelming tapestry of plant life. The next, I was standing on a limb, staring at a landscape that was unlike anything I had ever laid eyes on before. Vast rolling plains covered in snow rippled like a clean white blanket in every direction until they were interrupted to my right by mountains of gray stone with peaks crowned with white. Before me and to my left were more of the rolling plains as far as my eyes could see.

The wind moved fast over the flat land, and it was frigid— which was a totally alien feeling. I'd never seen snow, never smelled frost.

"Look there," one of the soldiers called to the rest of us. He was pointing to a small black smudge on the horizon off to our left. "Northwatch still burns."

Aubren's eyes flickered darkly. "We must assume the Tibran forces are still there, which puts us well within their striking distance. We will have to tread carefully."

"It would be safer to wait for the cover of darkness to move in the open," Kiran agreed. "You plan to make for Barrowton?"

"Yes." He nodded grimly. "But we can't linger there for long. We will press on into the mountains and try to make our way to Westwatch."

"That's a very long journey, Aubren, even with shrikes. They won't do well in the cold, either."

"Couldn't we get dragonriders to take us?" I suggested.

"Perhaps. But it might take a few days for them to reach us. There aren't any dragonriders housed in Barrowton. Usually, they're all kept at the Four Watches. Although my father has now recalled all of them to Halfax—except for those who defected and followed my sister. I'll have to dispatch a messenger to summon them." Aubren rubbed his chin, which was now sporting the beginnings of a beard. That and the dark, sagging circles under his eyes made him seem much older. "But dragonriders will undoubtedly draw the Tibrans' attention. Not to mention any time we spend in Barrowton will already be borrowed. I'm sure the city is attempting to prepare for a Tibran attack."

"You're short on alternative options," Kiran muttered. "And shorter on time if these Tibrans move as fast as you say."

Aubren's gaze locked onto him and there was confidence glowing in his eyes. "Then it's good we have a secret weapon on our side."

At dusk, everyone gathered to say our goodbyes. Some of the soldiers had made friends with our scouts, particularly the females. The men stared at them with mystification, like they'd never seen anything female before. And while the female scouts seemed to like the attention, I never saw any of them reciprocate the interest.

Kiran kept his farewells to Aubren brief. They both wore similarly somber expressions and exchanged quiet conversation, pointing to this and that and occasionally me.

At last, Kiran came over. "Are you ready?"

"Yeah," I lied, pretending to check the saddle on my shrike.

"Aubren will be counting on your instincts and skills. It's important, Reigh. Remember what I've taught you."

I nodded as I avoided his gaze. I didn't like goodbyes, and this one really sucked. There was a lot I wanted to say, but every time I thought I'd found the right words my throat seized up and I couldn't do anything but clench my teeth and look away.

Kiran's eyes steeled and his jaw went tense. Suddenly, he wrapped a hand around the back of my head and yanked me into a stiff hug. "You know that you are always welcome to come back home to me, boy."

"I know," I said.

"Keep them safe."

"I'll try."

Kiran reluctantly let me go and gave my shoulder an awkward, gruff pat. Then he looked at Aubren. Neither of them spoke, but I could sense an understanding pass between them as they stood apart, their expressions a mirrored image of grim resolution.

"You'll take these shrikes and make for Barrowton. Release them there and they will return to Luntharda," Kiran spoke at last. "May the favor of the gods go with you, Aubren. If I were a younger man, I most certainly would."

Aubren's smile was bleak. "I know. And if I didn't already owe you so much, I might ask you to go in spite."

Kiran closed his eyes.

The atmosphere was tense as the soldiers, Aubren, and I climbed aboard our shrikes and prepared to leave. The sun had disappeared behind the mountains, turning the snowdrifts orange and then red as blood. I tried to concentrate, to keep my focus on what we were about to do.

But I couldn't stop staring up at the sky as night closed in.

Stars, thousands and thousands of them, sparkled overhead. I'd never seen so many. And as the moon rose, it seemed so close I might be able to reach out and pluck it from the air.

Then Aubren, who was sitting behind me sharing my shrike once again, gave a whistle. It was time. My heart dropped into my stomach. I looked around for Kiran, having second thoughts. I was making a mistake—I was leaving behind the only home I'd ever known.

When I spotted him, standing at the back of the company of scouts who were waving farewell to us, I felt like I was going to be sick. He didn't look happy, or proud, or satisfied. He was looking back at me with his mouth set in a hard line and his forehead crinkled with worry.

That was the last glance at him I got. With a fierce burst of wind off the wings of our shrikes, we took to the open air.

The safety and cover of Luntharda was gone. There were no trees to shield us, no dangerous jungle to deter our enemies. Nothing but the cold, empty air lay between us and a small point of light on the horizon—the city they called Barrowton.

FOURTEEN

It was a sprint. The shrikes didn't like the cold air any more than they liked being out of the cover of the jungle. They hissed and chirped, complaining to one another and flocking close together as we zipped through the air. I wasn't exactly thrilled, either.

My first impression of Maldobar? I seriously needed some warmer clothes as soon as possible. My hands were going numb, and the blistering wind made my eyes water and my nose and cheeks feel raw.

Below, the landscape shimmered under the moonlight. The snow-covered hills rippled; rising and falling like wrinkles in a white blanket. It was beautiful, and strangely haunting. So much blank white emptiness was bizarre.

All of a sudden, a hard, violent chill bolted up my spine.

This wasn't from the cold. I sat up, heartbeat pounding in my eardrums as I looked around for Noh. I didn't see him.

But I heard him.

"*They're coming.*"

I twisted in the saddle, scanning all around. But there was nothing—no sign of anyone or anything for miles in every direction. "Who is? I don't see anything," I shouted over the wind.

Aubren was staring at me with eyes as wide as moons, like I was out of my mind. I guess he couldn't hear Noh.

"*Below. Underneath,*" he growled in my mind.

I shut my eyes tight and tried to feel if there were any other living spirits around us. Panic blurred my concentration and jumbled my thoughts.

Then behind us, someone shouted.

Aubren and I both turned, looking back as two of our comrades disappeared—snatched right out of the air by massive flying nets.

Far below, big trapdoors were popping up out of the hillsides everywhere. One second it was flat snowy ground and the next a dozen hidden panels flew open, throwing snow in the air, and revealing a strange wooden contraption that fired nets made of thick metal wire. The nets howled through the air at blistering speed and snagged two, three shrikes at a time, twisting around their wings and dragging them back to the earth.

"Spread out!" Aubren yelled right in my ear. "Fall back to the jungle!"

But it was too late.

All around us, our comrades were netted, one right after the other. The shrikes were in a frenzy of terror. I could hear the men screaming as they fell. Below, soldiers in weird bronze-colored armor were pouring out of the trapdoors like angry ants from an anthill.

Suddenly, we were the only ones left in the air. In wild desperation, our shrike did a quick twist and tried to make a break back to the boundary of the jungle. We were picking up speed, the wind moving with us.

Then the hillside directly in front of us exploded. Five trapdoors hidden under the snow opened with those net-throwers aimed right for us. I caught a glimpse of Aubren wrenching a golden signet ring off one of his fingers and throwing it away as hard as he could about two seconds before I saw a net hurling straight toward us.

I woke up lying on my back, the metal net mashing my face. I couldn't move. All I could do was look around at the unfamiliar faces that marched by. They were dressed in bronze suits of armor with a snarling lion's head engraved across the chest, and wore dark crimson cloaks and helmets crowned with a short mohawk of white hair.

Tibrans.

They were carefully removing the nets, working together to capture everyone who had survived hitting the frozen ground—including our shrikes. They tied the shrikes' wings down, strapped their jaws shut, and dragged them away one by one. The Maldobarian soldiers didn't get any special treatment. I watched them struggle and try to escape. But eventually everyone was caught and chained up as well.

A sneering face eclipsed my view.

It was a woman—at least, I *thought* it looked sort of like a woman. It was hard to tell past the black tribal tattoos that swirled around the left side of her face, her wide jawline, and the way her hair had been cut so that it was nearly down to her scalp. Her nose was crooked like maybe someone had broken it once or twice. She glowered down at me, her dark eyes studying me through the net.

"This one's alive," she rasped the human language in a gravelly, deep voice. "What about the other one?"

"Unconscious," someone answered. "But alive."

She leaned away, her eyes narrowing into black, calculative slits. "Very clever of them to abandon their human armor for these fancy savage scraps. It will make it more difficult to identify which one is the prince. But we have other means of discerning that. Strip them of their weapons and bring them to the interrogation chamber. Then I want these hatches recovered immediately." Her mouth curled into a menacing grin of excitement, as though the idea of getting to torture someone was a thrill.

"Mistress Hilleddi!" Someone shouted for her and she

went striding away, her hand resting on the massive, double axe that was hanging from a leather belt strung across her hips. She was wearing similar bronze armor as the rest of the Tibran soldiers around her, except hers had been modified. Instead of a breastplate, she wore something like a bronze bra. The shoulder pauldrons had long spikes sticking out of them, and there were similar spines running down the armor along her back and the sides of her legs.

As the woman moved away, shouting and cursing at her minions, I got a better look at the burly beast of a woman she was. She stood a solid foot taller than most of the men who scurried around her like scared puppies. Her neck was almost as thick as her waist, and her bare arms, torso, and thighs bulged with veiny muscle.

When I'd tried to imagine what human girls looked like—Mistress Hilleddi wasn't exactly what I'd had in mind.

The Tibran soldiers pulled the net off me. Right away, my instinct was to flee. I staggered to my feet and spun around, looking for a break in their ranks that I could sprint through, until I got tackled from behind.

I hit the ground so hard I lost my breath. My head spun and I was paralyzed with fear. A crushing weight bore down on my back, pinning me to the snow while my arms were wrenched around and cold metal shackles were clamped around my wrists. They took my kafki blades, my bow, quiver, and all my gear.

Someone grabbed my long braid and used it to drag me to my feet.

Next to me, I saw Aubren. He was lying on his back on

the snow, still unconscious, and already bound with chains. There was a deep cut across his brow that had stained some of the snow around him pink with blood, but except for that, he seemed okay.

Our shrike, on the other hand, wasn't getting up. We'd landed on top of him, as best I could tell, which is why Aubren and I had survived the impact. The shrike wasn't as lucky.

One by one, those of us who had survived were forced into the open hatches that had once been hidden under the snow, while those who were too wounded to walk, or still unconscious, were dragged by their ankles. Tibran soldiers flanked us on every side, armed with short swords, crossbows, or bronze-tipped spears.

As soon as we were all inside, the big wooden machines used to launch the nets were rolled back and the hatches were cranked closed again. A few hours of wind kicking up the snow would hide them again and no one would be the wiser. It would be liked we'd been wiped off the face of the earth.

The Tibrans had been very busy digging tunnels—lots and lots of tunnels. They weren't very wide, but they were tall enough to wheel those machines through with ease. Torches lit the way every few yards and I quickly lost all sense of direction as we were forced to walk through their dark, damp, earthy maze. Sometimes it felt like we were going down, sometimes it seemed uphill. After a few minutes, I gave up trying to remember.

"They'll kill us for sure," I heard one of the Maldobarian soldiers whisper.

"We're doomed," someone else agreed.

"Silence!" A Tibran soldier whacked me over the back of the head with what I suspected was the blunt end of his sword.

I staggered and almost fell, my vision going dark for a moment.

They took us into a big open chamber where stalactites dripped from the ceiling like long, jagged stone teeth. The walls were stone, too, as though their tunneling had accidentally intersected with a pre-existing cave system. Iron rings had been driven into the walls and connected by heavy chains, perfect for chaining up a string of prisoners—which is exactly what happened to us.

They propped Aubren and two of the more seriously wounded members of our group against the wall, but chained them nonetheless. As I looked around, I realized that only five of us, not counting Aubren and myself, had survived. The shrikes weren't anywhere in sight, and I didn't see any evidence that any other prisoners had been here.

Across the room, a line of Tibran soldiers stood against the opposite wall. They were all armed with crossbows primed and aimed right for us. It seemed like a lot of trouble to just bring us down here to shoot us, so I dared to guess they were insurance to prevent anyone from making a daring escape.

Minutes passed. Then hours. I was sore from the crash landing, but I didn't dare sit down or drop my guard. On either side of me, the Maldobarian soldiers didn't move, either. Their expressions were hard and focused, as though they expected that whenever this finally ended, it would end very badly for us.

A noise down the corridor made everyone stir suddenly. It

was a creaking, grinding sound like squeaky wheels. The light of torches lit up the passage and suddenly Mistress Hilleddi stepped into view. Behind her, being dragged on a low, flat cart by several of her soldiers, was another strange machine.

"Good evening, gentlemen," she purred as she walked slowly down her line of captives. She took her time examining each one of us. When she got to me, she stopped. The torches made her dark eyes glitter wickedly. "Perhaps you're wondering why you're still alive. Allow me to explain. You're here because of a rumor—a rumor Lord Argonox heard that the Prince of Maldobar was seen fleeing from battle into the wild wood."

She leaned down, putting her face uncomfortably close to mine. There was a stench of old meat on her breath. Or maybe that was just the way she smelled in general—I couldn't be sure.

"It was said he went to beg the help of the gods. Or perhaps to even seek help from your pointy eared neighbors to the north. Personally, I don't believe in gods, just as I despise rumors and those who run from battle like cowardly little children. But my brother is more superstitious. He believes in gods and magic. He commanded me to keep watch in case the spineless prince dared to show his face here again."

She grabbed my chin. Her fingers were too strong for me to pull away. "Normally, I would relish ripping the truth out of each of you one by one. But time is of the essence, so let me make this very easy. Since I'm sure your infantile prince is too cowardly to step forward himself, the first person to tell me which one of you he is will be set free. The rest of you will make excellent target practice for my new recruits."

No one said a word.

She was so close I could see my own reflection in her eyes. They were like bottomless pools of black tar—there was no color to her irises at all.

She squeezed my chin harder. "If you refuse because of some idiotic sense of loyalty to the gutless worm you call a prince, then I will greatly enjoy the alternative. Now, what'll it be, boys?"

FIFTEEN

No one was talking.

Minutes passed while Mistress Hilleddi paced in front of us like a hungry lioness, snarling and threatening us with what was going to happen if no one spoke up. Down our line, I could see Aubren out of the corner of my eye. He was still out cold. He must've taken a nasty blow to the head during our landing. Blood was caked all over his face from the gash on his forehead, but I could see him breathing every now and then.

"Time is up! No takers for my bargain, I see? This is why I love these noble kingdoms. They make for much better sport!" Hilleddi laughed in her throat and snapped her fingers to the soldiers behind her. They started moving that weird-looking machine into place in the middle of the room.

"Hmm. Who shall we take first? What about you?" She

lunged forward suddenly, grabbing one of the men down the line by the front of his tunic and yanking him up onto his toes so she could sneer into his eyes. "You positively reek of fear. Are you the prince?"

The Maldobarian soldier spit in her face.

The room was silent, as though everyone were holding their breath.

With her free hand, Hilleddi wiped the spit from her cheek and grinned. She dropped the man onto his knees, giving him one swift kick to the gut on his way down. Something that sounded a lot like a bone cracked.

I cringed. Behind me, I twisted my hands against the shackles.

I could kill her—I knew I could. Just one word to Noh and this would all be over. Except there were the other Tibrans with their crossbows to think about, not to mention I had no idea where we were or how to get out of the chains. Those things, however, weren't my biggest concern.

If I let Noh out again, if I let him kill Mistress Hilleddi and the rest of her bronze armored entourage, I wasn't sure I could get him to stop there. I'd never let him kill that many at once before. I could just as easily kill the rest of my companions. I was second-guessing myself. I didn't know how much control I really had over him. It was a weakness I couldn't escape, and one Noh might exploit.

I couldn't take that risk. Not yet. I had to hope there was some other way. Maybe if I could get closer somehow …

"Very well, then. Let's show the rest of them how the game

is played." Hilleddi twirled a finger in the air and pointed to one of her soldiers. "You there, come here. Remove your helmet."

The soldier obeyed. When he took off his helmet, I was stunned to see he looked about my age. His head was shaved to the scalp, and there was a marking freshly branded into the side of his neck. The skin still looked angry and swollen around it; I couldn't make out what it was supposed to be.

"Drop your weapons," Hilleddi commanded.

The soldier put down his round bronze shield and crossbow, then unbuckled his sword belt and placed them all on the ground.

"Good. Now get in."

Hesitation flashed in the young soldier's eyes. He looked at her, then at the machine, then back to her.

Hilleddi took a threatening step toward him. "I said, *get in*."

We watched him obey silently, standing up on the top of the rolling wooden platform. In the center was a wooden chair, which was where the other Tibran soldiers fastened him. It was tilted back uncomfortably far, like the sort of reclining chair Kiran used when he was going to extract a tooth. The other soldiers locked his arms and legs down with metal clamps. There was another that went around his forehead, holding his head firmly in place. I could see him shaking. His eyes were wild and his nostrils flared with fear as he watched Hilleddi approach.

Another soldier brought her what looked like a collar. It was bright gold and set in the center was a strange looking round plate, almost like a mirror. All around it were intricate designs made of that same gold, depicting twisted, tormented faces on one side and joyful happy ones on the other. When she fastened it around the soldier's throat, the mirror turned black. It seemed to churn with smoky dark movement and I got a chill I knew wasn't coming from Noh. This was something far more ancient.

"We've found many curiosities on our conquests, so many trinkets and artifacts from across the world. But this one, by far, is my favorite." Hilleddi stroked the collar affectionately. "The Mirror of Truth; that is what we call it. The only trick in demonstrating how it works is, well, you must tell a lie. And you are such a good, loyal servant, aren't you?"

The soldier nodded frantically, although he was beginning to fight the restraints.

"Yes, of course you are. Fortunately, there's one question all men lie about." Her voice became a whisper as she leaned in closer to him. "Do you love me?"

"Yes, Mistress," the soldier cried out desperately.

He must've known what was coming.

I couldn't bear to watch. It was bad enough to feel it the way only I could. Watching it was just too much. I turned away and squeezed my eyes shut until the soldier's screams finally went quiet.

While the Tibran soldiers unfastened their dead comrade's

limp body and dragged him down from the chair, Hilleddi began prowling down our line again. There was a fresh smirk on her lips as she sized each one of us up from head to foot, like she was selecting fruit from the market.

"The Mirror cannot be fooled. It is indifferent to crowns and kingdoms. Tell the truth, and it will release you. Tell a lie, and even if you don't know it's a lie, it won't matter. All the Mirror cares about is whether the words that leave your lips are true or not. But perhaps you think you'll give me no answer at all and that will save you." She hummed as she pulled a long, curved dagger from her belt and began flipping it in the air, tossing and catching it by the hilt every time. "Getting men to talk is my specialty. It's my favorite game. So the only *real* question is who looks the most princely, even in those tacky savage clothes?"

Down the line, I saw Aubren's head loll forward. His eyelids flickered and he started to groan. He was finally waking up.

And Hilleddi was walking straight toward him.

I didn't know how much Aubren understood about our situation. Obviously, it wasn't good. But as he drowsily sat up and looked at all of us, the Tibran death machine, and the already deceased soldier, I saw realization dawn on his face.

"Come on, little prince. We don't have all day. My brother grows impatient quickly. I tell you what, if the real prince is the first to step forward and reveal himself, then I will honor his show of courage and let the rest of you live."

She didn't have to be strapped to that stupid mirror for me to know she was lying. I seriously doubted any of us was going to be walking out of here alive if she had anything to do with it.

But I saw Aubren start to open his mouth. What choice did he have? If there was any chance he could save the rest of us, that idiot was going to take it.

"It's me!" I shouted suddenly. "I'm Aubren, Prince of Maldobar!"

Everyone stopped to stare at me.

Hilleddi's smile bloomed with wicked delight, as though she somehow knew I was lying and was just thrilled at the idea of using her favorite killing toy again. She made her way back to me slowly. Looming over me, she reached around to grab my long red braid and brought the end of it up to her nose. She took a few long sniffs and her eyes crinkled in the corners as her grin widened.

"Say it again, boy."

I clenched my hands into fists against the shackles. "Why? Did I stutter the first time?"

"Strange, I was expecting someone older. But I thought I sensed something different about you," she purred, and kept flicking the end of my braid back and forth under her nose. Creepy.

Behind her, I could barely make out Aubren's face as he gaped at me in horror. I tried not to focus on him. "So, you got what you wanted. Are you going to let them go?"

"Of course," she said and dropped my hair. "Right after I make sure you're telling the truth."

I did my best to look unfazed. I just had to get her alone, further away from everyone. Just for a second—if I could just get my hands on her for a second.

169

One snap of her fingers and the Tibran soldiers were on me like attack dogs. Aubren started to shout and fight against his chains, demanding they let me go and that he was the real prince. The other Maldobarian men did the same, shouting and declaring they were the prince, not me.

I guess they were trying to save me. I wished they'd knock it off.

"Noh," I muttered, "where are you?"

I got no reply. Uh oh.

"Noh! Answer me!"

Crap. My mind was empty. I listened for his voice or any clue that he was there, but got nothing except my own blinding panic. Maybe he couldn't get through to me. Maybe I was so overwhelmed I couldn't hear him—not that that had ever happened before. There's a first time for everything, right?

I fought as the Tibrans forced me down into the chair. They took off my shackles only to begin strapping down my arms and legs and closing that metal brace over my forehead. I couldn't move and couldn't see anything but the ceiling overhead. Aubren and the rest of my companions were still shouting, trying to distract Hilleddi.

Suddenly, her face appeared over me.

My body went stiff with fear. This wasn't part of the plan. Desperately I tried to wiggle one of my hands, just an inch or two and maybe I could reach her.

Just one touch, that's all I needed.

I felt the cold metal of that golden collar as she fastened it tightly around my throat. The places where it pressed against my skin tingled. I clenched my jaw and glared at her.

"Feisty, aren't you? You certainly have a royal's pretty face, even with that scar." She put her big ugly face in front of me again. "Say it again. Do it loudly, so they can all hear you."

Aubren was screaming at the top of his lungs. "No! He's not the prince! It's me! I'm the one you want!"

I felt the distinct prick and pressure of a blade against my forearm.

"Say it, or I start cutting off fingers," Hilleddi hissed. She dug the dagger in a little more, just to get the point across.

"I-I … " My voice broke.

"Come on, little prince. Don't be shy." Her dark eyes gleamed with pleasure, as though she knew what was about to happen.

I was about to die.

"It's me," I repeated. "I'm the Prince of Maldobar."

SIXTEEN

There was a loud metal clunk.

I could hear it because everyone else in the room had gone completely silent. Even Mistress Hilleddi was scowling down at me with her mouth scrunched up into a snarl of disappointment.

As soon as I spoke those words, the golden collar went slack around my throat, fell off, and clattered noisily to the ground.

I was alive. I didn't understand how or why, but I was alive.

Before anyone would argue or demand a redo, I heard a loud commotion enter the room.

"Mistress! There's been an attack on the entrance tunnels!" a man panted, like he'd been sprinting to get here. "It's the dragonriders! They've found us!"

Hilleddi growled a furious curse. She vanished out of my

line of sight and I was left staring up at the dangerous, dripping points of stalactites dangling overhead.

"Take them all to the containment block. Except that one—I want the prince brought to my chambers immediately!" Over the rattling of weaponry and armor, I could hear her barking orders at her men. Were they leaving? What was going on? I started wriggling in the chair again, but it didn't do any good.

A pair of Tibran soldiers appeared above me right on cue and began removing the restraints. They grabbed my arms, one on each side of me, and dragged me to my feet. I saw another soldier coming for me with those iron shackles in his hand.

Big mistake.

"*Noh*!" I shouted at the top of my lungs.

This time, his presence and power descended on me like a rush of cold wind. Darkness rose off my skin, boiling in the air like a column of churning black mist. From the depths of the darkness, Noh's menacing red eyes flickered. The hissing sound of his laughter filled the cavernous room, rattling the stalactites on the ceiling.

The Tibrans' ranks became chaos. Some of them began running from the chamber, while others drew their weapons or fired their crossbows at the cloud—which of course, did nothing. Hilleddi was apparently the only one who recognized that *I* was the actual problem.

I caught her gaze through the chaos, her dark eyes narrowing on me with intent.

I smirked back at her and winked. Better luck next time.

Before anyone else could remember me, I lashed out with

every shred of Kiran's training I could remember. I snatched my arms free of the two soldiers who held me, kicking into a roll and sweeping the legs out from under the third soldier who had the shackles. As he fell, I ripped the sword out of the sheath on his belt and kicked him the rest of the way to the ground.

Hilleddi was coming for me. The ground practically shook under each of her steps. She made a bellowing noise like an angry bison, her double-axe drawn and ready to chop me in half on the first swing.

I dropped down into a spring directly toward my Maldobarian comrades. I was aiming for Aubren.

She was right on my heels, the wind screaming off the axe as she swung it.

The axe came down so close it brushed my back—but I didn't stop at the wall. I ran *up* it, kicking off hard and launching myself into an aerial backflip.

I landed behind her just in time to see her mighty axe smash through the chain that held all my friends against the wall.

"Head's up!" I shouted to Aubren, who was already on his feet. I threw the sword to him.

He jumped, sweeping his shackled arms under his legs and catching the sword in mid-air. He didn't have long, but with that sword, at least he could crack the chains off our comrades.

"You!" Hilleddi yowled and spun around, her wild gaze meeting mine.

"Me, indeed. Shall we play?" I smirked and spread my arms wide, taunting her.

She screamed a curse and reared back her axe to take another swing at me. "You filthy little whelp!"

The axe came down, aimed for my head. I bared my teeth. I was going to destroy her, just like I had the surtek. All I needed was one touch—one touch and she was mine.

My rage boiled over. In an instant, I lost control. Something inside me snapped and Noh's power broke through my body, washing over me like an icy flood. It was different this time and so cold that I could barely breathe, my frantic breaths turning to puffs of white fog. Everything seemed to slow down.

Suddenly, Hilleddi stopped. Her gaze turned from me to something else—something behind me.

Something *bigger*.

Her expression blanched with terror under all those tattoos.

Noh rose up behind me, his form swelling into a monstrous black beast. It was as though we were one; I could feel his presence and power as clearly as I could feel my own body. When he moved, I moved. Our minds were melded, fused by the darkness. He let out a snickering laugh—or was it my laugh? I couldn't tell anymore.

I smiled. His smiling maw grew wider, as well. It was filled with jagged teeth. His smoky black body changed as it grew, beginning to resemble a hybrid of the surtek we had killed not long ago and a fox. His long tail lashed. One swipe took a line of Tibran soldiers and flung them across the chamber like toys.

Hilleddi's gaze met mine once more. From a few yards away, I could sense her thinking—considering me carefully. She may have looked like a barbarian muscle head, but she wasn't stupid.

She rushed at me again.

I shouted. At the same time, Noh let out a booming, screeching roar that rattled the chamber. Tibrans fled in every direction, clamoring to get out. Overhead, the stalactites started to fall like lethal stone missiles, crashing down all around us. Stones and boulders flew through the air. Dust choked out the light of the torches.

Something hit me hard over the back of the head and I was instantly dazed. I crumpled to my hands and knees, managed a few wheezing breaths, and collapsed.

I was still in a daze, my vision fuzzy. I couldn't see who was carrying me, but I could hear frightened voices shouting and the muffled sound of something roaring.

Noh? It couldn't be. I didn't feel his presence anymore.

As my mind cleared, I realized it was Aubren who was carrying me on his back like a limp sack of flour. We were running. All around us, the ceilings shook and rubble poured down on our heads like there was a battle raging on the surface.

Before us was a maze of dimly lit tunnels. Behind us were the shouts of Tibran soldiers. They were chasing us and firing their crossbows. Arrows zipped past us, bouncing off the stone walls or lodging in the dirt floor at our heels. We were screwed.

I squirmed on Aubren's back. "Put me down! I can run!"

He immediately dropped me and I fell into a sprint next to him.

We turned a corner, then another. The Tibrans were gaining on us. When we came to a four-way-intersection, everyone wasted a good four seconds arguing over which way to go. We took a right and kept going.

Right into a line of Tibran soldiers. They stood in a phalanx formation, using their bronze shields as a barrier.

We tried to turn around, to run back the way we'd come, but it was too late. The Tibran soldiers chasing us had caught up. More arrows launched from crossbow strings whizzed past my face. One of our companions fell immediately, and Aubren grabbed me by the scruff of my tunic and forced me to stand behind him to shield me from the fire.

So much for my great plan.

Then the whole tunnel began to shake. Overhead, rubble poured down over us like an avalanche as something huge broke through from the surface. The Tibrans fired at it blindly. Aubren threw himself over me.

Suddenly, two massive, scaly, clawed feet burst down through the ceiling of the tunnel. They snagged one of our friends and lifted him away. Another set of clawed feet appeared, and another, and another. One by one, they plucked us out of the ground and carried us up—up into the pale moonlight above.

"Hang on!" Aubren shouted. He grabbed me like a puppy and tossed me in the air so one of those big scaly feet could grab me. All I could do was cling to the toes and scream as I was swiftly yanked skyward.

I couldn't see what happened to Aubren. The moonlight dazed me, and I stared around at the blurred images of sky, snow, and scales.

Dragons.

There were dozens of them everywhere, soaring on powerful bat-like wings and spitting plumes of flame at the Tibran soldiers below. Their muscular bodies spun effortlessly through the air, their scales shimmering in the silver starlight as they dove and roared, attacking the soldiers who were firing at them with those net-throwing machines.

It took one net, sometimes two, to bring down a dragon. They were bigger than a shrike—much bigger.

I looked up at the dragon that was carrying me in its claws, ready to give a stupid grin and wave up to the rider.

Only there wasn't one.

The dragon wasn't even wearing a saddle.

The beast craned its head down, looking at me briefly with bright blue eyes. They were eerily intelligent, almost curious.

"H-hey there," I stammered. "You're not gonna eat me, right?"

The dragon canted its head and made a funny clicking, chirping sound. Its big eyes blinked and nostrils puffed like it was smelling me. Then it went back to flying with strong wings pumping furiously against the wind. It soared for the horizon and all around us I saw more dragons join in. They were all different colors and patterns. Some were red, while others were yellow, silver, or blue. Some had stripes. Others had markings like the big jungle snakes in Luntharda. Some were even spotted like a leopard.

The ones directly around us all had one thing in common, though. They were all carrying my companions.

"Reigh! Are you all right?" I heard Aubren shout suddenly. A huge blue dragon had him. It was bigger than any of the others with long black horns and spikes that ran all the way down its back to the tip of its long tail. The horns around its face were tipped with orange, and it had big yellow eyes that seemed to glow when it looked my way.

"I'm okay! For now," I called back. "What's going on? Where are the riders?"

Aubren was gazing around in awe. "There aren't any," he answered at last. "These dragons are wild."

SEVENTEEN

The dragons carried us away from the battle. They flew fast and so high up none of the nets the Tibrans launched could ever reach us. In the distance, I saw a spot of light on the horizon. Barrowton. We were nearly there.

We were carried almost to the city before the dragons finally began to descend. They soared in circles like vultures, taking turns swooping down and dropping us into the snow one at a time until Aubren was the only one left.

I stood back with the others, watching as the biggest dragon—a blue one with bright yellow eyes—landed with a *boom*. Aubren stumbled back away from it as the dragon let him go, slipping and landing on his rump in front of the rest of us.

It was unbelievable. I'd always imagined what dragons might look like. Kiran had tried to describe them many times. But they were incredible. None of the descriptions did them justice.

Their bodies were muscular and compact, built sort of like a mixture of feline and bat, with two front wing arms that boasted two toes crowned with curled talons. Their hind haunches had paw-like feet with long toes, big dew claws, and more of those lethal talons. Instead of looking like a serpent, their short snouts, pointed ears, and long tails made them seem even more feline— even if they were covered in scales and spikes.

The blue dragon lowered its horned head, looking at us with those dazzling yellow eyes. Everyone scurried back away from it, even Aubren, who was crawling backwards across the ground like a crab.

Now that we were closer, I could see there was a thick black blaze running down the length of the dragon's body. The rest of it, however, was a deep royal blue color. It also had two long fangs that dripped below its jaws, like a tiger.

The blue dragon didn't seem afraid of us at all, even if he was supposed to be wild. And it didn't seem threatened by us, either. It snorted and snarled at any of the other dragons that swooped down too close to us, like he was protecting us.

"Y-Your Majesty," one of our comrades stammered as he grabbed onto Aubren's sleeve. "Is that … ?"

Aubren didn't answer right away. His whole face was flushed and his eyes were wide with an emotion I couldn't identify. "Yes," he replied in a hushed, awestruck voice. "I think it is."

"Who?" I looked for anyone to clue me in.

"Mavrik," Aubren clarified. "The one ridden by Jaevid Broadfeather."

At the sound of that name, the blue dragon let out a thundering roar. He reared his head back and shot a plume of fire that lit up the night sky. I took a *big* step backward, just in case he decided to roast us on the spot.

The dragon apparently had other plans, though. He regarded us one last time with a snort, and then reared onto his hind legs, spreading his black wings wide, and sprang back into the sky to join the rest of his kind.

They circled a few more times and then soared away, Mavrik leading the flock. The sound of their wing beats faded into the distance. We stood there in the snow, only a mile or so outside of Barrowton, watching in silence until we couldn't see them anymore.

"But that was forty years ago," someone protested. "That would make him—"

"A king drake," Aubren finished for him.

"But why would they come save us?"

"Do you think it's possible? Did Jaevid send them?"

"Don't be ridiculous!"

"Well, how else do you explain a whole flock of wild dragons just showing up like that?"

"He did something like that before, didn't he? In the last battle of the Gray War?"

Questions started to fly. Things got heated. No one could agree on why the wild dragons had come to save us. For some, it was a miracle. For others, it was pure luck. To me, it seemed a little too bizarre to be luck. But I wasn't sure I believed Jaevid had sent them, either.

At last, Aubren raised his hand for silence. "There'll be time to debate later. We have to get to the city immediately. The healthy will help the injured. Let's move out."

Everyone began to obey.

It was an uphill walk through the snow to reach Barrowton. No one said much. I guess everyone was still processing what we'd just been through. I certainly was.

Somehow, I'd managed to beat Hilleddi's Mirror of Truth. Privately, I decided Noh must have had something to do with it. That's the only explanation that made sense to me. He'd helped me beat it and bought me enough time for … for the dragons to arrive? Argh, that didn't make sense, either. I couldn't summon dragons.

After a few minutes of trudging through the snow, I got the unsettling feeling I was being watched. Next to me, Aubren was staring in my direction.

"Scared of me now?" I muttered. I wasn't sure if I wanted him to hear me or not.

"Somewhat," he conceded.

"Sorry," I mumbled.

Aubren cocked an eyebrow like he was confused. "What for?"

"I would've done something sooner, but I was afraid of that."

"That I'd be frightened of you?"

"No, that I'd lose control and accidentally hurt you guys, too." I kept my head down. "That's why Kiran never wanted me to show anyone what I could do."

Aubren drew closer and fell in step right next to me. "I

can understand that. But I can also knock you out again. That seemed to neutralize things fairly well."

I rubbed the sore knot on the back of my head. "Yeah, I'll say."

"Reigh." He lowered his voice as though he didn't want anyone to overhear. "We aren't the only ones who know what you can do now. Hilleddi has seen it, which means Argonox will be looking for you, too."

"Why?"

"The Tibrans are fond of taking prisoners. Most of their army is made up of captured slaves from other kingdoms. They force them to fight under threat of death. They've done that very thing to some of our own men and even a few dragonriders."

"So, you think Argonox is going to try to make me fight for him?" I scoffed at the idea. "Yeah, right. There's no way I'd ever agree to that."

Aubren looked away. I could tell by his expression he wasn't so sure.

I had a hard time not taking that offensively since it was basically like calling me a liar and a potential traitor. Sure, I was new to this whole war between kingdoms thing, but I wasn't about to switch sides.

"At any rate, I'm grateful. Thank you for saving us," he said quietly. "I know Kiran would be proud of you, too."

I shrugged and shot him a quick, sulky scowl.

He caught me in the act. I expected him to frown back, but instead he just cracked a smile and ruffled my hair. "C'mon, don't look like that."

I swatted his hand away and tried in vain to smooth my hair back down. "Stop it! Geez, why do people always do that?"

"Do what?"

"Pet me like I'm a little kid, or a dog, or something."

"I don't know." He chuckled. "Maybe because you pout like one."

I was exhausted when we finally arrived at the gates of Barrowton. The city looked more intimidating up close—like a stone fortress perched on a snowy hilltop. Looking up at the tall gray walls made me feel insignificant. Gray elves didn't build walls that big. I'd never seen anything like it.

Far up on the ramparts, I spotted a few groups of soldiers. More were stationed on the turrets on either side of the gates. When they spotted us down below, they started shouting to one another. I heard the banging toll of a bell somewhere high in the towers. Slowly, the big gates groaned open and more Maldobarian soldiers stepped out to greet us.

Aubren greeted them first. As soon as he introduced himself, the soldiers bowed and saluted him with great respect. They looked happy to see us as they escorted us into the city. I turned to watch as they began to close the massive gates again, dragging them into place by two huge cranks that were being turned by teams of what I could only guess were horses.

I'd never actually seen a horse before—not live ones, anyway. I'd seen plenty of them in pictures. Kiran had told me humans liked to ride them, and some could run quite fast, although not as fast as our faundra. Others, like these, were bigger and stronger so they could be used to pull heavy things. Their legs where thicker and their bodies more muscular, and they had long manes of hair on their necks.

Inside the outer walls were another set of even thicker walls, like a double ring of protection. These had holes cut in them near the top with something that looked like a big rainspout sticking out. I wasn't sure what that was meant for, though probably not rain.

Through the second set of gates, the city of Barrowton was bustling with activity. There was a nervous energy in the air, so I stuck close to Aubren's heels and stared around at all the people who were walking the streets. Some of them were herding flocks of cattle while others drove big wagons pulled by more horses. Women walked with children in their arms and groups of soldiers marched back and forth. Their clothes were strange. The food displayed in the shop windows looked weird, too, although it smelled okay.

I expected to see humans everywhere. After all, Maldobar was a human kingdom. And while there were a lot of them, sweeping out the front steps of their shops or hanging laundry out the second and third story windows, I saw plenty of gray elves and even some halfbreeds, too. All of them stared at us as we went past—probably because of our clothes.

"Why are there so many gray elves here?" I asked Aubren quietly.

"During the Gray War, this city was burned to the ground and utterly destroyed. It was the site of a great battle that cost both our kingdoms immense casualties. My father wanted it to be the first site of our efforts for a peaceful future, so he ordered that the city be rebuilt. It would serve as a safe haven in times of trouble, and people worked year-round to build it. My father decreed that anyone who signed on to work and help with the construction, be they elf or otherwise, would be given their choice of a paid salary or a new home within the city. Many of the gray elves that had fled to Maldobar during the war came to live here for that reason," he explained with a smile. "It's become something of a melting pot since then."

"A melting pot?"

"Yes, it means a place where many cultures have mixed. After this place was such a success, my father decided to do the same thing with another city further to the east, called Dayrise."

I paused, turning in a slow circle to look all around as we walked through a city square. There was a large fountain in the center with a familiar figure sculpted into it. I knew his face now—and not just because it had the same scar over one of his eyes. I'd seen him plenty of times in Mau Kakuri in paintings, engravings, and tapestries. It was the lapiloque, Jaevid Broadfeather. In this sculpture, he was standing tall wearing a suit of armor, holding a scimitar regally against his chest and looking up toward the sky.

Aubren glanced at the fountain as we walked past, and I saw

his brow crease and his expression darken. "The whole city is made like a fortress and is highly defensible. The idea was that, if war ever came to Maldobar again, many people could come here for refuge," he went on. "The governing Duke is one of my oldest friends."

The deeper we walked into the city, the tenser the atmosphere became. Shopkeepers were boarding up their windows. People were stacking bags of sand in alleyways like makeshift barricades. Soldiers were going door to door, dressed in full armor and carrying battle-ready weapons.

Ahead of us, behind one last fortified wall, was the keep. It was a tall rectangular building, with turrets on every corner and narrow windows. Royal blue banners fluttered on either side of the iron front door, each of them stitched with the image of a golden eagle grasping swords in its claws. The door was opened for us as we got close and the soldiers who had been escorting us stopped, saluted, and turned to go back to the city.

"Aubren!" a voice called out suddenly.

We all turned to look.

A man who looked like he might be in his late twenties was running toward us, waving his arms. He wasn't all that tall—average sized, really, and a few inches shorter than Aubren—but he had a powerful build underneath his noble clothing and black leather jerkin. He had shaggy, wavy black hair that hung around his squared, firm jawline. When he glanced my way, I caught the glimmer of his fierce green eyes.

He grasped Aubren by the shoulders, laughing and giving him a shake. The two men embrace roughly, patting one another on the back. "Gods and Fates, it's good to see you." The man chuckled. "After Northwatch fell, I feared the worst. What on earth are you wearing?"

Aubren laughed with him. "It's a long story."

"Save it, then. I prefer to pair long stories with good ale." He looked around at all of us and when he got to me, he paused. The corners of his mouth quirked up. "And who is this?"

"Reigh," Aubren answered for me. "He's come from Luntharda to fight with us."

"Well that explains the hair," the man said. "A human boy taught to fight by the gray elves? Sounds lethal, indeed. A pleasure, Young Master Reigh. Welcome to Barrowton. I am Duke Phillip Derrick, but you can call me Phillip if you like."

He offered to shake my hand and reluctantly I obliged. I didn't think dukes were the kinds of people who shook hands. They were nobles, weren't they? Only, this guy didn't act very noble. He went around to each member of our group to offer a handshake and confident smile.

"Welcome, all of you. I wish we were meeting under better circumstances," Phillip said at last, and gestured for us to follow him into the keep. "But time is against us and there are far too many Tibrans on my doorstep for my liking."

EIGHTEEN

The rest of Aubren's men were excused to join the ranks preparing to defend the city. Phillip assured them they would be fed, given new armor and weapons, and a chance to rest before they got to work. Those who were wounded would go directly to the infirmary to be treated. The men seemed happy about this, and I sort of expected I'd be joining them, since I wasn't a noble. But Aubren insisted I stay with him.

I was given a room all to myself in the keep, and it was almost bigger than the whole house Kiran and I had shared in Mau Kakuri. The bed was huge and there was a set of brand new human-styled clothes spread out on it. I even had my own bathroom.

Phillip had invited us to join him for dinner, so I had to get cleaned up. A couple of lady servants in clean white dresses came in to help me get ready. I had to ask one of them to show me how the bathtub worked. There were all these knobs and I couldn't get the water to get hot.

"Sorry, it's different in Luntharda," I said as I stripped down out of all my filthy scout's clothes and undergarments, leaving them in a pile next to the door. It would all need a wash and some repairs now, anyway.

When I turned around, the servant girl who had been drawing the bath dropped the bar of soap she'd been unwrapping. Her whole face blushed bright pink and she covered her eyes. "Ah! Y-yes, of course. Please excuse me!"

Before I could get a word out, she darted out of the room and shut the door. Well, that was weird. What was her problem? I scratched my bare rear end and tried to figure it out.

Pfft, oh well. I had about made up my mind that all human girls were odd.

Scooping up the bar of soap she'd dropped, I climbed into the tub and started scrubbing the grit off my skin. Another servant came in, this one much older than the first one and her pudgy, wrinkled face sagged around her mouth and eyes. Her skin was like tree bark, textured with age, and her hands were knobby and callused. She sat down on the edge of the tub, pulled a wooden brush from her apron, and started trying to get the knots out of my hair.

"What's wrong with the other girl? Did she get sick or something?" I asked as I sank down and let the hot water sooth my sore joints.

The old woman gave a raspy laugh. "I assume she's not

accustomed to being flashed the private bits of a young man."

I winced as the brush snagged on a tangle. "Oh … wait, so humans don't have public baths?"

"No, child. We prefer to bathe alone. We also cover ourselves in the presence of young ladies, even if they are only servants, and we don't prance around naked. You might try to remember that next time."

Now I was the one blushing. "Oh. Oops. Uh, sorry about that, then."

The old woman sighed. "My goodness, all this hair. What a mess."

I blushed harder and sank down lower in the tub. "Gray elves don't cut their hair."

"I see." She didn't sound convinced that was a good excuse.

Once I was clean, the old woman turned her back long enough for me to climb out of the tub and wrap up in a towel. She followed me back out into my bedroom and waited while I got dressed. Then she sat me down at a dresser and started massaging some kind of oil into my scalp and brushed it through my hair. It smelled funny, but not in a bad way.

"It's cedar wood, tea tree, and olive oil," she rasped in her throaty voice.

I wasn't paying much attention. I was looking at my reflection in the fancy gold-framed mirror hanging behind the dresser. Kiran didn't have any fancy furniture at home. He had one mirror, which I used to shave sometimes, and I hadn't done that in several days now.

My chin and jaw were flecked with lots of dark stubble,

and I still had a pretty noticeable scar across the bridge of my nose from where the stag had slashed me with his antlers. I ran my finger across it, tracing the rough, raised skin while the old servant woman began weaving my hair into one long braid. The scar made my face look wild, even now that it was clean. Once she was done braiding it, my dark red hair hung all the way down to the base of my back. There were dusky circles under my eyes.

I looked almost as tired as I did savage—just as Hilleddi had said.

"Why such a sour face?" The old woman was eyeing me in the mirror.

I frowned and sank back in the chair. "I came here because I thought I'd fit in better than I did in Luntharda. I wasn't very good at being a gray elf. And now it turns out I'm not good at being a human, either."

"Why do you say that?"

"I keep embarrassing myself," I mumbled. "I just wanted to fit in, you know? Just once, I wanted to feel like I wasn't the odd man out. I thought maybe if I were useful … "

"Well, I'm no expert in gray elf culture, but I do know a thing or two about us round-eared folk. I don't think flashing your naked rear end to one servant girl is a ruinous mistake, considering you didn't know any better." The old woman chuckled and poked me in the back of the head. "You young men are all the same. You focus too much on what you're not— you forget to see what you are."

I glared up at my reflection again. I already knew what I was and it wasn't anything good. An orphan. A monster. Cursed. Haunted by an evil spirit I could barely control. The list went on and on.

"Up with you. It's nearly dinner time." The old woman poked me again, and when I stood, she muscled around me. She was surprisingly nimble for someone so ancient. She straightened the collar of my borrowed, human-styled tunic and picked a few bits of lint off my shoulders.

"Will you tell that other girl I really am sorry about before?" I rubbed the back of my neck and looked down.

She smiled, making her drooping mouth seem a little less saggy for a moment. "Yes, if you like. Now go on. It's bad manners to be late to dinner."

Big surprise—I got lost on the way to dinner. I didn't run into any princesses this time, though. And it wasn't completely my fault. As it turns out, human castles are much different than gray elf palaces, and the Keep of Barrowton was no exception. It was taller, narrower, and there were very few windows. A grand stone staircase spiraled to every floor, lit by chandeliers with hundreds of candles—and no one had bothered to tell me which floor the dining hall was on. Since you couldn't see out, the walls were adorned with big tapestries stitched with images of mountains, valleys, beautiful meadows, and scenes from great battles. The ceilings had paintings of clouds, dragons, and figures that I could only guess were gods and goddesses.

Following my nose and the fragrant aromas of a freshly cooked feast turned out to be the most effective tactic for finding my way around. The smells of freshly baked bread, roasted meats, herbal seasonings, and things I didn't even have a name for practically dragged me down the correct path toward the dining hall. Aubren and Duke Phillip were bound to be waiting for me. I was already late. I rounded another corner quickly, walking fast and not paying attention—and smashed right into a servant girl carrying a platter of fruit. Grapes went flying, apples rolled across the floor, and I got smacked in the face by the prickly end of a pineapple.

"I'm so sorry! I didn't see you there," she apologized and began frantically trying to recapture the grapes that were making a break for it down the hallway.

"No, it's totally fine. I wasn't paying attention," I said, attempting to help her pile all the runaway fruit back onto the tray. One of the apples had rolled away, making its escape to the far end of the corridor. I jogged in pursuit just as it came to a stop outside the dining hall's door. On my way to grab it, I heard Aubren and Phillip's voices faintly coming from the other side.

"So, she did come here." Aubren sounded relieved.

"Yes, only a few days ago. I was afraid we might suffer her rage when she found out you had gone to Luntharda without her," Phillip replied. "Not that I'm complaining. I find her most beautiful when she's angry."

Aubren chuckled darkly. "You're crazy. Crossing my sister is as good as a death wish."

"I know, I know. It doesn't matter, though. She still looks straight through me as though I'm not even there. All my compliments fall on deaf ears and she makes no effort to hide that she's using me for whatever value I might be to her and her riders. That cruel streak must run rampant in your family," Phillip complained. "I suppose that's why I was very surprised to find you letting that redheaded kid tag along with you. Taking up babysitting, are we?"

I froze with my hand around the apple, squatting down behind the door.

"Hardly," Aubren replied dryly. "Kiran found him as an orphaned whelp, or so he claims. Kiran might fool everyone in Luntharda with that shoddy story, but I've known him too long to be duped so easily."

"I didn't think Kiran had any children of his own. Granted, there was that one girl. Didn't she have red hair as well?"

"She did," Aubren agreed. "But I don't believe this boy is his child at all. He has none of the marks of a halfbreed."

"True. So what do you suspect?" Phillip's voice got quieter.

For a moment, no one said a word. I was afraid maybe they'd somehow realized I was listening to them. But after nearly a minute, Aubren took a deep breath. "Did I ever tell you how my mother died?"

"Only that she passed in childbirth. It wasn't so surprising, considering her age. I remember my own mother mourning for her. She said it was often too much for older mothers to go through a birth."

"Indeed. The pregnancy as a whole took a toll on her. I was too young to fully realize it then. It was only after that I realized how weak she had become, and how frail. She could barely walk across a room at the end. She hid it well. She kept smiling—I suspect because she didn't want to scare us. She pretended to be preoccupied with other things. She must have knitted a dozen blankets sitting in her bed."

"She was a strong lady, I do remember that."

"She was. But the night she went into labor, my father forbade my sister and I to enter their room. I think he must have known the delivery would be difficult. He didn't want us to see her that way." Aubren's tone was gravely serious. "I never knew exactly what happened; only that it had been too much for her. Jenna and I sat outside the door, trying to listen while Kiran watched over us. It sounded like chaos inside. I could hear my mother straining. And then there was silence—a strange silence. Kiran ran inside to offer his help, and it was as though utter chaos broke loose. My father began screaming like a wild animal, like he'd gone completely mad. I couldn't even understand what he said. Jenna and I were so afraid we ran back to my room and hid in my closet. We must've stayed there most of the night, scared out of our minds."

My face started to get hot. I was squeezing the apple harder and harder, not daring to move an inch.

"The midwife told us later that our mother had succumbed to the labor, that it was just too much for a woman her age to bear, and that the baby had been stillborn. It never even took a breath." Aubren was whispering now, his voice so faint I could scarcely hear him. I leaned closer and pressed my ear to the door. "I never had any reason to question it. My father, the midwife, and even Kiran told the exact same story—but without giving away any more detail. They wouldn't even tell me if the baby had been a boy or a girl. They buried my mother with the baby in her arms, wrapped up so no one could see it. But I couldn't resist. I wanted to see it. I wanted to know if it was a brother or a sister I had lost—to take just one glimpse of its face. So, I pulled back the blanket just to take a peek."

Aubren hesitated again. His voice caught like he was having a hard time getting the words out. "I remember when I saw it, I couldn't believe it was real. I'd never been so terrified in my life. It had only been a few days and yet the baby looked all wrong. It was tiny, shriveled, and shrunken. It was ... *mummified*."

The apple fell out of my hand and hit the floor. It rolled away, but I didn't go after it. I was staring at the door, barely breathing.

"What are you saying?" Phillip asked dubiously.

"He's the proper age. Kiran was very vague about where he'd come from. It was less than a week after that Kiran departed from Maldobar. True, he'd been talking about retiring for quite some time, but the timing is a little *too* convenient. You know as well as I do that after that night, my father was never the same. He's been all but mad with grief. If there was another—"

"Another what? Another child? Gods and Fates, Aubren. Think about it. How could that be possible?"

"I don't know. But that boy can *do* things, Phillip. Things you've never even dreamed of in your wildest nightmares."

"Like Jaevid?" His voice brightened with hope.

"No," Aubren replied. "Nothing like Jaevid. When I first met him, I thought that maybe he was. I thought maybe he could help us. But what I saw him do in Luntharda was only a small taste of his power." I heard a chair creak across the floor. "Now I am honestly afraid of what I have brought here. I am afraid of what might happen if I put him in battle and he unleashes the full extent of it. Even he admits that he can barely control the power within him. And worse, I am afraid that he might be my—"

"He doesn't look much like you or Jenna." Phillip was quick to interrupt. He still didn't sound convinced. "Although, your mother's hair did have a reddish hue, if I recall correctly. But let's be reasonable here, Aubren. You're suggesting that Kiran somehow stole a newborn baby with your father and the midwife standing right there and swapped it with a mummified one?"

"I don't know how or why he did it. But he was there—he was in the room."

Phillip's laugh twanged with anxiety. "So? That doesn't mean this boy has any relation to you. Why jump to that conclusion?"

"Because he said it himself," Aubren snapped in a soft but sharp voice, proceeding to tell Phillip about how we had been captured by the Tibrans, how they had interrogated us, and finally about the Mirror of Truth. He admitted that while he had taken a blow to the head, he had been able to figure out what was going on when I told Hilleddi I was the prince.

I should have died right then and there.

"Maybe it was just a fluke," Phillip suggested. "Magical

weapons and artifacts like that are faulty and inconsistent. You can't expect them to be accurate all the time."

"No!" I heard a banging sound as someone, probably Aubren, had slammed their fist down on the table. "I can't explain it. I've no real proof; I know that. I just *feel* it. He is my brother."

My heart was beating so hard I was afraid it might punch right out of my chest. I backed away from the door. I wanted to run. To get away before I had to hear anymore.

"And if he is?" Phillip asked quietly. "What then?"

"Then I have failed him in the most absolute and profound way one brother could fail another. I should have come looking for him. I should have been the one to raise him and take care of him, not Kiran. He's spent all his life pining for his lost family, thinking we had abandoned him, and I never knew he existed."

Suddenly, someone placed a hand on my arm. I flinched and spun around, almost knocking the servant girl over a second time. The platter clanged loudly again, and the conversation inside stopped.

"I-I'm so sorry, sir," she stammered. "You can go in, if you like. They're waiting for you."

I glanced at the door then shook my head. "Actually, I'm not feeling very good. Can you tell them I'm just going to stay in my room tonight?"

She gave me a hesitant, worried smile and nodded. "Of course. Should I have your dinner brought up?"

I backed away from her slowly and took one more, hard look at the door. "No. Thanks. I don't have much of an appetite anymore."

NINETEEN

I didn't go back to my room. Not right away, at least. I walked the halls of the keep, wandering from floor to floor while servants and soldiers passed me. Some of them stared, and I couldn't help but be a little paranoid. Maybe they knew who I was, what I could do, or that I was probably Aubren's—

No. I couldn't accept that just yet. If Aubren was right, if he was my brother, then I really was a *prince*. It was weird to even think about it. I didn't like the idea of being made into a social spectacle like that. The shadows were safer for someone with a problem like mine.

Unfortunately, there was only one person who could tell me if any of that stuff was true, and he was back in Luntharda. My blood boiled at the idea that Kiran had been lying to me all these years. Had he stolen me? Was it some kind of plot? Just what the heck was going on?

A familiar face caught my eye and made me stop. I was standing before another big tapestry. It was a scene from the Gray War.

I'd heard the gray elves tell this story many times, as though it were a legend. The lapiloque, Jaevid Broadfeather, was standing on what was supposed to be the temple grounds deep in the jungle of Luntharda. He and another man, who must have been Jace before he became the king, were bound up and about to be executed as traitors. At the last second, something amazing had happened. The tapestry showed Jaevid walking with his arms outstretched, directly toward the shining image of the ancient god, Paligno.

Paligno looked like a mixture of many animals. He had the body of a horse, the legs and wings of a bird, the tail of a lion, scales like a lizard, and long white horns sweeping back from his head like a stag. He'd been stitched in shining threads so the god seemed to be glowing and glittering with power. All around him were gray elves cringing away and shielding their eyes. Some were even bowing with their heads to the ground.

That was the moment when Paligno had chosen Jaevid as the lapiloque—officially, anyway. It was said a lapiloque's power wasn't complete until he was chosen.

I wondered if that went for evil gods, too.

"If anyone wants to choose or claim me, or however it works, now would be a great time," I muttered.

Of course, I didn't get an answer—not even from Noh.

I must have walked for hours. My stomach growled angrily because I hadn't eaten any dinner and I was so tired I found myself wanting to sit down in every chair or sofa I passed. Eventually, I wandered back to my room and found the door standing open. Aubren and the old servant woman from before were standing there, having a heated conversation.

"What do you mean he didn't come back here?" Aubren's voice was raised in panic.

"I'm deeply sorry, Your Highness. I didn't see him after he left for dinner." The servant woman bowed her head in apology.

"Miss Harriet, please, you must have some idea where he went. Did he say anything strange?" Aubren pressed her.

I scowled and cleared my throat. "I'm right here."

The two of them stared me down. Aubren looked surprised and relieved. Miss Harriet—well, honestly it was hard to tell. Her face was so wrinkled her subtle expressions were nearly impossible to interpret.

"You missed dinner." Aubren frowned. "What's going on?"

"Nothing. I'm fine." I muscled my way in between them to get into my room.

Aubren followed me inside. I saw Miss Harriet flash me a sympathetic look from the hallway right before he shut the door. Now we were alone and Aubren didn't look happy with me at all.

Okay, so I had ditched on dinner. And snubbing a dinner invitation from a duke and a prince probably wasn't a good thing. But if we were going to start comparing wrongs here, he wasn't exactly blameless.

"You don't look fine," Aubren said as he followed me into the sitting room. "You were listening to us, weren't you?"

I stopped. My hands clenched. Slowly, I turned back to face him. "And if I was?"

His expression fell. The hard lines in the corners of his mouth softened and he let out a sigh. "If I had any concrete proof, I would have said something to you first, Reigh. All I have is a suspicion. I didn't want to give you false hope."

"It's just as well. I don't want to be a prince." I stared down at the toes of my boots.

"Why not? I realize I'm no prize candidate for a brother but—"

"That's not the reason," I muttered. "You said it yourself; you really have no idea what you've brought here. I don't even know. But whatever I am, it's definitely not anything good. I'm a disaster waiting to happen, don't think I don't know that."

"Good can be a relative thing sometimes. What's good for the hunter isn't good for the deer," he said as he made himself comfortable in one of the parlor chairs. He leaned his elbow on the armrest and rubbed at his chin, his eyes gleaming thoughtfully.

"Noh said something like that to me once," I mumbled. "A spider is only a monster to a fly."

"He's not wrong."

"I know. I'd just rather not be a monster or a hunter." I sank into the chair next to his and slumped down till my chin was resting on my chest. "And I hate spiders."

"Well, let's not get ahead of ourselves." He cast me a tired smile. "The thing to do is ask my father. If you were stolen from us somehow, he's never said a word to anyone about it."

"What about Kiran?"

His gaze hardened. "He's spent a long time lying about this and trying to cover it up. I don't expect him to tell me the truth, even if I backed him into a corner."

My chest felt heavy. I couldn't decide if I was angry, upset, sad, or excited. There was a chance I had a family—one that truly wanted me. Maybe I hadn't been abandoned. Maybe I'd only been lost, or stolen. Aubren was right about one thing, if the King of Maldobar was my father, why hadn't he tried to find me? Did he know I was missing? Did he even care? I gnawed on the inside of my cheek while those questions rolled through my mind.

"What's he like?" I asked. "The King, I mean."

Aubren made a face like that was a loaded question. "He used to be a very good man, who loved to joke and tease us. He had a laugh you could hear from every corner of the castle. He was also very dedicated and straightforward. When I was a boy, much younger than you are now, he would take me on hunts and horseback rides. He taught me to wrestle, told me stories, and taught me everything he knew about navigation and tracking in the wild. Some nights he would sneak down to the kitchen with me late at night so we could have a midnight snack. A few times he let me ride a dragon with him—although I think that was to test if I'd make a good rider or not. Still, he was a very good father. I never had a doubt that he loved us."

That didn't sound so bad. "What's different about him now?"

"After my mother died, it was as though part of him died with her. He stopped talking to us. He didn't laugh or smile anymore. We didn't play games, or go on hunts, or even have dinner together. He didn't leave their room unless it was for business. Sometimes I didn't see him for weeks on end. He became like a phantom in the castle." Aubren took in a deep breath. "Then a lot of things seemed to go wrong. Jenna and I became a constant source of disappointment to him. Whenever we did speak, it always ended in an argument. I hated those days. I did everything I could to avoid fighting with him," he recalled. "Jenna wasn't as mindful of his temper as I was. She didn't back down when he would raise his voice. He couldn't break her. I doubt if anyone can."

I swallowed hard and looked at the fireplace. A few thick logs were smoldering and crackling in a nest of white ash. The heat from it warmed my face even from across the room. "Hilleddi is going to come looking for me, isn't she? She's going to come here and attack Barrowton."

Aubren didn't answer. He was staring at the fire, too, the flames flickering in the centers of his dark blue eyes.

"We need to have a plan," I said. "Something better than just blockading ourselves in here and hoping the dragonriders show up before they burn the whole city down."

He flicked me a quick sideways glance. "What did you have in mind?"

"Something crazy," I muttered under my breath. "Something absolutely insane."

The broad side of a sword's hilt came smashing right against my face, knocking me into a daze. I stumbled, tripped, and fell flat onto my back. Before I could come to my senses, the point of the sword was pricking against the end of my nose.

"You've got to stay off your heels when you take a blow. You do that and a follow-up strike will knock you flat on your back, like so. That's as good as a death sentence." Aubren leapt back a few paces to reset the match, his wooden sparring sword raised at me. "Again."

I groaned and sat up. My whole body screamed in protest. There weren't many parts of me that didn't hurt. We'd been stuck here two days. Two days waiting for word to come from Aubren's sister and the rest of her dragonriders. To pass the time, Aubren had decided to test my skills in battle.

"Tibrans don't fight like elves, Reigh," he warned. "They fight more like humans—like us. But their armor is thick. Their shields are heavy. They will hit you hard and from all sides. They outman us on the battlefield five to one, on a good day."

I grabbed my own practice sword, which had been knocked out of my hand at least a dozen times this morning, and dragged myself to my feet. "Can't we take a water break?"

He smirked. "I thought you were the Queen of Luntharda's

most honored scout?"

"Yeah, maybe in Luntharda. Here I'm just … existing." I touched my nose gingerly, testing to see if it was broken. "Am I bleeding?"

"No, not yet. You gave it your best try, though. Come on," he urged and poked me in the arm with the tip of his wooden sword. "One more round. Then we'll take a break. I'd like to see you win one match."

I narrowed my eyes. "Fine."

I dove in, swinging wide to feint an assault. He saw it coming, and stepped in to make a strike of his own while my guard was down. I pitched backward suddenly, bounding off the floor and hurling myself into a backflip. I pulled my knees in close to my body and kicked him square in the chest as I went over.

I landed in a low crouch, my sword still clenched tight in my hand, and immediately rushed him again. Rearing back my blade, I aimed for the winning blow.

Aubren blocked. The impact made my teeth rattle. And too quick for me to react, he swept my legs out from under me. I dropped my blade when I hit the floor again, but that didn't mean I was out of the game yet.

"That's cheating." I snarled. "I'm not used to a human sword."

He smirked. "There's no such thing in a real battle, kid. Those fancy elf blades of yours are as good as gone now that the Tibrans have them. So you'll have to improvise."

"Okay, then."

I curled my body into a ball for a kick up. When I landed, I slowly stood and rolled my shoulders, one by one. I flexed my empty hands, spreading my fingers wide, and summoning just a *tiny* bit of my power. Darkness gathered around my open hands like swirling clouds of black. They took form, boiling inwards and morphing into the shape of two long, black scimitars. It only took a few seconds and there they were, just as I visualized in my mind—two blades as dark as night and as sharp as razors resting comfortably in my grip.

Aubren's eyes went wide.

I rushed him once again, and this time I wasn't faking. I struck hard, tearing through different combinations and strikes in a flurry that kept Aubren on the defensive.

His jaw clenched as he strained to match me. Something had changed. Uncertainty and panic wafted off him so strongly I could practically smell it.

A grin wriggled its way up my lips. I just couldn't help it. This was *fun*.

I came down hard, knocking Aubren off balance. While he stumbled, I swung an arm out wide. The scimitar in my hand exploded into a puff of black mist, swirling and instantly snapping back into a new shape—a long black whip. I snapped it in the air, letting it wrap around one of his arms. One solid yank and I brought him face-first into my knee.

The blow rattled him. Aubren crumpled slowly to the practice mat and dropped his blade. He stayed on his hands and knees, breathing heavily, trying to collect himself. Then I saw him raise one of his hands in a gesture of surrender.

"Talk about cheating," he panted.

"You said to improvise." I let my shadow-hewn weapons dissolve into the air and crossed my arms smugly.

"That's not really what I had in mind." Slowly, he started to get up. He had a round, raised, knee-shaped lump beginning to swell on his forehead. "How long can you sustain those weapons? Doesn't it drain you to use that power?"

I shrugged. "I'm not sure. I've never tested it. Kiran didn't want me to. It does drain me a little, but not as much as when Noh ... well, you know."

Out of nowhere, the doors of the small sparring gymnasium we'd been using flew open. Duke Phillip burst in, red faced and out of breath. His eyes looked at both of us with frantic desperation.

"What is it? What's happened?" Aubren was already halfway across the room, running toward him. "Is it the Tibrans?"

"N-no," he stammered. "I mean yes! I mean—your sister is here!"

"What?" Aubren and I both asked in unison.

"They've come to warn us! The Tibrans have attacked the western border. They're marching this way!"

TWENTY

We left our sparring equipment behind and followed Duke Phillip out into the front courtyard of the keep. There, other soldiers and people from the city were gathering, crowding around to watch as five dragonriders landed. It was difficult to see. Everyone was pushing and shoving around me, and I was too short to catch a glimpse of what was going on. The thunderous beats of dragon wings and roaring filled the air. The crowd started shouting.

Aubren's strong hand grabbed the back of my neck. He was looming over me, his expression tight and fierce as he started muscling his way through the crowd. He kept his hand on me, trying to make sure I didn't get lost.

When we broke through the front of the crowd, I immediately got a blast of angry dragon breath in my face. Not the fiery kind, thank the gods. Just a big snort of stinky, hot breath that made me gag. The dragon snarled, showing rows of jagged teeth that might have had a few bits of his enemies still stuck between them.

"Keep back," Aubren warned as he steered me out of the way.

Five dragons stood together, fully dressed out in their battle gear. They wore big, beautifully crafted saddles between their wing arms and the base of their necks. Each saddle was made to fit flush against their bodies, over their spines and rippling scales. I didn't see any kind of bridle or reins, but the saddles did have a peculiar looking pair of handles on the front, and deep leather pockets on the side where the riders stuck their legs from the knee down.

The dragons hissed and bared their teeth at the crowd while their riders dismounted. One after another, dragonriders dressed in gleaming armor stepped off the beasts. They each wore helmets and long, royal blue cloaks with collars made out of white fox fur. Swords hung on their belts and their breastplates were engraved with Maldobar's royal seal depicting the eagle with its wings spread wide.

I assumed they were all men—which was dumb considering I should have known better—until the rider in the center of the gathering took off her helmet. Hair like bolts of golden silk fell, flowing down her back. Her eyes were a dangerous shade of stormy blue, and her heart-shaped face turned to pan the crowd with a bold, indifferent expression. She was tall, staggeringly beautiful, and looked about as friendly as the dragon that had snarled at me just a few minutes earlier.

The crowd booed, yelled curses, and called her names, and some even hurled rotten fruit in her direction. One of the other riders quickly moved to stand in the way, holding his cloak out to protect her from the garbage. Some of the soldiers from the keep were trying to keep the angry mob back, using their shields like a barrier.

None of it seemed to bother her. Or if it did, she never let it show. She strode proudly through the crowd with her head held high, shoulders back, and gaze focused squarely ahead. She walked straight toward us and stopped, slipping a hand free of her riding glove so she could shake hands with Duke Phillip and exchanged a stiff nod with Aubren.

Then her gaze fell on me.

Her brow furrowed slightly. She tilted her head to the side slightly, studying me up and down without ever saying a word.

Suddenly, some of the crowd broke free of the soldiers who were battling to keep them back. They were flinging potatoes and screaming, calling the dragonrider princess vile names Kiran never taught me.

The princess's dragon, which also happened to be the one that had growled at me, let out a bellow of rage and a blast of flame into the air. It made a few members of the angry mob stop, some even ran away in fear, but others pressed on, undeterred.

"Hurry, we must get inside." Aubren squeezed the back of my neck harder.

Together, Aubren, Phillip, the princess, and I walked quickly into the keep, while the rest of the dragonriders followed behind, but stayed by the doors to stand guard until the mob was dispersed. Duke Phillip barked out orders to his own men inside the castle, commanding them to do whatever was necessary to make them go—even if that meant locking them out of the city altogether. He had an angry flush to his face as he led us to a private parlor on the second floor. Servants had put out a long table of snacks for us and were still pouring four goblets of wine when we arrived. Phillip dismissed them and commanded that the doors be shut. We weren't to be disturbed.

The parlor was quiet. The atmosphere was tense. Aubren had taken a seat in one of the wingback chairs, and was scowling as he gripped the armrests in quiet rage. Phillip was pacing back and forth like a panther in a cage.

Only the princess seemed calm. She didn't look bothered that the crowd outside had just tried to mob rush her. She sat her helmet down on the coffee table and began removing the heavier pieces of her battle armor. She tossed them all onto a sofa and unbuckled the cloak from around her neck, folding it and placing it on top of the pile. Under all that metal, she wasn't very big. She was tall, yes, and she did have broad shoulders. But her body was lean and long-limbed. She had a slender neck and elegant arch to her back. When she walked, it was like she floated with her long golden hair spilling down all the way to the base of her back.

She looked up at me all of a sudden, catching me red handed gawking at her. A small, impish smile put dimples in the corners of her mouth. "You're a bit young to be a soldier."

I blushed. "I-I … "

"He's not a soldier." Aubren's voice was quiet and sharp. I couldn't decide if that should offend me or not.

The princess blinked. "Oh?"

"My name is Reigh." I decided to speak up. "I came from Luntharda. A-as a volunteer, I mean. To help."

Her smile widened. "That explains the hair, then."

My face got hotter. "It's traditional for gray elves."

The princess nodded as she walked over to me, planting her hands on her hips. I could sense her sizing me up and almost had a heart attack when she thrust a hand out for me to shake. "I am Princess Jenna Farrow," she said. "But Jenna will do. An ally of Maldobar is a friend of mine."

My hand must have felt like a limp noodle as I shook hers. Her grip was like a snagwolf's jaws.

"Why do you look so embarrassed?" she teased. "Don't tell me that's the first time you've seen a princess get pelted with garbage?"

I swallowed. It totally was.

"I was the first woman to ever join the dragonrider ranks officially. I went through the same training as any other rider. There are many people in Maldobar who don't agree with that. I know in your kingdom, women may fight and become warriors if they choose, but that isn't the case here. My people despise it, and hate me for it, as well." Her gaze flicked to Aubren while she explained. "Even more so because of my social standing. They think a princess should wear beautiful gowns, sit still, behave, and always look pretty."

"O-oh."

Jenna giggled and winked one of her dark blue eyes at me. "But between us, sitting still is overrated and I'd rather wear pants any day."

Things calmed down after a few minutes and everyone got something to eat. I could still feel tension in the air, though, and it took me a little bit to realize that *I* was the problem. They wanted to talk business and war strategy—just not in front of me.

"Maybe you could go and make sure they are taking good care of Phevos for me." Princess Jenna was at least trying to be discreet about telling me to scram. "He's very temperamental and doesn't like being cooped up. Make sure they feed him well; he hasn't had much to eat in a few days."

"Right." I knew it was a bogus errand. Sure, I was probably close to ten years younger than everyone else in that room, but I wasn't five years old anymore.

As I left the parlor and closed the door behind me, I felt like I'd just been kicked out of a secret clubhouse or something. I wondered if Aubren would tell her about me, or rather, how much he would tell her. Knowing they'd probably be discussing me only made me more anxious and frustrated as I dragged my feet through the halls of the keep.

One thing was certain: I wasn't going to see about her dragon. No way. That thing would probably do worse than snort at me if I got close to him again. I wasn't going anywhere near any more dragons.

I decided to go up to the roof. I wanted a breath of fresh air, to clear my head, and maybe I'd be able to see Luntharda in the distance. I climbed the stairs up, going all the way to the top level of the keep. Past a pair of reinforced iron doors, I found the roof. It was wide and open. A few soldiers were stationed along the corners to keep watch. Each one of them carried a big bronze horn, and they ignored me completely as I walked past.

The wind was strong and cold. It snatched at the flags hoisted to the top of tall poles on each of the four corners of the building. Overhead, the sky was bright and as blue as a bird's egg. Clouds like puffy clumps of cotton floated over the valley to the east, casting shadows on the snow below. To the west were the mountains, still crowned with white. To the south, I could see more mountains in the distance, and to the north the distant solid green wall of jungle that I knew was Luntharda.

Seeing it put a pang of sorrow through my heart. I wondered what Kiran, Hecate, and Enyo were doing right now.

Out of nowhere, the whole building shuddered under my boots. I spun around, expecting to see some form of a Tibran attack hailing down upon us. What would it be this time? A catapult? A monster? I didn't have a weapon—no sword, bow, or scimitar.

I ran right into the end of a short, scaly snout. Two familiar, big, blue eyes the same hue as the sky stared at me.

I gave an undignified, I'm about to die, please someone save me scream. Thank the gods Aubren and Jenna weren't there.

Scrambling backwards, I flailed my arms and tried to get away. The heel of my boot caught on an uneven stone tile and I went down, landing flat on my back.

Those big eyes appeared over me again. Cat-like pupils widened and that short snout sniffed me so hard it sucked up some of the front of my shirt.

"Gods and Fates," I squeaked. "Please don't eat me."

The dragon made a humming, purring noise. It pulled back some and perked its small, scaly ears. Wait ... Why was that look so familiar? Then I realized—this was the same wild dragon that had pulled me out of the Tibran's tunnel and saved my life. It was back, and alone this time.

"What do you want? Look, I'm really grateful for before. You saved my life, and I appreciate that. But I don't have any food." I tried to bargain with it as I cautiously sat up.

The dragon flopped onto its belly in front of me, making the roof shudder. I swallowed, my heart still pounding in my ears as we stared at one another. What was this? A greeting? Not that I was any sort of dragon expert, but there was something impatient about the way it was staring me down.

This dragon was smaller than some of the others I'd seen. It had a more slender body, and its scales were shiny like they had a pearlescent coating on them. Their lime green color faded gradually into electric yellow along the dragon's belly. Its back, snout, tail, and legs all had dark green stripes like a tiger, and there was a line of long yellow spines down its whole body. Two big horns on the dragon's head curved back and sloped inward, like a stretched-out S-shape.

The beast was looking up at me and twitching the very tip of its tail, like it was waiting on me to do something.

"I … uh … " I tried taking a step backward, away from it. "I'm just gonna go back inside now, so you should probably go back home."

The dragon scooted closer and lay flat again, making a chirping sound.

"I'm not sure what you want."

It snorted. Its hind haunches wiggled, like a puppy trying to get someone to play.

Crap.

It scooted again, this time intentionally bumping its big nose against my knees. I tripped and fell forward, landing square on the dragon's head. The monster yipped in delight and immediately stood up, tossing me backward so I landed right on its neck. Thankfully, I didn't get impaled on any of those spines. I landed right between two of them, and barely had time to hang on for dear life as the dragon rose, spread its wings, and took off.

The last thing I saw were the four watchmen at the top of the tower rushing in to try to help me. They yelled and waved their arms, blowing their horns—but they were too late.

TWENTY-ONE

I screamed until I was hoarse.

Clinging to the dragon's neck, I squeezed my eyes shut and tried to pray to whichever of the gods might be listening that I wouldn't fall or be carried back to a dragon nest and devoured.

"Reigh!" someone shouted suddenly.

I cracked an eye open. At first, I thought maybe I was dead, or terror was making me hallucinate. But I recognized Jenna sitting astride her big dark purple dragon, soaring right next to us.

"Help me!" I shrieked. I wasn't sure she'd hear me over the rush of wind. I could barely hear her even when she swooped in closer.

"Calm down! She's not going to hurt you!"

She? I looked down at the dragon underneath me. It was peering back with big, curious blue eyes.

"Just get me down!" I yelled again.

"She's chosen you, Reigh! She wants you to be her rider! You have to talk to her if you want to get down." Jenna was grinning like a madwoman as she steered her own dragon away, soaring back toward the keep.

Talk to her? Great. Fantastic.

"Hey, c-can we land somewhere and talk this over? I'm not really, you know, cut out for this kind of thing. It's nothing personal, but I don't want to be a dragonrider." I felt stupid. This was ridiculous. As if the dragon was actually going to be able to understand me.

She let out a ferocious little grunt, snapped her wings in suddenly, and we went rocketing toward the ground like a lime green comet.

I screamed again, and it was even less dignified than before. Wrapping my arms and legs around her scaly neck as far as they would go, I hunkered down and tried not to sob. "Stop! Please!"

She did the opposite of stopping. The green dragon started spinning like a top, swirling through the air, and slinging me around like a ragdoll. I could barely keep my grip. My legs started to slide off.

"O-okay! You win! You hear me? You win! I'll be a dragonrider! Whatever it takes! Just put me down!"

Suddenly, she slowed down. The ride became smoother. When I finally dared to open my eyes again, we were soaring in a slow circle around the keep. Jenna and her dragon had landed on the roof to watch us. She was waving at me and still smiling from ear to ear.

"Easy, girl." My voice shook and my teeth chattered. "Be gentle with me."

The dragon finally spread her wings and cupped them, making a few graceful flaps as she stretched out her hind legs and landed on the roof.

As I scrambled down from her back, one of my boots snagged on her spines. I fell the last few feet and landed in a heap.

As I lay there, on my back again, staring up at the sky and trying to figure out why I wasn't dead, I felt something warm and slimy swipe the side of my face. Dragon spit. She'd *licked* me.

"Yuck!" I bolted to my feet and started wiping the thick, sticky goo off the side of my head.

Jenna was gripping her sides, howling with laughter. "Aw! You've got a girlfriend."

I glared up at the green dragon, who was making content purring sounds. "You have got to be kidding me."

"You should see your face!" Jenna was still cackling.

"How do you even know it's a girl anyway?"

"Look at the dewclaws on the hind legs," she explained through giggling breaths. "Smaller ones mean it's a female."

I tried wiping the dragon spit onto my shirt, but it only made my hand stick to my tunic like wet paste so I had to peel it off. "Ugh. Gross. Out of all the soldiers here, why did she pick me?

"You'll spend the rest of your life asking yourself that question." Jenna's expression had gone misty and distant as she beamed at us. "Welcome to the ranks, Master Reigh. What'll you name her?"

"Nothing. I'm not naming her and I'm definitely not riding her again," I growled. My face was burning with embarrassment and I couldn't wait to get out of there—just as soon as I got the rest of the dragon spit out of my ear.

I turned around to leave, looking for the exit doors, when the floor in front of me erupted into flames. I stumbled to a halt and glared back over my shoulder. The dragoness was glaring back at me, her nostrils flared and her ears slicked back.

"I don't think she's going to let you just walk away, Reigh," Jenna warned.

"She held me hostage!"

"She chose you. It's an honor, one of the highest to be had in Maldobar," Jenna said firmly. "By right of our laws, it means you are a dragonrider."

I crossed my arms and faced the green dragon again. "Fine. You want me to be your rider? Then you better promise not to do that to me again. I don't negotiate with kidnappers."

She gave another snort, licking her toothy chops. I took that as an agreement.

"So, what does this mean? I have to go to the academy or something?" I glanced at Jenna, who was giving me another one of those appraising stares. It was different than before, though. I wondered how much about me she knew now.

"Maybe, in time." She sighed and came over, grabbing one of my arms to drag me closer to the dragon. "Normally, Blybrig Academy, where all dragonriders are trained, would welcome you and train you. But this war is far worse than our kingdom has ever seen before. The academy has been closed for a state of emergency. So, for now, ride her ... forge a bond with her. The closer your bond, the better you will fight together."

Jenna forced my hand against the dragon's nose. She held it there and gave me a hard look. "You are *very* lucky, Reigh. Most riders don't even sit in a dragon saddle until their first day of training. Anything you can learn now will be of great use to you. Being chosen by a dragon is a high honor. She will be loyal to you until the day she dies. It's a bond stronger than love. I can only compare it to the connection between a mother and child. It's soul-deep. Do you understand?"

I didn't, but I nodded anyway. When I looked at the dragon again, meeting her sky-blue eyes, I got a strange tingly feeling in my stomach.

"Being a dragonrider does not mean you simply have the option of zipping around on a dragon, doing as you please. It's much more than that. To be one of us means you stand with us. We are a brotherhood—a family bound by honor. We defend our own and we hold tightly our oaths to do whatever it takes to protect Maldobar. That is our legacy."

I could feel the gravity of her words settling over me like a heavy weight—the weight of hundreds of years of tradition. I couldn't comprehend being a part of that. Who was I? Why would I be chosen? How could I possibly live up to that kind of standard?

"What will you call her?" Jenna asked softly.

I thought for a moment and then decided out loud, "Vexi."

"Is that a gray elf word?"

"Yeah." I smirked. "It means 'troublemaker.'"

Barrowton's keep housed the dragons in a stable that had been built into a highly secure vault hidden underground. As we walked across the open courtyard that was secluded behind the keep and blocked off by tall iron bars, Jenna explained to me that while it would have been better to have the dragons up high, inside the keep, where they could take off more easily, it also made them an easier and obvious target. According to her, the Tibrans had war machines unlike anything else they had seen before. Their range was extensive. And they knew the strength of the dragonriders was the greatest threat to them.

"As soon as we appear in battle, all focus of the enemy's assault is on us. They know that if we can be disabled, the rest of the army will quickly fall into chaos," she said as she guided us to a place in the rear of the keep where a wide, open tunnel seemed to slope gradually downward. It looked almost like the mouth of a cave, only there were steel tracks laid into the floor. They reminded me somewhat of the mining carts the gray elves used to haul gems out of the ground; only these were much larger.

"The launching system here in Barrowton is unique and untested, for the most part. It works out well enough on paper, and in the few trial runs that were done when it was constructed.

But we've yet to use it in battle. This whole place was designed to be an impenetrable and highly defensible fortress, you see."

Yeah, I was beginning to grasp that now. It was obvious from the outside that it was meant to be defensible. It had two outer walls, an inner set of walls, with turrets and ramparts teeming with soldiers and a whole network of underground tunnels.

Jenna led us down into the dark through the wide opening. Vexi didn't seem to like it, even if there was plenty of room for a dragon twice her size to get through. She stuck right on my heels like a stray puppy, lumbering along with her head so close that I could feel her damp breath rustling the back of my hair. Occasionally she made uncomfortable chittering noises and nudged me roughly with her snout.

Jenna's dragon, Phevos, didn't seem to care. He followed us from a distance at an indifferent pace, and his presence only seemed to make Vexi more nervous. She kept herself between me and the other dragon.

At the end of the sloping passage was a big, cavernous room. Soldiers were bustling back and forth, rolling carts and driving wagons full of supplies. The distant bellow of another dragon echoed from somewhere in the distance.

"This is the launch dome. Here the riders are prepared to go into battle," Jenna explained. She pointed out two huge cranks on either side of the passage. They reminded me of the ones pulled by horses to open the gates of the city. "The launcher is spring-loaded with tension. It can deploy only one dragon at a time, but the speed should be more than enough to get them airborne. Then the launcher is quickly reloaded. We estimate it can launch one dragon every two minutes."

"Whoa." I turned in a slow circle, taking it all in.

"This way." She waved me on. "I'll show you where you can keep Vexi."

I had a lot of questions. I just didn't know where to start with any of them. How was I even going to be a dragonrider? I didn't have a saddle or any money to buy one. According to Kiran, dragonrider gear didn't come cheap. I didn't have any armor—I didn't even have my own weapons anymore.

Jenna brought us to the dragon stables. The stalls were spacious and the air was warm. It smelled like new hay and animal musk. Vexi crouched down low behind me, curling her tail around her legs and slicking her ears back. Her big eyes peered around at all the other dragons, some of whom had poked their head out of their stalls to get a look at her.

I patted her head. "Guess you're the new kid, huh?"

She made an uneasy grumbling sound.

"It'll be okay. I'll stay down here with you, if you want."

Her gaze met mine and she pressed her head harder into my palm. It made me smile. Okay, she was still a troublemaker, and I didn't quite trust her not to take me hostage again, but it was hard not to like her.

Jenna showed me how to guide Vexi into an empty stall and get her settled. Vexi chirped at the nest of hay and immediately began nosing around in it. She turned around four times and curled up, lying her head down and letting out a big dragon-sigh.

"Good, eh?" I chuckled.

She chirped.

"Workers come by to feed them fresh meat daily. Dragons are quite efficient eaters. They prefer their food whole, and are partial to fish, but they are scavengers and in desperate times will eat just about anything to stay alive. They can go months without eating, if necessary. But of course, we'd never make them wait more than a day. They get pretty cranky when they're hungry."

"I don't know much about them," I admitted as I sat down next to Vexi's head. "I grew up in Luntharda. We don't have any dragons there."

Jenna was leaning in the doorway with her arms folded over her chest. She was watching us, a distant, thoughtful expression on her face. "Aubren told me. He told me quite a lot about you."

I looked down.

"He said you've saved his life more times than he could count. He also insists that you're quite brave for so young a person and perhaps a better sword fighter than he is. He seems to have a great deal of faith in you."

"I wish he didn't," I mumbled. I started tracing my fingers over Vexi's bright green scales, outlining the stripes on her head. She purred with delight.

The hay crunched and when I looked up again, Jenna was sitting across from me. "It's okay to be scared, you know."

I met her gaze.

"I'm scared," she said. "Right now, right this second. When I left Westwatch, the rest of the dragonriders there were deploying to try to stop the Tibrans from burning the port cities along the western coast. Many of them are my friends. I've known them for years. I think of them as brothers. And I don't know how many of them will survive. I'm scared for them. I wanted to go with them, to fight alongside them, but I have a duty to the kingdom. I had to come here to warn Aubren, Phillip and the others."

"You could go back. Maybe it's not too late," I suggested.

Her delicate brow furrowed, her jaw stiffed, and her lips puckered slightly. "I want that more than anything. But Aubren tells me that the Tibrans are practically on Barrowton's doorstep. I must stay here in case the city is attacked. With the dragonriders at Westwatch already engaged, we can't expect any reinforcements from them if things should go badly. There are a lot of people living here depending on us to protect them."

"The same people who hurled rotten food at you and cursed you?"

The corner of her mouth turned in a half-smile. "Yes. I fight for them, too, even if they are too foolish to see it. It's true; there are lots of people in Maldobar who still don't think women should be allowed to be soldiers or dragonriders. But I was chosen, just as you were. Phevos chose me, and not even my father could refute that. I was meant to be a dragonrider—so I will be the very best one I possibly can, even if no one ever blesses me for it."

"Aubren doesn't seem to mind it," I said. "In fact, he seems really proud of you."

She laughed quietly and looked away. "Yes, well, over the years we've learned to encourage, support, and protect one another through anything—whether we agree with it or not. Our parents either can't or won't, so it's what we have to do." She fidgeted with a lock of her hair, winding it around her thumb. "Since they came here, the Tibrans have been hell-bent on kidnapping someone from the royal family to hold as hostage. I can only assume that's so my father will be forced to negotiate the surrender of the royal city and, in essence, the whole kingdom."

I rubbed the prickly stubble on my chin. That must have been why Hilleddi was so determined to figure out which one of us was the prince. She wanted a hostage to deliver back to Argonox.

"My father wanted Aubren and I to stay with him in Halfax, to hunker down and hide like rabbits in a hole." Jenna's jaw tensed as she bit down hard on every word. "But I refuse to hide. I won't abandon my people to suffer and perish. I will fight for them until my very last breath."

We sat quietly for a few minutes, watching Vexi drift off into dragon dreamland. I was thinking about what an epically huge mistake that poor dragon had made by choosing me. Couldn't she sense that there was something wrong with me? What would she do the first time she saw Noh?

Jenna must have been thinking about her comrades in battle. There was a grim heaviness in her demeanor and a dark sense of worry in her eyes. It put a crease right between her eyebrows.

She looked a lot like Aubren. They had the same eyes, similar color hair. But where Aubren's features were more squared and broad, Jenna's was distinctly feminine and almost angelic. Her face was deceptively gentle looking for someone who could have crushed my fingers to dust with one handshake.

"My brother tells me you have a touch of destiny in you." Her voice was barely a whisper. "I wasn't sure what he meant until I saw her choose you."

"Destiny," I replied. "Or darkness."

"Maybe in your case, the two go hand in hand." Jenna was staring me down once more, determination like dragon fire flickering in her eyes. "But that doesn't mean you don't have a choice about the path you take—as long as you're prepared to live with the consequences."

"I guess." I sighed and looked back down at Vexi. "She is pretty awesome. Too bad I can't ride her. I don't have a saddle."

Jenna grabbed one of my cheeks, stretching and pinching it. She had another one of those wry, teasing grins on her face. "We'll just see about that."

TWENTY-TWO

"Jenna, wait! You can't do this!" a familiar voice shouted in the hall.

Groggily, I raised my head off my pillow and squinted into the dark. Two seconds later, someone kicked down my bedroom door.

One of my feet snagged in my sheets as I scrambled out of bed. I fell flat on my face just as Jenna appeared in front of me. Smooth, real smooth.

"Get up, Reigh. Get dressed. We're leaving." She started barking orders, still wearing her nightgown.

"Jenna, please! Stop and think for a moment. We have to talk about this." Aubren pleaded with her as he followed her into the room—also wearing his pajamas. Geez, why was everyone having a pajama party in my room?

"They are my brothers! More so than you ever were!" She spun on him, her eyes blazing with rage. "I will not abandon them!"

She turned on me next, picking my boots up off the floor and flinging them at me one by one. "I said get dressed, idiot!"

"Uh, what's going on?" I ducked for cover as a boot whizzed past my head, missing me by mere inches. Something told me she'd missed on purpose.

Aubren's expression had gone cold, as though Jenna's words had struck a kink in his armor. "Westwatch is burning. We just received word," he replied quietly.

Jenna was picking up my clothes and throwing them at me. "If we hurry—"

"*It won't matter!*" Aubren roared with a fury I'd never heard before. "You heard the report. The tower has fallen."

Jenna stopped dead in her tracks.

He clenched his fists, his thick shoulders bowing up as he faced her. "It took at least a day for that messenger to make it here. You know that as well as I do. He said the tower was already under siege. It wouldn't matter if we left right now. They are already gone!"

"My men can hold longer than a day," she fired back.

"They didn't at Eastwatch." He took an aggressive step toward her. "And not at Northwatch, either! Leaving this fortress would be idiotic and you know it. Here, we have a chance. And any one of your men who survived at Westwatch will know it, they'll come, and we need to be here to receive them."

The two were practically nose-to-nose, although Jenna was

about half a foot shorter than her older brother. I cringed and waited for the fists to start flying as they snarled at one another.

"*He* could have done something." Jenna threw her arm out to point at me. "You know it. He could have stopped them, or at least given them a fighting chance. You should have taken him—"

"How was I supposed to know they would attack us from the western coast? They've only come from the east until now! I'm not a fortune teller, Jenna!"

"G-guys?" I tried to break things up.

It didn't work. Or maybe they just didn't hear me.

"He came here to help. So, let him help! Let's take him out there right now and let him slaughter them like the barbarian cattle they are!" She lunged at me faster than I could evade and seized my arm. "You've got that demon magic inside you, right? Can you do it? Can you kill them all?"

"I-I-I—"

I squirmed and tried to get away, but she just squeezed my arm harder. She was much stronger than I was, and it scared me. Her eyes flickered with wild emotion as she stared me down, waiting for me to do something.

"Let him go," Aubren warned.

She ignored him and twisted my arm harder. "Show me. Prove that you can do it."

A cold chill tingled up my spine. I bit back a curse and tried to will Noh away. It shouldn't have surprised me—with so much anger and negative emotion swirling around. He always did like a good fight.

"No," I growled, both to her and Noh. "I'm not some mutt you can order around. You have no idea what you're messing with, or what you're asking me to do. I can barely control this thing inside me as it is. If I go out there and try something like that, there's a good chance it won't stop with Tibrans. I'd probably end up killing more civilians than enemy solider before it was over."

Jenna let go of my arm, her eyes wide. I couldn't tell if she was surprised or on the verge of a nervous breakdown.

"Aubren's right, we need to stay here and prepare. It sucks. I know you feel like you're turning your back on them. But now we have Tibrans coming at us from two sides. Did you ever stop to think that maybe this was their plan? They're probably hoping to draw you away from here, and me too. It would make this place even easier to conquer, and you'd be running out of places to hide. Think about it—you're the one who said what Hilleddi and Argonox really want is to take one or both of you hostage."

Across the room, I saw Aubren's demeanor soften. His shoulders relaxed and he bowed his head slightly. "If you're right, we should anticipate an attack very soon."

I sincerely hoped I wasn't. It wasn't like I was some great war-planning mastermind. It just made the most sense to me, one monster to another, to try to lure all the best fighters away from the one place where they stood a chance to make a meaningful stand.

Fresh tears rolled down Jenna's face. Her jaw trembled, and she hid her face in her hands.

Aubren put his arms around her and hugged her tight. She curled against him and started to sob. He patted the back of her head, comforting her like he would a small child.

I let out a breath of relief.

Aubren narrowed his gaze on me. He didn't say anything—but he didn't have to. I got the message. Time was running out. I needed to get it together and figure out how to use my power without losing control.

I might be the only chance they had of surviving this.

I couldn't sleep.

Aubren managed to convince Jenna to go back to her room and try to rest. He was going to talk to Phillip and make sure that first thing in the morning the city began lockdown procedures. The gates of Barrowton would be shut permanently. The civilians would be advised to stay inside and take cover until further notice.

I was supposed to be resting, too. But after a few hours of tossing and turning, watching the moon silently sail past my bedroom window, and asking myself if I could do this or not—I finally gave up. I got dressed in a basic dark blue tunic, black pants, and my boots. I didn't even bother putting on my belt. After all, it's not like I was going outside. Not technically, anyway.

I crept out into the hall and snuck from shadow to shadow, dodging guards, soldiers, and servants until I got down to the sublevels of the keep. Things were quiet upstairs. Down here, however, the Maldobarian soldiers were on high alert. It wasn't easy sneaking my way past them all—lucky for me, being sneaky was a vital part of being a gray elf scout.

Vexi lifted her head drowsily when I cracked open the door of her stall and slipped inside. She chirped happily and flicked the end of her tail.

"Shh!" I pressed a finger to my lips. "Don't let them know I'm here."

She canted her head to the side, cocking her ears like she didn't understand why I had to worry.

I trudged across her nest of hay and flopped down beside her, propping myself up against her neck. "It's a long story. Basically, I just don't want anyone to come down here and preach to me about what I have to do anymore."

I felt the heavy puffs of her breath in my hair as she sniffed me.

"You know, I seriously don't get why you picked me," I said as I scratched her under the chin. "But it's kinda nice to have a friend. You know, one that doesn't want me to kill people for them, anyway."

She purred happily and wrapped her tail around me as she plopped her big head back down into the hay.

I tried not to think about it. There was so much going on. I was far away from the only home I'd ever known and all the people who'd cared about me there. It was moments like this, when I was feeling especially crummy, that Enyo always seemed to pop by to cheer me up. I missed her a lot. It made the center of my chest ache like there was a big hole in it.

And Kiran … Where did I even start when it came to him? I missed him, yeah. He was the closest thing to a father I'd ever known. At least, that's what I'd always thought. Now I was forced to question why he wanted me in the first place. Had he stolen me from the castle? From my real parents? Why would he do something like that? It obviously wasn't because he was dying to be a parent because he refused to let me call him my father. So why?

And now I had Aubren trying to treat me like a kid brother, or just a kid—honestly, I couldn't tell which. I had no idea how much he'd told Jenna about me, and I was too afraid to ask. She apparently knew about my power, so he'd told her that much. She wanted me to use it to avenge the dragonriders and kill the Tibrans, which wasn't all that different from what Aubren wanted, as well.

I growled angry gray elf curses under my breath and scratched the back of my head. The hay was itchy. I was anxious. I couldn't get comfortable here, either.

So, I did something stupid.

"Noh," I muttered. "Are you there?"

At first, there was no answer. Then I felt that shiver of cold. I could see my breath in the air. Around me, Vexi stirred. Her nose twitched and her ears perked. Suddenly, her head shot up and her eyes focused on a corner of the room where the shadows were especially thick.

"*Yes, master?*" Noh's voice echoed like a whisper in the air.

Vexi started to growl softly.

"When we were captured by the Tibrans, you know, and I was bound to the Mirror of Truth … " I hesitated and scratched the back of my head again. "Did you do something to make the mirror go screwy? What I mean is, did you save me then?"

Noh stepped from the darkness like he was just passing through a doorway. This time, he didn't look like a wolf. He looked like a darkened reflection of me. It caught me off guard. He was even wearing the same clothes as I was, although they were all black. His skin was a dark gray and his hair, while it was still a long, braided mess like mine, was as black as a moonless night. His bottomless red eyes flickered as they stared me down from across Vexi's stall.

"*No.*"

I pushed Vexi's tail out of the way and stood up. Gathering my courage, I walked toward him. "So, the mirror didn't kill me because I was telling the truth?"

Standing eye-to-eye with him was beyond creepy. He even had the same scar across the bridge of his nose. Geez, no wonder everyone treated me like a kid, I really did look like one.

"*So it would seem,*" was his reply.

"We have to come to an agreement here, okay? I need to be able to use this power without it getting out of hand."

He smirked, showing off his pointed canine teeth. "*You still don't understand, do you? Silly master.*"

"Understand what?"

"*It is not me you cannot control, it is yourself.*"

I frowned. "What is that supposed to mean?"

"*You think you desire control, but what you need is understanding. You cannot have one without the other. I am you, what hides within you, what you hope no one else sees. The darkness of your heart. The thing all men fear.*" He stretched out a hand and touched a finger to the center of my chest. A pang of violent cold ripped through my body, leaving me breathless. "*We are one, you and I. Two souls, one body. That is our inheritance.*"

I tried to push his hand away from me, but every time I touched him, my hands passed right through him like mist.

"*Don't fret. Soon, she will claim you—and hers is the only family that will matter. The ritual must be done, you see. Without it, our power will never be complete and you will never have the control you seem to crave.*" He laughed and tapped a finger against his temple. "*We cannot sync until it is done.*"

The memory of that woman's voice that had whispered to me in the dark—right after saving Aubren and his men from the snagwolves—resurfaced. I hadn't heard her again since then. Was that it? Was that the key?

She'd said something about a ritual, too. And blood … pure blood.

"Until what is done? What is the ritual? Who is she?" I started to yell. "What the heck are you talking about!"

It was no good. I dove at him, but Noh had vanished and I wound up tackling nothing but empty air. I stood in the stall, breathing hard and looking around in case he reappeared somewhere else.

At last, I met Vexi's worried gaze. Her blue eyes blinked,

regarding me cautiously.

"Sorry, girl." I sighed as I sank down to sit in the hay far away from her. "I should've warned you there was something seriously wrong with me. It's not too late, right? You could leave and find someone better."

A heavy, scaly, green dragon snout landed in my lap. Vexi stared at me with eyes the size of dinner plates, making worried chittering sound as she pushed her snout against my chest.

My eyes got misty. I ran a hand across her head and gave her a scratch behind the ears. "Guess you're pretty stubborn, huh?"

She closed her eyes again and scooted the rest of her big dragon body close to wrap around me again. I leaned back against her side and listened to the deep, muffled *thump, thump, thump* of her heartbeat right in my ear. It was soothing, like a soft dragon lullaby, and eventually it lulled me into a deep sleep.

TWENTY-THREE

I awoke to the sensation of the whole world shuddering around me like an earthquake. The stacked stones of the walls and floors groaned. Little bits of debris and rubble showered down upon my face and dust swirled in my eyes. Geez, how long had I been asleep?

Behind me, Vexi unfurled from her nest and let out an uneasy growl.

People were shouting outside her stall. Commotion and the faint tolling of bells accompanied the low blast of warning horns.

Oh no. That could only mean one thing.

I ran to the door of Vexi's stall and rolled it open, sticking my head out into the corridor just in time to see Jenna and her company of dragonriders rounding the corner. They were fully outfitted from boot to helmet in their battle armor, long blue cloaks fluttering behind them. They each carried their helmet under their arm and walked single file, parting the flurry of panicked soldiers who were running up and down the corridor.

Jenna and I locked eyes as she strode past, but she didn't stop.

"H-hey! What's going on?" I called after her as I jogged to catch up.

"Isn't it obvious?" she snapped back. "The Tibrans have finally come to lay siege to the city. They're attacking from both sides and they've brought more war machines than ever before."

"You can't go out there! There's only five of you." I grabbed her arm and dragged her to a stop. "You'll be killed!"

Her steely gaze met mine and for a second, I thought she might backhand me across the face. Since she was wearing her riding gauntlets, it would have left a mark and maybe even knocked a few teeth loose.

She put a heavy hand on my shoulder instead. Her gaze softened and her mouth curved into a faint, bittersweet smile. "This is what we do, Reigh. This is what it means to be a dragonrider. Every person in Barrowton is counting on us. Live or die, we have to fight for those who can't."

Jenna pulled away, leaving me standing in the corridor while she and the rest of her men went to mount up. I was numb. All around me, the keep shuddered again, as though being hit by something enormous. Men shouted. Rubble sprinkled over my head.

I looked back to the stall were Vexi was peeking at me,

leaning her big head out so she could watch me with one big eye.

For a moment, everything seemed to stand still. Something clicked in my brain—like a switch had been flipped. Now was the time. I didn't have any weapons. I didn't have any fancy armor. Heck, I didn't even have a saddle. But I did have a dragon and a few wicked tricks up my sleeve.

I made my choice.

I hid in Vexi's stall, peering through a crack in the door while the other dragonriders rode past on their way to the launch dome. I waited until they had all gone around the corner and out of sight before I rolled Vexi's stall door all the way open. Racing down the hall again, I grabbed the first piece of rope I came across and darted back to begin tying it around Vexi's neck.

"This is nuts. Yep. This is crazy. I am insane," I muttered as I crawled onto her back, trying to find a good place between her spines to sit. My hands were sweating and shaking as I tied the other end of the rope around my waist. It wasn't a saddle. Not even close. But maybe it would keep me from dying if I fell off? Here's hoping, anyway.

"Okay, girl. Are you ready to do something stupid?" I leaned down to pat her neck.

Vexi gave an answering snarl. I felt her strong body flex under me as she stood and immediately bounded out of her stall.

The last dragonrider was being deployed from the launching system when we arrived on the scene. They had him standing on a big wooden sled while the cranks held tight, pulled by draft horses. The dragon hunkered down, wings folded in tight, and the rider was sitting low in his saddle with his body flush against his mount.

Then, together, the soldiers released the ropes binding the horses to the crank wheels. The huge wheels spun and the wooden sled went rocketing up the passage toward the blaze of daylight. It fired the dragonrider and his beast out of the tunnel like an arrow. The dragon spread its wings, catching the wind, and soared out of sight.

"Okay, that's terrifying." My teeth were chattering.

Vexi crawled forward while the cranks were hooked back to the horses and pulled tight again. The soldiers quickly began winding the wooden sled back down the ramp and into place.

I got a few hesitant looks from the soldiers manning the launcher as I went past. Probably because I wasn't dressed for battle. I didn't even have a jerkin on, for crying out loud. But I did have a dragon, so for them I guess that was good enough.

My hands were slippery from sweating; I couldn't get a good grip on Vexi's already slick scales. My heart was pounding so fast I could barely breathe. I tried to get as flat against my dragon's neck as possible, wrapping my arms around her in a bear hug.

Vexi flattened herself down on the wooden sled just like the dragon before her had. She folded her wings in close to her body and lowered her head, her ears slicked back and her eyes narrowed.

Somewhere in the back of my mind, my common sense reminded me that this was an *extremely* stupid thing to do and I was probably going to die in the next two minutes.

Good thing I've never been all that smart.

"Okay, we can do this," I whispered. "We can totally do this. No big deal."

It was a *very* big deal.

The cranks released and suddenly we were being hurled out of the end of that tunnel like a projectile into the midday sky. Vexi twisted her body into a spiral and then spread her wings wide, catching the wind and soaring upward.

Below me, the scene of battle was nothing short of horrific. Under a gloomy sky, the Tibran army had surrounded the outer wall of Barrowton. There were so many soldiers it was like looking at an angry ant colony. They were using massive catapults to throw black orbs over the walls, which exploded into a spray of liquid inferno.

"Dragon venom." I guessed. Kiran had told me all about dragon fire. It wasn't really fire—it was a sticky, highly acidic venom that combusted explosively whenever air got to it, making it almost impossible to put out. You had to wait for it to burn itself out once all the fuel was used up.

The soldiers inside Barrowton were firing volleys of arrows, but the effort seemed futile. The Tibran soldiers had come in overwhelming numbers. Another explosion of fire and burning venom rocked against the keep. In the distance, I saw Jenna and her dragonriders making calculated passes. They were trying to take out the catapults.

I leaned down to call up to Vexi. "I've got a plan. Ready for this?"

It was hard to tell how much she really understood. I didn't know how dragonriders usually communicated with their mounts. Kiran had never explained that to me—although he'd told me that Jaevid could speak telepathically with his. Part of being the lapiloque, I guessed.

I wasn't that lucky. So, I had to improvise.

I smirked and set my eyes on the closest of the catapults, squeezing the rope tighter. "Time to fight fire with fire."

I guess Jenna was surprised when Vexi and I went zipping past her into battle. I couldn't see her face because of her helmet, but I got the impression from the way she started frantically waving her arms that she wasn't exactly thrilled about me being here.

We didn't pull over to debate it, though. Vexi darted through the sky, spinning and rolling, dodging arrows and nets that were being fired from below. We did a wide pass, circling one of the catapults closest to the city wall. It was firing shot after shot at the keep, trying to break it down.

I squeezed my legs around Vexi's body to get her attention and pointed at the black orbs being hurled through the air. "Let's go for it!"

She snorted in agreement, pumped her mighty wings, and went in for the strike.

The timing had to be perfect. As the catapult's long arm was cocked back, I watched the Tibran soldiers roll another huge black orb onto the spoon-shaped bucket at the end of the arm. I clenched my teeth. We just had to wait for the right moment.

"Now!" I yelled at the top of my lungs.

Vexi whirled through the air, picking up speed and falling into a steep dive. I felt her sides swell as she took a breath. The catapult's arm released, beginning to fling the black venom-filled orb into the air.

The air around me exploded. There was an acrid smell and a flash of heat as Vexi detonated the orb like a bomb with her breath before it could even leave the bucket, sending burning dragon fire spraying through the air and all over the Tibran soldiers.

And all over my back.

I cried out in pain as Vexi wheeled upward again, a hailstorm of arrows zipping past us and glancing off her scaly hide.

I couldn't see how bad the damage was, but it felt like my whole back was ablaze. I tried to twist to see, but the movement was almost more than I could stand. That's the problem when you decide to play with dragon fire—you gotta be ready to get burned.

Below us, the catapult was in cinders. Unfortunately, there were dozens more being slowly positioned all around Barrowton. Sure, my plan had worked, but we'd only taken out one. Trying it again might actually kill me.

In the distance, I heard another huge explosion. Fire belched into the air and I saw Jenna and her dragon soaring upward as another catapult was destroyed. She had seen what we did—and now she and the rest of her riders were copying us!

Catapults started going up like torches one after another. The Tibrans scrambled to regroup and tried desperately to shoot down the dragonriders.

"Let's go again," I called down to Vexi.

She turned her head to look back at me disapprovingly.

I didn't have to be the lapiloque to figure out what she was thinking. I was already hurt. It was beyond dumb to take that chance again, right?

Why does everyone keep expecting me to do the smart thing?

"Not with fire this time," I bargained. "I wanna try something new. Just trust me!"

She did. Or at least, enough to give it another try. She began beating her wings faster, picking up speed as we set our sights on the next catapult.

As we got close, I let go of the ropes and let my weight fall back against the tension of the knot tied around my waist. I spread my arms wide, closing my eyes and drawing my focus inward. Just moving my arms made my back feel like it was being scalded.

I bit down hard and forced myself to concentrate through the pain as I called upon the darkness within me, drawing out my power like I had in my fight with Aubren. It was hard with so much chaos and the rocking motion of Vexi's wing beats bouncing me all over the place. Yet I could feel it, like a spot of cold pressure between my open hands.

I reared back, visualizing the swirling mass of darkness taking the shape of a spear. As soon as I felt it go solid in my hand, I opened my eyes and hurled it straight at the black orb about to be launched from the catapult bucket.

The shadow spear hissed through the air, leaving a trail of black mist behind it. Vexi immediately did a mid-air about face and started to retreat, but I wasn't about to miss it. I turned back just as my shadow spear struck the orb.

The explosion sent out a blast wave of darkness that spread through the air like ripples on a pond. It blew the catapult apart in a shower of burning venom. Then it tore through the surrounding Tibran ranks, reducing the soldiers closest to it to nothing but heaps of black ash.

Vexi was fast—but she wasn't *that* fast. She couldn't outrun the blast wave. When it struck us, it sent her flipping end-over-end through the air. I felt the rope tethering us together snap.

I tried to grab onto her, reaching for any part of her I could, but my sweaty hands slipped right off her neck. I caught a glimpse of her green scales hurtling away from me as I twisted in the air, plummeting straight toward the ground.

TWENTY-FOUR

I shut my eyes tightly and told myself it was okay to die. It wouldn't be so bad. Sure, I was young. There was a lot of stuff I hadn't done yet—including kissing a girl. But hey, at least I'd have a few good stories to tell when I got to the other side, right?

Then a strong arm snagged me around the waist and snatched me out of midair. I wheezed as the sudden impact knocked the breath out of me, looking up into the frenzied glare of the last person in the world I expected to see.

"Hang on," Kiran shouted as he hauled me over onto the back of his shrike with him. He pulled my arms around his waist tightly.

All around us, other gray elf warriors riding shrikes were streaking through the air like tongues of lightning. I couldn't believe it. They were joining in the fight!

"You came?" I called up to him in disbelief.

He didn't answer. Now wasn't really the time to chat, though, so I tried not to take it personally.

"Watch out for the machines throwing nets!" I warned, pointing below. "We have to stop them from tearing down the wall!"

Kiran nodded and heeled his shrike into more speed. He drew back his bow and started firing arrows in rapid succession, taking out the Tibran soldiers who were trying to reload one of the net-throwers.

Right on cue, Vexi dove in for a strike. One burst of her burning breath demolished the machine. She flashed me a toothy dragon smile as she soared away, following us from a distance as we began making more passes.

We made quick work of six more net throwers, although in the sea of Tibran forces that were crashing against Barrowton's outer walls like the sea against the shore, it didn't seem to make much difference. We couldn't keep this up forever.

We didn't even get the chance to try.

The sudden, panicked screech of a dragon made my insides go sour.

I whirled around just in time to see a net snag around Vexi's head. She clawed and tried to hover, but another net wrapped around one of her wings. She started to go down, kicking and clawing to get free until she landed with a thunderous boom in the middle of that boiling sea of Tibran soldiers.

"No!" My whole body pitched violently and I kicked away from Kiran, leaping out into the open air before I could even think about it.

"Reigh!" Kiran shouted and reached for me, missing by inches.

I was falling again—but I wasn't scared this time. I wasn't going to die.

I didn't have to concentrate. My power came to me instantly, snapping in the air around me and taking the shape of two huge black bird wings. I could move them, like extensions of myself, and I used them to fly straight for her.

The Tibrans were prodding at her with spears, trying to find the right place to stab to kill her quickly, before she could shower them with flame.

Right as one of them went in for the killing blow, I kicked down and snapped the staff of his spear in half. With one punch from my shadow-coated fist, the soldier went flying backwards and crashed through a stunned line of his comrades.

I landed next to Vexi, spreading my black-feathered wings and snarling at them. Raw dark power sizzled off my body. I wasn't myself. I could see and hear, but my body was out of control.

I flexed, spreading my arms outward and sending out a pulse of darkness much like when my shadow spear had detonated the black orb of venom. More Tibrans went flying, and the ones closest to me were reduced to heaps of ash.

That got their attention. Some of them immediately dropped their weapons and ran. Others tried to form ranks, linking their bronze shields together and pressing in.

"Go ahead," I growled. "Just try to touch her."

They fired bows. One flex of my hand sent a focused blast

that made all the arrows disintegrate in the air long before they could ever touch Vexi or me.

"Care to try again?"

They threw spears—and I did the same thing.

"I don't have time for this."

I couldn't stop. It was like Noh had taken over my body completely. He was the one talking, the one suddenly cutting through the Tibran ranks like chaff. The sensation of so many deaths made me reel and left me totally delirious. I couldn't concentrate at all. I was out of my mind.

And I had no idea how to make it stop.

Terror gripped me like a chokehold. What if I couldn't stop? What if it stayed like this forever? What would happen to me? What if—

I felt someone grab me from behind. Powerful arms wrapped around me, pinning my arms to my sides.

"Reigh, you have to stop this now!"

I knew his voice. But I couldn't stop it. Another wave of power surged out of me, tearing past all my willpower.

His arms went slack.

I whirled around, looking straight into Kiran's eyes. He seemed surprised at first, like he wasn't sure what had happened. Then I saw realization come over his features. He gave me a warm smile as one of his hands brushed over my cheek.

"I am so sorry, my son."

His whole body faded, instantly dissolving into a fine black mist right in front of me.

Kiran was gone.

Whatever happened next, I couldn't remember. The roar of battle, the heat of flames, and the dull gray sky all turned to a muddy blur. I blacked out.

The next thing I knew, I was waking up, lying on my side in my bedroom at the keep. I bolted upright, my body pouring a cold sweat as I called out for Kiran. The fight with Jenna, the battle—maybe it had all just been a nightmare.

"Reigh, please, you have to lie down," a soft voice cooed to me. "Careful. Don't lie on your back."

I was still dazed when I looked over to find a beautiful gray elf lady sitting on the edge of my bed. Something about her was eerily familiar. Only, I was sure I'd never seen her before. That is—until she smiled.

"Enyo?"

She nodded slightly.

"W-what happened to you?"

I looked her over slowly, carefully. She wasn't anything like the small, dark-headed little girl I'd left behind in Luntharda. She had *changed*. Her black hair was now the color of freshly fallen snow, and her once childish frame had transformed into that of a slender, elegant woman dressed in the cream-colored robes of a healer. Her smooth, oval face reminded me of the sculptures of goddesses I'd seen in the gray elf temples. And yet, I could see ghostly traces of my childhood friend in her features as she arched one of her brows at me. It was her, the girl I ...

"Don't be ridiculous, you know how gray elves mature." She rolled her eyes. They caught the candlelight like diamonds.

"I'm sorry, I just had a terrible dream," I said as I started to lie back on the bed. Moving again sent a pang of sharp pain through my body, pain from the where the dragon venom had burned me.

I knew, even before I saw her expression fade from that exasperated smile to a look of sorrow. It wasn't a dream.

"N-no," I stammered and choked. "I-I didn't. I wouldn't."

Enyo closed her eyes and bowed her head. Resting in her lap, I saw Kiran's bow.

Suddenly, I couldn't breathe. Tears blurred my vision. I wanted to scream but nothing, not a single sound would come out.

"Your dragon is safe," Enyo said softly. "We came when we learned that Westwatch had fallen. King Jace wouldn't stand to see the dragonriders fail. He made a proclamation that he would be joining the fight and many others followed him. He is here now, speaking with the other nobles."

I still couldn't speak. Inside, it felt like I had swallowed a mouthful of dragon venom. My whole body burned. I squeezed my eyes shut as I tried to keep it in. I didn't want to lose it. Not now—not in front of her.

"The battle is over. Barrowton's walls still stand and its people are safe, for now. The Tibrans who survived fled in fear. But it is expected they will return very soon in far greater numbers. For now, you need to rest. You were badly injured."

"Get out," I rasped.

"Reigh?"

"Just go."

The bed shifted as Enyo stood up. I felt her take one of my hands and place Kiran's bow into it, gently rolling my fingers closed around it. "I'll be right outside if you need me."

Her footsteps retreated. When I dared to look again, I saw her hesitating in the doorway—like she wanted to say something else.

Whatever it was, she never said it. Her eyes fluttered closed and she turned away, closing the door behind her.

TWENTY-FIVE

The damage was much worse than I'd anticipated. By the time I managed to hobble across my bedroom floor to the dressing table and turn around to see my back in the mirror, I was in so much pain I nearly fainted. I peeled back the corners of the bandage to assess how bad it was.

My skin was scorched, blistered, and raw. There were a flew places where it had been melted away, revealing spots of naked flesh and muscle. So yeah, it was severe.

I couldn't do anything, couldn't go anywhere. I collapsed on my way back to the bed, crumpling to my knees, and buried my face in my hands to stifle my own screams. My body shook out of control. Every fiber of my body cried out in agony, but I bit down hard. I didn't want Enyo to hear. I didn't want her to come in here again and see me like this.

I didn't deserve anyone's comfort.

She and Aubren found me there the following morning. I was still sitting on the floor staring out my bedroom window, feeling nothing as I watched a red sun rise over the mountains. Part of me had hoped I wouldn't live to see that dawn. It only seemed fair after what I'd done.

Aubren helped me get back in bed so Enyo could change my dressings. She talked, making idle conversation that I guess was supposed to distract me from the fact that it felt like she was peeling my skin off every time she removed a bandage. Apparently, Kiran had hired her to take my place as his assistant and was beginning to teach her all his healing methods.

"The job seems to suit you," Aubren said with a friendly smile.

"I've wanted to learn to become a medic for a long time. My mother was a very talented scout, and she hoped I would follow in her footsteps. I tried to for years, but it never felt right. The moment I woke up after my change, I knew I had to be honest with her. Being a scout wasn't what I wanted. And as soon as I started to learn about the healing arts, making medicines, and caring for patients—it was like coming home. This is what I was meant to do," she replied. "Of course, my mother was a little surprised. I'm not sure she's convinced I made the right choice, yet."

I had nothing to say about it. It was taking every bit of concentration I had to keep from yelling curses as she began applying what smelled like a healing herbal salve to my back. It would speed the healing process, cutting the time in less than half. That's what I kept telling myself. And the sooner I was able to walk around, the sooner I could …

"Kiran began learning the healing arts here, when he served in my father's court as an ambassador and advisor. There was a very talented medic in the city named Holly. She trained him for years." Aubren rubbed his chin thoughtfully.

"That explains why so many of his medical texts are in the human language. I wish I could read them. Kiran was a very good teacher, but I still have so much to learn." Enyo was applying new bandages, carefully covering each of the open places where the dragon venom had melted away my flesh.

"I'm sure you'll do fine," he reassured her. "You speak the human language very well."

"O-oh, thank you!" Enyo's voice had an excited, girlish tremor in it. I'd heard that before whenever she talked to one of the older male scouts.

"Will you both just shut up," I growled.

Aubren stared at me with his eyes wide.

Behind me, I felt Enyo pause in her work. "Reigh, I'm sorry, I didn't think ab—"

"I said *shut up*!" I snarled louder.

Aubren's expression had gone cold. His eyes narrowed at me dangerously, like he was silently daring me to make a scene. "Calm down. I know you're in pain, but don't take it out on her."

"Get out. Both of you just get out!"

They did. It took a few minutes because Enyo had to gather up her medical supplies. But eventually, she hurried out of the room with tears in her eyes and Aubren's hand on her shoulder. I couldn't decide which upset me more.

By evening, I could tell the pain was starting to subside. I could sit up without wanting to vomit, anyway. The next day, I could finally stand up and walk across the room. Enyo came back in every morning to change my dressings, just like before, but she didn't try talking to me again. She was sulking. Or she was afraid of me. Either way, it was probably for the best. I didn't have anything to say to anyone.

Kiran's bow sat on my bedside table, right next to the one the Queen had given me, until the morning of the third day when I felt well enough to get up, change my clothes, put on my boots and belt, and begin packing what few belongings I had. It wasn't much, just a few changes of clothes. I slung the bag over my shoulder and reached for the bow—*his* bow.

My hand hesitated, hovering over it. I couldn't stop my face from screwing up. Tears blurred my vision and I bit down hard on my tongue to keep from making a sound.

No. I couldn't use it. I didn't deserve to even touch it.

"What are you doing?" I heard Enyo's voice from the doorway. "You should be resting. You aren't well."

"I'm fine." Gritting my teeth, I picked up Kiran's bow and quickly disassembled it, packing it away with the rest of my gear. Then I picked up the one the Queen had given me, slung it across my shoulders, and started for the door.

"Reigh, wait." She grabbed my arm.

Enyo was standing so close that I found myself staring directly down into her eyes. Her brow was drawn up into a look of desperation, tears welling in her eyes. I tried not to notice she was gorgeous, or that the feeling of her hand on my skin made my heart race.

"Don't you trust me at all?" she pleaded. "You are my best friend. Please, just talk to me."

"It's me I don't trust," I muttered as I pulled away.

I made it all the way out of my room and into the hallway before she caught up with me and planted herself in my path. "But where are you going?"

"Home, where I should have been all along."

"You mean you're—?"

"Going back to Luntharda." I sidestepped around her and kept going down the hall.

"But what about the Tibrans? What about Aubren and the others? They still need you."

I stopped. "No. They don't."

"Reigh, that's not—"

"No!" I whirled around suddenly, fixing her with a scorching glare. "I never should have come here. It was a mistake. It's been a disaster from the very beginning. I'm done. I'm not fighting in anyone else's wars. I can't stay here any longer, not for one more minute."

Enyo's eyes narrowed and her forehead crinkled slightly as she glared back at me. "So, you'll go back and do what?"

"Run the clinic, what else? I'm the only one who's qualified."

Her lips parted and she blinked slowly in surprise.

I started walking away, but I only got a few more feet down the hall before I heard her running to catch up.

"I'm going with you, then," she declared.

"Pfft."

"I am!" She crossed her arms and pursed her lips stubbornly. "You can't do it on your own. You'll need help."

I rolled my eyes. "Fine. Just stay out of my way."

I didn't tell anyone else I was leaving. I didn't want to have to explain myself and it wasn't hard to guess how Aubren and Jenna were going to feel about this. I was a convenient pet for them to have around. A useful tool of war. They'd have to find another blunt object to wail the Tibrans with.

I wanted to get out of this place without someone pinning me down to interrogate me or tell me what I *should* be doing. And as I led the way down through the keep's maze of corridors, I got the impression that Enyo was hoping I would change my mind. She followed close behind, flicking me worried glances whenever she thought I wasn't paying attention.

I pretended to ignore her.

Nothing was going to change my mind.

When we arrived at the big door of Vexi's stall, Enyo started to fidget. She stood back as I began to heave the heavy door open, groaning as the wounds on my back burned in protest. My vision spotted. I felt lightheaded. The door was halfway open when I felt my legs go numb and I started to fall.

Something warm and scaly caught me. I looked up, realizing that Vexi's big head was under me, keeping me from falling the rest of the way to the floor. She made a worried murring sound.

I let her help me back up, using her head to steady myself on my feet again. "I'm fine, really."

Vexi snorted like she didn't believe me.

"She's so beautiful." Enyo whispered, her face the picture of awe. "Can she really understand you?"

My dragon and I exchanged a glance. "I guess so."

Kiran had always told me that dragons weren't like horses or faundra. They weren't even like shrikes. They were smarter than other animals. They had thoughts, opinions, and personalities like people.

I walked around to Vexi's back and eyed that place between her spines where I knew I could sit. I hesitated again. The last thing I remembered from the battle was ... well, let's just say Vexi had still been trapped under the net and we were surrounded by Tibran soldiers.

But what about after that?

"You said the Tibrans were afraid of me," I said as I turned enough to watch Enyo's expression. "Why? They weren't running from me before everything went dark. What happened? What do I not remember?"

She swallowed hard. Her eyes flickered with fear. She was afraid of me, or at least of whatever I'd done. "Reigh, does it really matter?"

It did. However, if she didn't want to tell me, fine. So be it.

I grabbed Vexi's spines and pulled myself onto her back, then stretched out a hand to help Enyo up.

She still hadn't put a toe across the threshold of Vexi's stall. She stared at me, at my dragon, and at my outstretched hand. Her cheeks flushed and she shook her head. "I ... "

"If you want to go with me, then hurry up."

Enyo paused, thinking it over. Finally, she muttered a gray elf curse under her breath and quickly trotted over to grab my hand and climb up behind me. Her arms snaked around my middle, clinging to me and squeezing handfuls of my shirt. Great, now I was the one blushing.

She squeaked with alarm when Vexi stood up, hugging herself against me tighter as my dragon began prowling out of the stall. I was having second thoughts the whole way to the launch dome. It was rude to bail out without even telling Aubren or Jenna where I was going. I hadn't exactly been a shining example of honor here lately, though. Cowardice and humiliation weren't so far fetched for someone who had just murdered their own father.

The soldiers working the launcher didn't ask any questions. I guess if you are riding a dragon, everyone does their jobs and doesn't bother you with questions. I could get used to that.

"Hold on tight," I told Enyo as Vexi positioned herself on the wooden sled.

She hugged me harder.

I hadn't bothered with a rope this time. After all, I didn't have any intention of doing any fancy aerobatic flying. This was strictly a transport mission. But as I heard the cranks draw tight and one of the soldiers give the order to release the launcher, my stomach churned with nerves. Crap. I should have grabbed a stupid rope.

The launcher released and hurled us through the tunnel toward the daylight. I squeezed my whole body against Vexi's neck as hard as I could, trying to lie down flat against her as the wind whipped past us. Behind me, Enyo was gripping me so hard it was killing my back.

Suddenly, we were in the open sky. Vexi spread her wings, caught the wind, and began wheeling in a gentle circle. I let my body relax.

Enyo was still clinging to me, her face pressed against the back of my neck, her frantic breaths puffing on my skin. It made my insides feel like jelly. She'd held onto me before, but things were different now. She was different.

I didn't enjoy it for long, though. The higher we climbed, the more of Barrowton I could see. The Tibrans were gone—or at least, the living ones were. What was left behind, all around the city, was a sea of black like the earth had been scorched. Even some sections of the city walls were stained black. I thought it might be left over from the catapults or the dragonriders, but as we swooped low, I saw the black dust swirl. It wasn't scorch marks. It was *ash*. Scattered throughout it were empty helmets, breastplates, shoes, and shields—and not just from Tibran soldiers.

My heart went cold.

Gods and Fates ... what had I done?

TWENTY-SIX

I got Vexi to land at the boundary where Maldobar and Luntharda met. We touched down gently, and I helped Enyo climb down before I swung my leg over and slid down to the ground. Traveling by dragon was a lot more convenient than a shrike. Her flight was much smoother and she could go higher—so high no Tibran net thrower could possibly catch us.

Standing before the looming tree line, I caught a waft of all the familiar smells of the jungle. The damp smells of rotting wood, rich soil, humid air, and exotic flowers. It smelled like home.

I started for the trees.

Vexi let out a shriek of unhappiness, leaping over me and landing right in my path. She stamped and puffed, growling like she didn't want me to go.

"I'm sorry, girl. I'm leaving. And I'm not coming back." I started walking around her.

She zipped back into my path again, blowing a furious dragon snort right in my face.

I glared up at her. "I said no! Look, I appreciate the gesture. But you picked the wrong guy. I'm not a dragonrider. I'm not even a good person. So, move!"

Her scaly ears slicked back and she showed me her teeth, belting out a roar of defiance.

Fine. So, we were doing this the hard way.

"I don't want you," I yelled. "Get out of my sight—*now*."

She stopped growling and blinked her owlish blue eyes at me in confusion. Her ears swiveled and her snout twitched.

I stormed around her, marching straight for the tree line. I could hear Enyo's footsteps crunching along right after me. As soon as we crossed into the jungle, I heard Vexi let out another frustrated roar.

I didn't look back.

We hadn't exactly come prepared for a journey. Fortunately, Enyo had said that King Jace was at Barrowton. That meant he had brought a company of warriors with him—and that meant there would be more of them camped out near the boundary waiting for marching orders and to relay news back to the Queen.

Finding them was easy, mostly because they found us first. Scouts running perimeter patrols escorted us to their base camp. They knew who we were, although they were surprised to see us, and granted my request to borrow a shrike and enough provisions to get us back to Mau Kakuri. I didn't mention Kiran, even when they asked me how he was. When my back was turned, I overheard Enyo delivering the news that he had fallen in battle.

She didn't tell them *I* was the reason.

We left as quickly as possible. It was a long journey back and I didn't want to waste any time. Even being back in the jungle, shielded under the canopy of trees, I didn't feel any more at ease. My soul was restless inside me. I couldn't sleep. I couldn't sit still. Every second we wasted might be one I decided to look back, reconsider, or really think about what I was doing.

We flew hard during the day, breaking only twice to eat and let the shrike rest. At night, Enyo and I slept on separate bedrolls. I faced away from her, not wanting to run the risk of idle conversation.

She changed my bandages in the morning and slathered my back down with healing salve, all without saying a word. Privately, I wondered how bad the lasting damage would be. I'd have scars, of course. I might even lose some of the sensation back there.

I kept thinking about how if that spray had killed me, Kiran would still be …

We arrived at Mau Kakuri three days later. The city was the same as I remembered—still tucked away in a tranquil part of the jungle under the misty ambience of the falls. I guided the shrike to the front of the clinic where Kiran and I had lived ever since I was a baby. It hadn't changed—not that I'd been away all that long.

So why did it feel like I'd been gone for ages?

I climbed down but stopped Enyo before she could do the same. "Just go home. I'm sure your parents will be glad to see you're back."

She frowned. "Won't you need help settling in? We have to prepare to receive patients again."

"There'll be time for that tomorrow." I swatted the shrike on the rump, sending it off in a flurry of mirrored scales and fluttering wings.

I just wanted one night alone without someone's sad, sympathetic stare pinned at my back.

I unlocked the front door of the clinic and stepped inside, quietly closing the door behind me. I locked it—just to make sure Enyo didn't try to come sneaking in when I wasn't paying attention.

The house was a tomb of memory. The air smelled strongly of herbs that were hung up to dry so they could be made into medicines. Kiran's shoes were lined up neatly in the foyer along with a few of mine, as though he'd expected I would come back someday. He'd cut lots of firewood and left it piled in its usual place on the far wall. His books and texts were stacked by the side of the fire pit where he always sat to read and smoke his favorite pipe.

Sitting on top of the stack was a crumpled piece of paper— an old drawing of two wobbly looking stick figures holding hands. The taller one had silver hair, while the shorter one had red. It was something I'd made for him when I was a child.

I choked out loud and covered my mouth to stifle the sound.

Tears welled in my eyes and I turned around to slam my fist against the door. I did it over and over, until my knuckles were bashed and bleeding and there was a deep dent in the wood.

"Reigh!" Enyo's voice cried out from the other side of the door. She'd come back. "What's going on? Let me in!" She knocked furiously.

I let my head fall forward until my forehead came to rest against the door. "Go away." My voice broke.

There was a long pause and I started to suspect she'd gone.

"I know you're ashamed," she said quietly. "I know you don't want anyone to see you this way. I know you're hurting. You miss him."

I closed my eyes.

"So do I," she whispered. "I miss him, too."

My hand fumbled at the door lock. As soon as it was open, Enyo pulled the door back and pounced at me. She threw her arms around my neck and drew me in against her. I buried my face against the side of her neck.

We held each other for a long time. I wasn't sure how to let go. I was afraid if I did, she might disappear, as well.

At last, Enyo pulled back enough to brush my bangs out of my eyes and wiped the tears from my face. "Don't think for a single second that you're alone now, you hear me? You're not. I'm right here. I'm not going anywhere."

I cringed at those words.

She kissed my cheek gently. "Come on, let's get your hand cleaned up. I know you haven't been sleeping. You need to rest."

Enyo insisted on staying at the clinic with me. It looked

bad, most likely, but I swear we slept in separate rooms. Or rather, she stayed up sitting by the fireplace, reading one of Kiran's medical technique journals he'd translated into the gray elf language.

I went to my room, and stretched out on my old bed. It felt too small now. The whole room did, in fact. The window was open and outside I could hear the constant rumble of the falls. Usually, it was the perfect white noise to lull me quickly to sleep.

I was exhausted. I wanted to rest. But sleep came restlessly. I tossed and turned, staring at my closed bedroom door for what felt like hours until at last I drifted off.

And a nightmare swallowed me instantly.

I opened my eyes to the inside of a dim cave. Overhead, stalactites dangled like stone fangs. Before me was nothing but darkness, as though the cave went on forever in every direction.

My pulse raced. For a moment, I thought I might be back in that awful Tibran interrogation chamber. I took a step back, and my boots sloshed and splashed noisily. There was standing water on the floor.

When I looked down, I saw my reflection rippling on the surface.

I looked like Noh—or rather, some twisted version of him.

My hair was black and my eyes were glowing like red fires, just like his. I had two immense black-feathered wings on my back, and black spiky horns poking out of my hair. They started just above my ears and went all the way down my back. My hands were stained black all the way up to my elbows and my fingernails had become hard and long like claws.

I staggered back in panic, turning in a circle as I attempted to wipe the black stuff off my hands. It wouldn't budge. It was as though my skin had been stained with ink.

"Hello? Is anyone there?" My voice echoed off the cavern walls. "Where am I?"

Out of the corner of my eye, I saw a point of white light. Without thinking, I ran for it. Maybe it was a way out.

It wasn't.

A square, milky-colored slab of stone stood only a few yards away. I couldn't be sure, but it looked like it might be a gray elf sarcophagus. There was a bust of a person engraved on the top of it, and the whole thing seemed to emanate a soft white light.

Sitting on top of it with his back to me, was a guy in a dark blue tunic. At least, I assumed it was a guy. I couldn't see his face. But his muscular build and the broadness of his shoulders made me think it was a man. He had shaggy ash-gray hair that came to his shoulders, and he was leaning over like he was resting his elbows on his knees.

"Hey, are you stuck here, too? Do you know the way out?"

He didn't answer. He didn't even move. It was as though he couldn't hear me. I got a weird feeling, like pins and needles under my skin.

I started walking up to him. "Hello? Can you hear me?"

"*I've been waiting for you.*" A woman's voice suddenly filled the cave, sending out ripples across the water.

I staggered back. I knew that voice. It was the same one from before.

"M-me?"

"*You've been lazy, boy. You've been reckless and stupid.*"

"Hey!" I shouted, looking around to try to find where the voice was coming from. "Who are you?"

"*But no more. You are my chosen one. My champion. My harbinger. Soon you will carry the staff of my judgment and all will bow before it.*" The woman's voice oozed with delight and she gave a wicked laugh. "*But first you must complete the ritual. You must find the crystal, harbinger, and give an offering of pure blood.*"

"What are you talking about? Who are you?"

"*I am your Matron. Your mother. Your master. You will call me Clysiros,*" the voice replied. "*Now go and do as I command. Awaken he who sleeps and complete the ritual.*"

I turned back, looking over my shoulder and past one of my black wings to see the guy still sitting on top of the sarcophagus. His head fell forward slightly, as though he were hanging it in anguish. I still couldn't see his face, and I didn't get the impression that I knew him.

"I don't understand," I shouted at the empty air. "Tell me what's going on! Who is that? Who are you? What do you want from me?"

I didn't get an answer.

Suddenly, the ground fell out from beneath me. I was

swallowed up by a vortex of swirling black water—falling farther and farther away from the light until there was nothing.

Just the darkness and me.

"Reigh, wake up!"

Enyo was shaking my shoulders. I felt it an instant before she smacked me hard across the face.

I bolted awake, dazed by the candlelight. I looked around frantically, my gaze finally settling on her. I was in my room, still in my bed. My sheets were soaked with sweat and my heart was trying to pound out of my chest. A dream? I checked my hands just to make sure.

They were back to normal. The black marks, claws, wings, and horns were all gone. Slumping forward, I buried my face in my hands with relief.

"Reigh, what happened? You were yelling. I couldn't get you to wake up." Enyo's voice trembled with concern.

I tried to remember. It was all a haze now. I just remembered that voice, a woman's menacing voice calling to me in the dark. And something about a crystal.

"I'm sorry," I rasped. "I'm fine. It was a dream."

Her mouth drooped into a frown. "About Kiran?"

I caught myself before I could answer. Should I tell

her? Studying her face, I could see the evidence of worry, apprehension, and fear.

"Yeah," I lied. "It's fine now. I'm okay. Sorry for freaking you out."

"You're sure?"

I rubbed my cheek. "Well, my face stings now."

"Don't worry. I went easy on you; it won't leave a bruise." She brushed one of her cool palms over it, making me go stiff.

"*Har har har*, so funny."

"Seriously, are you sure you're okay?"

I forced a smile, purely for her benefit. "Yeah. I'm gonna try going back to sleep."

She seemed to buy it. Her face brightened and she gave me a cautious smile as she left, taking the candle with her. I almost asked her to leave it. The light was a comfort. But I didn't want her to suspect that I wasn't okay. I waited until after she closed the door behind her to lie back down and rub my forehead with the heel of my hand. I was hoping I could rub that voice out of my mind.

No such luck.

Clysiros—the name was stuck in my brain like a thorn. I'd never heard it before. I didn't know if she was someone important, but I had a feeling I knew exactly where I could find out.

TWENTY-SEVEN

Early the next morning, I got up and got dressed. The clinic was quiet. There weren't any patients here, yet. Now was as good a time as any.

I crept downstairs, tiptoeing through the main room where Enyo was curled up on a sleeping pallet next to the fire. There was a book still open, resting in her hands, and she was breathing softly. I paused as I passed her, studying her placid expression. Her lashes fluttered as she dreamed.

I couldn't leave her like that.

Squatting down, I slid my arms under her back and knees and carefully lifted her off the floor. I carried her up the stairs, into Kiran's room, and laid her down on his bed. I tucked the blankets in around her snugly.

As I brushed my fingers lightly over her cheek, she sighed and mumbled something I couldn't understand. A strange pressure settled in my chest, like a hand was squeezing around my heart. It hurt—in a good way—which made absolutely no sense to me.

I closed the door and went back downstairs. I sat on the front step and tied up my boots. Around me, the jungle made its waking up sounds. Birds, bugs, and frogs sang. The city was just beginning to rouse. As I walked the streets, I saw shopkeepers beginning to open. Bakers were already putting out their fresh pastries. Street merchants were rolling out their carpets on the sidewalk and arranging their wares on them.

I'd seen it all before, hundreds of times. Some of the shopkeepers even waved at me as I went by. I tried to smile back, but I couldn't find the strength.

I made my way to the front gates of the palace. There, two royal guards stopped me and demanded to know what I wanted.

I frowned at them. "I need to see Queen Araxie."

"Hah!" One of the guards laughed in my face. "You think you can just waltz up here and demand to see her?"

"I'm her favored scout. Or maybe you don't remember? Kiran is my father. I've come all the way from the battlefront in Maldobar to see her." I bit at the words angrily, narrowing my eyes at them. "Stand aside."

"What proof do you have? You aren't even dressed like a scout. You're just a kid!"

I flexed my arms, flinging them out wide. One small blast of my power sent both royal guards flying through the air like scarecrows. They landed on their rear ends on either side of me, mouths agape in horror.

I straightened my shirt collar, dusted off my sleeves, and stepped through the gates. Neither of them said another word.

Nobody else gave me any trouble as I walked into the palace. The other guards who saw me stood perfectly still, gripping their spears and bows hard, watching me carefully for a false move. Lucky for them, I hadn't come here looking for trouble.

I remembered the way to the throne room, and I was nearly there when I heard someone calling my name.

"Reigh! It is you!" Hecate walked toward me, her mismatched eyes fixed right on me. "I felt it the moment you came through the gates. You came back?"

I looked down, my face burning with embarrassment. She couldn't see me—I knew that. Still, I had been hoping she might not be anywhere nearby to hear what I'd come to say to her grandmother.

"It's a long story." I tried to be vague.

She stopped a few feet away from me with the lengths of her long, white and pink gown pooling around her. Her expression became tense as her brow furrowed ever so slightly. "What you did outside, I felt that, too."

"I'm sorry." Only, I wasn't.

"What's going on? That voice … the whispering voice … it's so much louder now. I can hear it." She tilted her head to the side slightly, as though she was listening. "What does it mean? Who is the harbinger?"

My jaw dropped. "I-is it a woman's voice?"

Her head bobbed slowly.

I gulped. "Maybe you're the one I should be talking to."

"About what?"

"I need to know if there's anything in the royal library about a woman," I replied. "A woman named Clysiros."

Hecate led the way through the halls of the palace, guiding me to the royal library where all the ancient texts and scrolls were kept. She explained that it was one of the few rooms she knew how to get to without her attendants. "It's been much easier to come and go as I please with my grandfather away. He's so stiff about the rules. He doesn't want me going anywhere without an escort, not even the library."

"Not to be mean, but why do you like the library. You can't read the books, right?"

She gave a small, haughty smile. "Not to be mean, but I think I use them better than seeing people do. I don't *read* the books. I *listen* to them."

"How exactly does that work?

"It's difficult to explain. I told you, I hear things—things no one else can." Her brow creased as we stopped where two halls intersected. She thought for a moment, and took an abrupt left and kept going. "It helps for me to make physical contact. It makes things much clearer. When it comes to books, if I hold them, I can hear the voice of the writer. Sometimes I can even ask them questions."

Okay. That was weird even by my standards.

"Here," Hecate said. She stopped right in front of a tall door with a rounded top. There was a silver half-moon shaped panel with the head of a stag engraved on it hanging over the door.

I opened the door and took her arm to guide her inside. "So how long have you been able to do that?"

"As long as I can remember. My cousins had the same ability. We were all born this way. But eventually it became too much for them. It drove them mad."

"What did?" I studied her troubled expression.

"It's like listening to a chorus that never ends. Some days are better than others. If I try, I can focus on one voice, like yours. It's easier if it is especially strong. But most days I am overwhelmed. Day or night, sleeping or awake, I always hear them. It's exhausting. And no one seems to know any way to make them quiet." Her brow creased with distress as she turned her face away. "I've tried everything. My grandfather seems convinced that sitting alone in my room undisturbed will make it better."

"Does it?"

Hecate shook her head. "He cannot hear them, so he doesn't understand. What sounds like silence to everyone else is a raging orchestra of chaos to me."

I felt bad for her. That didn't sound like fun at all. Somehow, though, it was comforting to know I wasn't the only weirdo walking around these days. "So, does anyone know why?"

"Why what?"

"Why do you hear these things?" I clarified.

She drew her bottom lip into her mouth, nibbling at it for a moment. "I don't know. Some have theories. My grandmother suspects it's something to do with the gods, maybe even a punishment for the things our family did during the Gray War. But no one knows exactly."

"Oh."

"Reigh, did he …" She started to ask, but her voice fell silent before she could finish the question.

"Did who what?"

Hecate swallowed, her mouth pressing into an uncomfortable frown. "Did Prince Aubren say anything about me?"

"Uh, um, well." This was *not* something I wanted to get caught up in. Since when was I qualified the middleman in their relationship?

"Did he find me disappointing?" She asked again.

"What? N-no! Of course not," I rasped. "He didn't give me that impression at all."

"He never spoke directly to me while he was here, except for that one moment at dinner. And only then because my grandmother insisted upon it. I don't even know if he looked at me." Her tone had gone soft, as though she were ashamed or afraid someone else might overhear. "I was afraid he might find me … less suitable as a bride than my cousins. I'm younger. I don't know if I'm as pretty. I was hoping he would at least introduce himself, or let me touch his hand so I could hear him. From afar, his sound was so conflicted and wrought with worry, I couldn't get a clear impression of him."

I rubbed the back of my neck. Was I supposed to tell her everything Aubren had said? Was that even fair? Love games were not my thing. I had my own problems in that department. "Look, I'm no expert here, but I think Aubren's a nice person. Honestly, he's kind of worried you'll be disappointed with him, too. Maybe there's a lot you two have in common."

"Maybe so." Hecate's expression brightened slightly. "Come, let's see if we can find that name."

The library was a literal labyrinth of shelves and cubbies crowded on every wall. There were rows upon rows of them, all crammed with papers, scrolls, rolled up maps, and dusty tomes. I stared at it in awe. There was no way we'd ever have time to search every shelf. It would take a lifetime just to get down one aisle.

"Clysiros." Hecate repeated the name. Her whispering voice sent chills over me, like there was some sort of spell to it. Her sightless eyes panned the room and she took a small step, then another. She started walking slowly down the center aisle of shelves. Her lips moved, making shapes like she was repeating the name over and over.

I hung on to her arm, eyeing the long shadows that were cast by the huge stained-glass window overhead. Something about them felt off, as though they were quietly mocking me.

Hecate stopped suddenly. She turned, going down an aisle to the right and taking very slow, careful steps down it. When she stopped again, she faced the shelf and reached into one of the cubbies. I heard papers crinkling inside.

She shrieked and drew her hand back like she'd been bitten by something.

I stepped between her and the shelf, ready to smash whatever might come popping out. All I saw was the corner of an old, yellow, ragged-looking piece of paper. I carefully pinched it between my fingers; dragging it the rest of the way out like it might bite me, too.

It was just a piece of paper, though.

Once I was sure about that, I held it up to the light.

"That voice," Hecate whimpered. "It's the same."

The paper had no words on it—at least, none that I could read. They had been written ages ago, so the ink had almost completely disappeared over time. What I could see, especially when I held it up to the light, was a drawing. It was a picture of a woman in a long black gown adorned with tiny pinpricks of white, almost like stars. Her eyes had been colored in so they were completely dark. Black spiked horns protruded from her head, peeking out of her flowing dark hair, and she had three sets of feathered wings—two of black, and one of silver.

Resting in her hands was a jewel. The picture was so old; I had a hard time discerning what it really looked like. It was just jagged, black, and oddly shaped like a cluster of … crystals.

My stomach went sour.

"She keeps saying the same thing." Hecate groped forward until she found my hand. She clutched it and I could feel her shaking with fear. "*Awaken he who sleeps and complete the ritual.*"

I squeezed my eyes shut.

"What does it mean?"

When I opened them again, I set my gaze on the face of that woman in the picture and growled, "It means I have to leave now."

TWENTY-EIGHT

Hopefully the Queen wouldn't add theft to my growing list of crimes. I'd blown her guards over, entered the palace without invitation, met in secret with Princess Hecate, and now I had that piece of paper with the drawing on it folded up in my pocket—and it wasn't even noon yet. At this rate, I'd be burning the jungle down by dinnertime.

But first, I had a bone to pick with "he who sleeps."

There was only one person in the world I knew she might be talking about. And frankly, I was sick of him. It was time to put an end to this once and for all.

I already knew the way to the stable where the royal family kept their prized shrikes. I'd been there before with Aubren and King Jace. It wouldn't hurt to borrow one for a little while, right? I mean if I was going to be arrested for any of that other stuff anyway, this would just be a good story to tell the guy in the cell next to mine.

I slipped into the stable without any of the guards seeing me. Then I nabbed a saddle, crept into one of the stalls, and got the shrike ready to go. It was kind of bittersweet. I wished I could be riding Vexi instead. Hopefully she was okay and had gone back to wherever her home was with the other wild dragons.

The shrike gave an excited trill as we took off, which alerted all the guards and stable hands nearby. We were already long gone by the time they came dashing over to try and stop us. I gave them all a smirk and a wink as I zipped away into the jungle.

The trees whipped past us as the shrike's translucent wings hummed in the air. It sprang from limb to limb, kicking off the branches and tree trunks as it flew. The sun hadn't been up for long. I could make it before dusk if we pushed hard and didn't pause to rest.

There was no stopping me now.

My blood was on fire. I gripped the saddle so hard my palms ached. I kept my eyes sharp as the shrike took a brief dive above the canopy, bursting through the foliage into the sunlight. There, looming in the distance, was the prize—the lapiloque's tree.

"Faster," I urged the shrike. I wanted to get there before I changed my mind or my better sense caught up with me.

The sun had just begun to set when the shrike finally landed on a branch on the edge of the temple grounds. The beast was tired. As soon as I was out of the saddle, it flopped down to pant and growl in complaint.

"Sorry," I muttered. "Don't worry, the trip back won't be

anything like that."

If I even went back.

Honestly, I had no idea what I was doing here. From where I stood on the edge of a branch, I could see the overgrown temple grounds below. The tree was still there, enormous, and not budging.

My whole body flushed with anger. Beyond this forest, his kingdom and everything he'd claimed to love was being destroyed. And yet here he was, the lapiloque, the great Jaevid Broadfeather—chosen one of the god Paligno—doing absolutely nothing about it.

I climbed down to the jungle floor, which was a terrible idea considering I didn't have any weapons on me. Luntharda's vast assortment of hungry predators wasn't my concern right now. My boots hit the ground and I started running, smacking fern fronds out of my way and jumping over boulders. I scurried across the temple grounds until I came to the base of the tree and skidded to a halt.

The monstrous tree was just as we'd left it. I could feel the faint aura of power wafting off it, pulsing like a heartbeat.

My lip curled. My insides writhed and anger crackled over my tongue. Stupid tree. Stupid legends and myths, giving people false hope. Enough was enough.

"I'm sick of you!" I yelled at it. "You hear me, Jaevid? *I hate you*! None of this would have happened if you had kept your promise. You're a liar."

I curled my hands into fists, drawing upon my power for what I sincerely hoped would be the last time. I hated it—being this monster. I didn't want it. After this, I never wanted to use it again.

"This is it. No more," I growled under my breath. "You hear me, Clysiros? You stay away from me. I'm not your harbinger. I won't be anyone's weapon. I'm finished."

I thrust both of my hands against the tree trunk and poured into it every ounce of power in my body. I gave it all, every last drop. It felt like my insides were being scrambled. My head swam—but I didn't stop. Not until I felt that pulse within the tree suddenly stop.

I jerked my hands away and stumbled back.

There was an unnatural silence, nothing in the jungle made a sound. No birds. No insects. No wind.

Only my heartbeat thrashing in my ears.

Then, right where I had touched the tree, its bark began to turn black. The blackness spread, growing bigger and bigger until it surged over the entire trunk. Far overhead, the leaves turned brown and began to shrivel. One by one, they began dissolving into black ash.

The trunk came next. From top to bottom it began to fade away, dissolving into ash that slowly faded away in the air. I couldn't stop it. In a matter of minutes, the tree was completely gone.

The only thing left was a deep, dark, open pit.

With my knees shaking, I wobbled to the edge of the pit and peered down. It was so deep I couldn't see the bottom. But there was an old, cracked stone staircase that spiraled around the chasm, leading down into the gloom.

I had the weird sensation I had seen this before somewhere. I just couldn't remember where. For some reason, I just *had* to go in there. I needed to see what was at the bottom.

Before I knew it, I was walking down that staircase. The deeper I went, the more the sunlight and jungle became a distant memory overhead. The air was cool and damp. It smelled of old soil, roots, and rotting leaves.

I raked my sweaty hair out of my face as I stepped off the last of the stairs. I was standing before the gaping mouth of a tunnel and, far at the other end, I could see a faint glow of light. It made my entire body shiver and every hair on my body prickle.

Slowly and cautiously, I crept down the tunnel. It was so quiet. The air was musty, like no one had been down here for a long time, which probably had something to do with the giant tree that had been covering it until a few minutes ago.

Part of me expected to find that dark woman, Clysiros, waiting for me on the other end of the tunnel. But when I got to the other side, I stared around at a massive cavern chamber. It looked a lot like the one from my dream.

And just like in that dream, dead in the center of the chamber was a white stone sarcophagus.

Only, there wasn't anyone sitting on top of it this time. There wasn't any water on the floor, either, which was a huge relief. I kept an eye out just in case as I hedged toward the gravesite. The white stone shimmered in the dark like pearl. It filled the whole room with a soft, ethereal glow.

"This is it?" I asked myself out loud as I stood over it.

The stone vault didn't look like anything special. It just looked like a normal burial vault that the gray elves used to bury their loved ones before the Gray War. There were plenty of them in the older cities.

On the top was an engraving, an extremely detailed bust of Jaevid lying on his back, his expression serene and eyes closed, with his arms at his sides. He looked younger in this sculpture than he had in any of the others I'd seen. He had that same scar over one of his eyes, which was a fairly easy way to be sure of who it was.

I didn't know why, but seeing him look so calm and content pissed me off even more. I curled my lip in disgust and reached out to thump his statue in the cheek—just for spite.

The stone cracked under my fingertip like an eggshell.

I bounced back in terror. I-I'd barely touched it!

The place on his cheek began turning black, just like the tree's trunk had. The darkness spread, consuming the whole sculpture of Jaevid and beginning to dissolve it. Black ash boiled into the air, swirling and curling like a plume of smoke that stung my eyes. I covered my face and looked away.

Then I heard someone cough.

My eyes flew open wide and I gaped at the place where Jaevid's bust had been. Lying there in its place was a person—a live person. His mouth opened wide and he sucked in a deep, desperate breath. Then he coughed hard, like he'd been holding his breath for a long time.

About forty years, to be exact.

I was paralyzed with shock, my mouth still hanging open. It wasn't possible. Seriously, I'd barely touched it. I hadn't done anything. I hadn't even used my power on it.

I watched Jaevid try to roll over and sit up. He was weaving drowsily, squinting around, and still coughing and gasping for breath. Suddenly, he started to topple forward.

I immediately rushed forward to catch him.

"Whoa, there. Take it easy." I helped him sit down at the base of the marble slab. "Deep breaths."

He blinked up at me, his brow drawn up in a confused daze. He kept looking around as though he were expecting to see someone else in the room.

"W-where are they?" he asked in the human language. His voice was weak and hoarse.

"Who?"

His pale gaze seemed to focus for an instant. He—Jaevid Broadfeather—looked me square in the eye. "I don't remember. I just thought there would be someone else."

"Sorry, it's just me." I wasn't sure if I was supposed to apologize or what. I'd just murdered his sacred tree and, well, raised him from the dead—accidentally.

"You're him, right? You're Jaevid?" I wasn't sure. After all, it could have been a trick.

It certainly looked like him, though. At least, mostly. He seemed way younger than he did in all the paintings, sculptures, and tapestries I'd seen over the years. In fact, he looked like he might be close to my age. He also didn't look very chivalrous, knightly, or regal like he had in all those sculptures.

His black cloak was ratty and dirty like it had seen better days, and his silvery-gray hair was a wavy, shaggy mess. He had that distinct halfbreed look to him, with pointed ears that were a little shorter than a normal gray elf's peeking out of his hair. His skin was a dark bronze color like theirs, too, and his features were sharp and defined. But his jaw was wider and more human looking. And his eyes, well, they were such a light shade of blue they almost looked like ice.

"That was my name, I think." He seemed to be sizing me up, as well. "Who are you?"

"Reigh." I wasn't sure if I should try to shake his hand or not. Did you shake hands with legendary war heroes? Not to mention I'd come here to, you know, destroy his final resting place.

He glanced around the room again, his eyes panning everywhere like he was still hoping to see someone else. "Where am I?"

"Luntharda," I answered. "At the old temple ruins. You mean you don't remember anything?"

He reached up to touch his face, exploring it like he had no idea what he even looked like. He did the same thing with his clothes, looking them all over and dusting the black ash off where it was still stuck to him. When his hand struck the hilt of his scimitar, I saw him hesitate. He gripped it firmly, then drew it slowly from the sheath and brought it close so he could examine it. He brushed his thumb over the stag's head engraved on the pommel.

"I'm not sure," he answered quietly and slipped the scimitar back into its sheath. "It's like trying to remember a dream. Some things are clear. But others ... " He closed his eyes, his brows drawing together and his mouth set into a hard line.

"Hey, just take it easy. You've been down here a while. It might just take some time to—"

"How long?" he interrupted.

"Uh ... " I wasn't so sure I should tell him that.

Jaevid staggered to his feet, leaning against the marble slab behind him for balance. He was still weak; he could barely stay upright. And yet he looked at me with a fierce desperation blazing in his eyes. "How long?" he demanded.

"Forty years, give or take."

His chest shuddered with a frantic breath. He started to wobble forward, but didn't make it two steps before his legs buckled. I dove out and caught him again to keep him from falling. I looped one of his arms around my shoulders and helped him sit back down.

"N-no," he pleaded. "No, I can't stay here anymore. Please, you have to help me. I have to find them."

"Who?"

His eyes got cloudy. He looked lost and confused, staring around us at the dark until he finally admitted, "I can't remember."

"We're the only ones here. But you're right; we can't stay much longer. It'll be dark soon. I don't know how much you remember about Luntharda, but being on the jungle floor in the dark is the last place anyone wants to be."

TWENTY-NINE

It was well past nightfall by the time I helped him hobble up out of the pit, going up all those steps one at a time, and making our way across the temple grounds. The best scenario we could possibly hope for was making it to the tree without being found by anything looking for an easy midnight snack. Jaevid had a weapon, but I seriously doubted he could use it. He could barely put one foot in front of the other.

Jostling him a little bit to steady my balance and adjust his weight on my shoulder, I focused on the tree. "Just hang in there, okay? We're almost there."

"I ... I feel something," he said hoarsely as his head bobbed and lulled against me. "It's coming this way."

"What?"

I stopped dead in my tracks, looking around as the haunting

sounds of snagwolves yipping to one another echoed through the darkened jungle. I caught glimpses of their glowing eyes winking at us in the dark.

They had us surrounded.

"No," I growled under my breath. "No, no, no. Not now."

The snagwolves started to close in. One popped out of the foliage directly in front of us, its mossy hide bristled. Then another came from behind. More and more emerged from the thickets, circling us and baring their jagged teeth.

One of the snagwolves lunged, jaws open wide for the kill.

I squeezed my eyes shut and braced for it. There wasn't time to do anything else. We were goners.

Suddenly, I heard a deep, concussive sound like the low toll of a bell. Green light exploded in the air, blinding me even through my eyelids. The snagwolves howled in fear. The sounds of them yipping and screeching in terror faded into the distance.

The flash of light left me seeing spots. I rubbed my eyes and when I could see clearly again, I realized Jaevid wasn't leaning against me anymore.

He was standing tall with his shoulders square and one of his hands outstretched. His palm was still glowing with a faint greenish light and his gaze sharpened into a lethal glare. Slowly, he lowered his arm and turned to look at me—about two seconds before he fainted. His eyes rolled back and he toppled backwards like a puppet with its strings cut.

"Hey! Don't you dare die on me!" I rushed over to check his pulse.

He wasn't dead, thank the gods. But he was completely out

of it, so I had to pick him up and fling him over my back. It set the sensitive areas where my wounds were ablaze with a painful reminder that I wasn't fully recovered yet.

I struggled to scale the tree, foot by foot, inch by inch. My body burned with exhaustion. My hands trembled and slipped and my legs cramped. I stopped to catch my breath, to curse Jaevid for weighing so much, and then I started climbing again.

It probably took an hour or more. When I reached the limb where my shrike was still waiting, I collapsed face-first onto it. Jaevid's unconscious body was on top of me and I roughly pushed him off, lifting my head to spit out dirt and leaves.

This day was *not* going as planned.

After lying there for a minute or two to catch my breath, I forced myself to get up again. Grabbing him by the ankles, I dragged Jaevid further onto the branch. I took off his cloak and rolled it into a bundle that I used to prop up his head. That was the best I could do for him at the moment. I didn't have any water, food, or even a blanket to make either of us comfortable.

Sitting down next to Jaevid, I crossed my legs and stared up at the big empty hole in the jungle canopy where his tree had been. Moonlight poured through it, illuminating the ground where the pit was. It made the dew-covered plants sparkle like they'd been sprinkled with diamonds. I could even see a few stars, which was kind of nice. It gave me something else to think about in between doing life-checks on Jaevid every few minutes.

I'd come here intending to put an end to all the myths about Jaevid ever coming back to life. Now he was lying about two feet away from me. I couldn't decide if this was a stroke of good luck or a huge mistake. I did decide one thing, though, and that was that I absolutely—without a doubt—could not tell him why I'd really come here. He was the chosen one of the forest god, lord of all living things. That wasn't the kind of guy you wanted on your bad side.

"Not to mention he wouldn't approve of our differences, don't you agree?" Noh's voice whispered in the back of my mind. *"The lord of life and the harbinger of death. What a recipe for disaster!"*

Next to me, Jaevid's face twitched. He stirred, almost as though he could hear Noh, too.

I clenched my teeth and tried to will him to be silent.

It was already going to be a long night without Noh making it worse.

Jaevid woke up before dawn. He rolled over onto his side and groaned loudly, clutching his head. It made me jump and have a tiny heart attack since I had been nodding in and out of sleep for the past few hours.

"Where am I?" he croaked.

"Still at the temple grounds. Sorry, but you weigh a ton and carrying you up this tree was about all I could do."

He pushed himself up slowly and went on rubbing his forehead. "My head is killing me."

"Yeah, I don't doubt it," I mumbled. "Nice trick with the snagwolves, though."

My borrowed shrike began to stir, making heavy puffing sounds. It was eager to get going. I hadn't brought anything to feed it.

Jaevid's eyes went wide as he stared at the creature. "That's a shrike," he said.

"Yep. So, you do remember some things, after all."

He turned to stare at me next. "Who are you?"

"I already told you, my name is Reigh."

"No, that's not what I meant." He shook his head. "Why did you awaken me? How did you do it?"

Those were two excellent questions and I didn't want to answer either of them. "It's kind of a long story. Maybe we should start with what you do remember and go from there."

He frowned suspiciously, his eyes crinkling at the corners. "I remember … faces. There was a war. Someone was trying to … " His voice faded to silence and I saw his shoulders curl forward, withdrawing as though he were afraid. "It's still too hazy. None of it makes any sense, like scattered puzzle pieces in my mind."

"Look, it really doesn't matter right now. Don't worry about it. What's most important is getting you to Mau Kakuri as soon as possible. Queen Araxie will know what to do." I showed him a confident grin.

He smiled back, but it looked painfully forced. "Araxie— that name does sound a bit familiar."

"Good. See? It'll be fine. She'll know much more about how to help you than I do."

"I suppose I owe you a debt of gratitude, Reigh, for awakening me." He slowly turned his head down and away, staring vacantly at the end of his scuffed-up boots. "Thank you."

I tugged at my shirt collar. It felt too tight for some reason. "That's really not necessary. It was kind of an accident."

"Forty years," he muttered. I could hear the weight of those words even as he said them.

Until that moment, I'd never really thought about how waking up was going to be for him. He was a hero. A legend. He was supposed to be someone we could all count on to come riding in on his famous blue dragon and save us from whatever happened to be destroying the world that day. Tibrans, in this case.

But forty years was a long time. Odds were, anyone he'd known before was either dead or so old they'd be dead sooner rather than later. I studied his profile, watching as his eyes rolled closed and he bowed his head slightly. He was alone in a way I knew I couldn't understand.

"We should probably get going," I suggested.

"Yes," he agreed and began to stand. He wobbled a little, but the more he moved around the more stable he seemed to get. At least I wasn't going to have to carry him anymore.

"Ever ridden a shrike before?" I asked as I climbed up into the saddle.

He approached the creature with uncertainty. For a few awkward seconds, Jaevid and the shrike stared at one another. Then he smiled, petted it on the head, and climbed into the saddle behind me.

"Not that I remember," he replied.

Weird.

"Okay, well you better hang on tight, then. We're going fast. It'll take all day to get back to Mau Kakuri."

"Whatever you say, Reigh," he agreed and grabbed on to the back of my belt.

I nudged the shrike with the heels of my boots. The animal gave an excited screech as it crouched down low, its strong legs coiling for takeoff. I stole one last glance back over my shoulder to where Jaevid Broadfeather was sitting behind me. He flashed me another forced smile. Then we took off into the jungle like a comet, leaving the old temple grounds far behind.

THIRTY

Under any other circumstance, returning to Mau Kakuri after I'd basically broken into the palace, assaulted a few guards, consorted with the princess in secret, and stolen one of the queen's shrikes, was probably an extremely bad idea. I would have been better off staying as far away from there as possible. Not to mention, the rest of the gray elf citizens in Luntharda were probably going to notice that a certain enormous tree-shaped landmark was now missing on their horizon. Whoops.

However, with Jaevid sitting in the saddle behind me, I had more than enough reason to think that past transgressions might be overlooked. Or, at the very least, they wouldn't kill me for it.

Hopefully, anyway.

Three scouts intercepted me before I could cross the boundary back into the city. They were probably one of many who had been put on patrol to watch for me in case I did come back. They surrounded us from every side, their mounts snarling and snapping bony jaws dangerously. Their bows were drawn, arrows pointed right at Jaevid and me.

"Wait a second," I protested. "I can explain!"

"Silence," one of the scouts shouted back. "Dismount immediately and drop all your weaponry!"

"All right, all right. Just don't shoot." I got down first and Jaevid followed. We both stood between the scouts with our hands in the air in a gesture of surrender. I hadn't brought much in the way of weaponry with me. Jaevid, on the other hand, was relieved of his scimitar and a long hunting knife before the scouts were satisfied.

Then one of them actually looked at the blade Jaevid had been carrying. I watched him studying it, surveying the peculiar design, and noticing the royal seal on the pommel. That wasn't just anyone's scimitar.

Suddenly, the scout's gaze shot up to look right at Jaevid. He paled. The other two men with him quickly noticed his reaction and came over to see what the problem was. All told, it took them about five minutes to work it out.

"Lapiloque," they gasped in unison.

Two fell flat on the ground, prostrating themselves before Jaevid—who honestly looked bewildered. The third inched forward, his knees shaking as he offered the scimitar back. "Y-you are truly him? You are lapiloque?"

Jaevid seemed unsure, but he gave them another one of those thin, uncomfortable smiles as he took his blade back. "I am."

The third scout dropped to his knee in reverence. "May the

gods be praised!"

"That's really not necessary." Jaevid was blushing slightly and patted the man on the shoulder. "Stand, please, all of you. We need to go to Mau Kakuri. I need to see Queen Araxie as soon as possible. Can you take us there?"

"You, yes." The scout nearest to him confirmed with an eager smile. That smile immediately vanished when he looked at me. "He is a criminal, my lord. He broke into the palace and stole from the royal stable. He must be taken to stand trial."

Great. What a way to make a first impression. Granted, it wasn't exactly offbeat from my usual antics, but Jaevid hadn't known that. Fantastic.

He shot me an exasperated look. "You might have mentioned that before, Reigh."

I forced a chuckle. "Yeah, well, it didn't seem relevant at the time."

He rolled his eyes. "We can address his crimes later. For now, I require his presence. Please, take us to the palace."

The scouts exchanged quiet murmurs and unsettled glances, but they didn't question him. They did, however, decide to make me ride with one of them—my hands bound behind me—just for good measure. I guess they weren't willing to take it on divine faith that I wouldn't try to run if I got the chance.

It was impossible to tell from Jae's expression what he might be thinking as we crossed the final distance and broke through the last line of foliage into the city itself. Mau Kakuri was breathtaking, even for a jungle paradise. He didn't smile, though. In fact, he appeared to be even more confused as the scouts landed in the city street right before the palace gates. Two of them ran on ahead to alert the rest of the palace. The last stayed behind to guard me. He grabbed the cord that had been tightly tied around my wrists and shot me a punishing glare.

I thought about elbowing him in the gut, just for good measure. He had a lot of nerve, treating me like that. If he was a scout, then he knew who my father had been.

I shuddered at the very thought of Kiran. Thankfully, it didn't linger for very long because Jaevid was slowly approaching the palace gates just as a chorus of horns blew throughout the complex. It started a chain reaction and within minutes, bells, chimes, and horns were ringing out all over the city. People came running out of their shops and houses, crowding into the streets and clamoring in our direction. They gathered in throngs, hundreds of men, women, elderly, and children—all pushing and shoving to see him.

And Jaevid, well, he looked lost.

Standing in front of the city gates in his tattered, dirty clothes with nothing but a cloak and a scimitar, he stared back at everyone with wide eyes. His forehead crinkled and his brows drew up in a look of distress. I could see him breathing faster, backing up step-by-step until the gates opened suddenly behind him. Startled, he spun around to face the front steps of the palace itself.

The royal family came out one by one. First Queen Araxie, then King Jace. Behind them was Princess Hecate with a few of her personal bodyguards. I knew she couldn't see what was going on, but the look on her face me told me that she probably knew more about it than the rest of us who could. Her misty eyes were welling with tears and she had a fierce grip on the arm of her nearest bodyguard.

Everyone was composed for about six seconds.

Then, the Queen suddenly broke into a run. She sprinted down the paved walkway from the front of the palace to the gate, moving faster than I thought an old woman in those kinds of clothes possibly could. I guess she hadn't lost all her spirit, yet.

She stopped barely a foot away from Jaevid, the wrinkles in her face lifting as her eyes widened and her mouth opened. She didn't speak. No one dared to breathe a word. Around me, the crowd and city bells had all gone eerily silent—as though everyone was holding their breath and hanging on the one and only question that mattered:

Was this really him?

The Queen raised a trembling hand to touch him, cupping his cheek tenderly as her whole face twitched with emotion.

Slowly, Jaevid's tense brow relaxed. He stared back at her, his mouth opening slightly and then closing again. Placing his hand over hers, he held her palm against his face and closed his eyes. "It's been a long time, cousin."

She let out a loud, frantic sob and threw her arms around Jaevid tightly.

A deafening cheer went up through the crowd all around us. It was like the whole city of Mau Kakuri exploded into celebration. People threw ribbons and flowers in the air like confetti. Women sobbed against one another, shedding tears of relief and joy. Men beat their chests and shouted war cries. Children danced to the sounds of the music as the tower bells began ringing again.

Jaevid Broadfeather had returned.

ACKNOWLEDGEMENTS

Thank you to all my friends and family who helped me so much with all the ups and downs going on in our lives while I was working on this book. Being a new mom in a foreign country is difficult, but doing it alone would have been impossible.

A big thank you to all my readers and fans who have been so faithful to encourage me! You all make the months of hard work and stress totally worth it! I hope you'll enjoy this part of Jaevid's journey as much as you did the first.

Thanks, as always, to my wonderful husband for listening to me ramble endlessly about characters, plotlines, and imagery worlds. I'll always love that you embrace me for the humongous nerd I am!

HUGE thanks to my beta readers and members of the Dragonrider Legion Fan Club –having your support and enthusiasm is priceless! I can't wait to share the rest of this journey with you guys! Thunder!!

NICOLE CONWAY

Nicole Conway is the author of the children's fantasy series, THE DRAGONRIDER CHRONICLES, about a young boy's journey into manhood as he trains to become a dragonrider. Originally from a small town in North Alabama, Nicole moves frequently due to her husband's career as a pilot for the United States Air Force. She received a B.A. in English from Auburn University, and will soon attend graduate school. She has previously worked as a freelance and graphic artist for promotional companies, but has now embraced writing as a full-time occupation.

Nicole enjoys hiking, camping, shopping, cooking, and spending time with her family and friends. She lives at home with her husband, two cats, and dog.

Introducing

HARBINGER

Book 2 in
The Dragonriders Legacy Series
(unedited sample chapters)

Nicole Conway

PART ONE

JENNA

ONE

I heard him before I saw him—which was nearly always the case with Phillip.

"Good morning, my love!"

I stole a quick glance over the top of the book I was studying, one centered on aerial battle techniques, as Duke Phillip Derrick swaggered into the parlor and leaned against the arm of the sofa beside me. He peered over my shoulder, invading my space to see what I was reading. Or maybe he just wanted to see what I would do if he let his cheek brush mine.

"I've asked you not to call me that," I muttered, fully aware of the futility of having this discussion *again*.

"I'll stop when it stops being true," he replied.

He probably thought he was being clever, using lines like that.

Calling him *ridiculous* would have been the understatement of the century. It was just a cruel, inconvenient coincidence that he also happened to be one of the better-looking men I knew. That hadn't always been the case, however. When we were children, which hadn't been all that long ago, he had been tall, gangly, and awkward. He'd had buckteeth, a face covered in freckles, and a regular riot of loose black curls on his head that stuck out all over the place.

Now, in his late twenties, he'd changed quite a bit. He didn't have the buckteeth anymore. In fact, his were obnoxiously perfect and straight now. I got a good look at them every time he flashed me one of those roguish, coy smiles he most likely thought were charming.

There were still a few freckles dusted across his cheeks and nose, almost invisible now because of his darkly-tanned skin. His hair, however, was no less a mess than it had been when we were little. It was still as black as pitch, wavy, and tended to poke up if it was even the least bit humid. He wore it a bit longer now, almost to his shoulders, so that those loose curls framed his squared jawline in a pleasing way. Something about how they shone in the light made you want to run your hands through them, just to see if they were as soft as they looked.

—Not that I'd ever tried it, myself. I had a firm no-touching policy with Phillip. The cheek brushing was a test, I knew. If he tried that again, I'd be forced to smack him to reinforce my rules.

"More battle plans?" he asked.

"We know the Tibrans will strike again soon," I replied. "Without Reigh here to help even the odds, we'll have to try some new techniques. I only have four riders at my disposal, counting myself. That doesn't leave us with much hope when the next attack comes. If the Tibrans have proven anything, it's that they bounce back quickly and fiercely. We can wager with confidence that their next assault on this city will be far more brutal."

"Ah." Phillip shifted and looked down at his boots. "Well, for what it's worth, I have the utmost faith in you."

So much for keeping the conversation light.

Truth be told, I was no good with that sort of thing. Social grace and appropriateness might as well have been foreign tongues. Being a princess didn't grant me an innate sense of grace, and when it came to interacting with other nobles, I had a long track record of embarrassing myself.

It was easy to play it off like I didn't care what they thought about me, most of the time. I think many people, even my own brother, believed that ruse—that it really didn't bother me not to be very refined when composing myself in court. But there were moments when I wished I could come up with the right things to say; moments when I wished I had just a single ounce of social confidence. Half the time, whenever I opened my mouth, it was the soldier in me who spoke rather than the princess.

I managed to smile back at him slightly, which was a huge mistake.

Phillip grinned and leaned in closer like he was trying to dazzle me with his sharp, vibrant green eyes. "You're so lovely when you smile, Jenna."

I immediately scowled. "Stop that."

"Stop what?"

"Whatever it is you're trying to do." I raised my book up again and all but buried my nose in the crease of the pages. "Go away, please. I'm very busy."

He sighed. I felt his presence withdraw from looming over my shoulder. For an instant, I dared to hope he really had gone away.

I should be so lucky.

The couch where I sat minding my own business and hoping for a few minutes of quiet to read and plan, suddenly lurched. Phillip flopped down onto the opposite end of it, reclining back and staring at me while he scrunched up his mouth and rubbed his chin.

"You'll fall for me one day, you know." He sounded so sure. "Maybe not tomorrow, or next month, or next year—but eventually. My love for you knows no limits. I'll wait forever, if that's what it takes."

I resisted the urge to hurl my book at him. One well-aimed shot and I was pretty sure I could break his nose with it. If I'd thought for even a second that might humble him a little, I might have tried it. "You're impossible."

"Impossibly handsome, maybe." I could hear the smirk in his voice without looking.

I rolled my eyes. Like I said—ridiculous.

His antics weren't a recent development, though. Phillip had been antagonizing me this way for years, baiting me for any response he could possibly get. I think he honestly just liked getting me riled up and he'd discovered that flirting with me shamelessly was an easy way to do it.

This game of his had started when I turned thirteen. I'd grown from my own awkward childhood body into adolescence and finally become a figure of interest for young men in the court. Hooray for puberty, I suppose. Most girls would have been delighted to suddenly be regarded as beautiful. I was cautiously intimidated by those kinds of compliments, however, especially from the boys my age.

I wasn't sure how many of them actually saw *me*—or were just looking for an easy leverage point to get to the crown. Fortunately, my father, King Felix Farrow of Maldobar, was protective. He wouldn't allow most of the suitors who wanted to spend time with me to come anywhere near our family. I was grateful for that. It felt like I might be safe to make some of my own life choices, after all.

And then Phillip began professing his undying love for me.

He was older, the son of a long-time family friend, and I'd known him literally since birth. He and Aubren, my older brother, had been partners in crime for as long as I could remember. We'd all played together as children. He was already inside my father's barrier of family trust, so when he started to show interest in me, everyone just seemed amused by it. Perhaps they assumed we would be married eventually, anyway.

I found it completely annoying and humiliating—like he was making a joke out of me.

Now, more than ten years later, nothing had changed in that department. Phillip was one of the only men in my father's court who still didn't seem thrown by my determination to follow what I knew to be my destiny and become a dragonrider. It wasn't a womanly thing to do—hefting swords, smiting enemies, riding in a dragon's saddle. At least, it wasn't in Maldobar. I was undeniably good at it, though, and that only seemed to make my father even more irate. He'd been staunchly against it from the very beginning. But when my dragon, Phevos chose me—that left no room for anyone's objection, not even the king's.

I was born to be a dragonrider—in body, in heart, and now in destiny.

"Would you go for a walk with me?" Phillip asked suddenly.

I lowered my book so I could glare at him. "Why?"

He put on one of his rare, businesslike frowns. If he'd known I found that look slightly less annoying than any of his other expressions, he might have used it more often.

Of course, I would die before I ever told him that.

"I'm having the catacombs under the city opened for anyone who wants to begin moving there in the event of another attack. Those with young children who might have difficulty getting there should we fall under siege. I've also opened up two of the escape tunnels for anyone who may want to escape to the mountain passes. We know those paths are clear of Tibran forces, so far. They should be safe," he explained. "Like you said, we have to accept the reality that the Tibrans are going to come back. I'd like to go see how everything's progressing."

I arched a brow. "That's so ... *responsible* of you."

His brow puckered with a wounded expression. "I can do my job, you know. My love for you hasn't blinded me from all the things your father expects of me as duke. I mean to take care of the people here as best I can."

"And that's the only reason? Worry for their welfare?"

Phillip made a snorting sound, as one side of his mouth curled up into a half smirk. "That and the remote chance you'll hold onto my arm or hand while we walk."

I closed the book and narrowed my eyes. "Don't count on it."

***

I told myself this had absolutely nothing to do with Phillip—I needed to get out of that stone fortress for a little while, breathe the free air, and think about the battle plan that was taking shape in my brain. So as soon as we stepped outside the front doors of the keep, I took a deep breath. The smell of smoke was still thick on the wind. The courtyard before us was crowded with soldiers working to refortify the walls, bolster the gates, and arm the catapults that had been lashed onto the ramparts.

We weren't going to win this fight. I knew that. One look at the somber, focused frown on Phillip's face and I suspected he was aware of that fact, as well. Our forces had been all but devastated by the first Tibran attack. Barrowton had endured, but that was only because of Reigh.

Aubren had been right about him—he was a dangerous boy. Useful, but very dangerous. He'd killed almost as many of our own troops as he had Tibrans with his demon magic.

I had no illusions of glorious victory here. I only had three riders, besides myself, to work with. They were good men and seasoned riders. But we were still going to lose, so the only question was how.

Phillip was right to invite his people to begin evacuating and taking safety measures now. The smart ones would accept and be long gone by the time the hammer fell. For the rest of us, who had no choice but to stay and fight it out to the bitter end, things looked grim.

I chewed on my bottom lip as I walked beside him, down the steps and through the gates, into the city beyond. Here, the cobblestone streets sloped steeply downward. Barrowton had been designed to be the stronghold of the north, a place of safety and refuge, and a great amount of care had gone into the design. The city itself sat on a manmade, cone-shaped hill with the keep at the very top. It was difficult for an invading enemy to move uphill, and it gave us a sight advantage on all sides. Archers could rain down arrows from any of the three sets of high stone walls that encompassed the city like rings around a bull's eye.

"The outer wall was severely damaged during the last attack," Phillip said as he stopped in the center of an intersection. Around us, four streets came to a large square where a fountain stood in the very center. "My men are doing their best to repair the damage, but I think it's safe to say that we will have to fall back behind the second wall next time. I've asked them to focus their efforts on making sure the second and third walls hold for as long as possible."

I nodded. Walking slowly around the huge fountain, my eyes were involuntarily drawn up to the all too familiar image of Jaevid Broadfeather engraved into the granite, high upon a pedestal. His statue stood tall and proud, dressed in dragonrider armor and holding a scimitar against his breastplate as he gazed toward the north—toward Luntharda. The lengths of his cloak had been cut to look as though they were blowing in the wind, and the detail on his face was so lifelike it was nearly haunting.

"Still hoping for him to return?" Phillip asked suddenly. He'd snuck up behind me again.

I quickly looked away. "No."

"He insists he's given up, but I think Aubren still believes Jaevid will come back."

"He's always believed it, even when we were little. That's just who he is; a believer." A bittersweet smile crept over my lips. I looked up at Jaevid's stony face again and tried desperately not to hope. "My father told us stories about him every night. He made it all seem so real."

Phillip sighed. He was standing right next to me, his arms crossed and those raven black curls blowing around his face. His annoyingly perfect brows were furrowed ever so slightly.

"What about you? Do you believe?" I asked quietly.

He flicked me a look with those electric green eyes. It might have made any other girl swoon when he grinned like that. "I believe the universe always balances itself out. Every right, every wrong, in the end it will all even out. We may not live to see it happen; but it will."

"So Reigh appearing instead of Jaevid is the universe balancing itself out?" I snorted and turned away to continue walking down the sidewalks.

He shrugged as he fell in step beside me. "Maybe so."

I wasn't so sure I agreed. I still didn't know what to make of Reigh. My brother had dredged him up from the depths of the jungle when he'd gone on that desperate and futile errand to try to get help from the gray elves. I knew they wouldn't help us—not that I blamed them. Ours was becoming more of a lost cause every day.

Still, finding Reigh had seemed like it might be a brush of fate. He was a human teenager who had apparently been raised with the gray elves since infancy. Odd? Yes. I'd never heard of such a thing. Not that gray elves were incapable of that kind of compassion, but the one who had raised him was a man I knew well from my own childhood. Kiran had been an ambassador in my father's court for years. He'd taught me to fight, to meditate, and to appreciate the value of nature's balance. But Kiran taking in an orphaned infant was ... shocking. He'd never been married, as far as I knew. I couldn't even picture him changing diapers and handling a baby—especially on his own.

Perhaps that's why Reigh was strange, too. That boy couldn't even speak the human tongue without an elven accent. That and his wild red hair, cute childlike face, and somewhat cocky demeanor all hid a powerful darkness I'd now witnessed lurking inside of him. He was *very* dangerous. Aubren had brought him here hoping he would fight for us, but you only had to gaze out beyond Barrowton's outermost wall to see exactly what kind of devastation he was capable of.

I didn't dare say it, but his mysterious disappearance might have been a blessing in disguise. That is, so long as he didn't show up fighting for the Tibrans. If that happened—Gods and Fates—I shuddered to think of what that would mean for us.

When at last we reached the outermost wall, Phillip led the

way up into one of the turrets so we could stroll along the high ramparts, examining the work being done to repair it. Outside, beyond the wall, was a scene of utter desolation beyond words. That was Reigh's handiwork. The smell of the smoke was intense, tinged with the sharp flavor of smoldering dragon venom and singed flesh. It made my eyes water.

Phillip covered his nose and mouth with his hand. He didn't look out across the battlefield for long, and gagged as his face went a bit pale. He wasn't used to these things. He'd never seen death like this.

Until recently, I hadn't either. Now I was beginning to learn that this sight—endless burning fields of death and despair—was what the Tibrans had always left in their wake. And if they had their way, all Maldobar would be this way.

I couldn't allow that to happen.

TWO

"You're suggesting that we just leave you behind?" Aubren had gone stiff. Sitting across from me at the dinner table, I could see an angry little vein standing out against his forehead.

"I'm suggesting that the only chance the citizens who still remained in the city have of safely making it to the mountain passes is if the dragonriders hold the Tibrans back and then destroy the tunnels on this end so they cannot pursue you," I replied. "That includes me."

My brother's mouth scrunched up and his nose wrinkled. "I won't do that. I won't just run away while you and your men stay here and—"

"This is what we are meant for, Aubren," I snapped. "And we will do our job with pride. It is an honor to die protecting the people of Maldobar."

"Guys, please, let's take this down a notch. I've known you both long enough to know that your arguing will never solve anything. You're like two angry cats in a bag," Phillip interrupted. He cleared his throat and took a moment to rub his hand across his forehead. "Based on what we saw today, I think Jenna and I can agree that a good number of Barrowton's citizens have taken my advice and are already either evacuating, or taking refuge in the catacombs under the city. I'll issue a decree in the morning warning those who remain to be ready to fall back behind the third wall at the sound of the warning horns. We'll save as many as we can. But should the third wall fall, this keep will be the only safe place left. We'll have to evacuate, as well."

I poked nervously at the prongs on my fork. "The dragonriders and I will hold the Tibrans off for as long as we can," I promised.

"You're sure that's the only way?" Phillip studied me carefully.

"Yes. I've been over the plans a hundred times. It's the only way to be sure the Tibrans can't follow you. You'll be able to make it to the mountains."

Aubren slammed a fist down on the table, rattling the china. "I will *not* go without you, Jenna. What will I tell our father?"

"Tell him that if he'd spared even a dozen of the rider's guarding Halfax, maybe we would have stood a chance." The words tasted bitter on my lips, and I couldn't keep my voice from sounding punishing.

It was too much. I didn't like having both of them staring me down that way. Without ever touching the food on my plate, I stood up and left the dining hall.

I waited until I was behind the closed doors of my private chambers to let out a ragged breath. It was almost impossible to keep the emotions from surfacing. All the uncertainty, the fear, the dread, and the burning resentment of my father—all of it ate away at my insides. I didn't understand how he could just stand by and allow the Tibrans to burn city after city without sending any of his forces to help us. He had almost every dragonrider in Maldobar guarding the Halfax, the royal city. Meanwhile, his people burned. Soon, his children would burn, too.

My face flushed and my hands were sweaty. I was terrified. I leaned against the door for a moment until I could catch my breath. Breathe—I just had to breathe.

Wandering further into the room Phillip had lent me, I rang for a servant to draw a bath. I waited until it was done and the servant had gone to undress, though. I wasn't fond of this part. To me, it seemed most women were proud of their bodies. It was their social weapon, something they could use to manipulate and coerce.

My body wasn't like that. At least, not anymore. Perhaps it could have been, but I'd chosen a different path—a path riddled with scars.

I tried not to look at my reflection in the mirror on the wall as I closed the bathroom door and began to undress. I unlaced the sides of my leather jerkin and pulled it over my head, slipped out of my tunic, and stepped out of my boots and pants. Out of the corner of my eye, I saw the edge of the jagged, gnarled, freshly-made scar that zigzagged down the curve of my back. It went from the back of my shoulder all the way down to my hips. Gruesome hardly did it justice. Just the sight of it made my heart wrench. No man—not even Phillip—would be able to look at that without cringing. It wasn't beautiful.

Pair it with the rest of me, which was flecked with nicks, cuts, and scrapes, and you weren't left with someone whose body would be alluring to most men. Not the noble, wife-seeking sort, anyway. My face and neck were protected well by my armor, so they were still fairly unmarked. But my hands weren't soft or slender. They'd been hardened by the hilt of a blade, and I knew I could trust their strength, even if I couldn't trust anything else.

Sinking into the fragrant, steaming waters of the bath, I sat back to let the warmth relax my muscles. It took a long time to wash and detangle my hair. Despite having chosen what was deemed in my kingdom as a "man's profession," I still preferred to keep it long. Just because I'd elected to wear a dragonrider's gauntlets instead of lace gloves didn't mean I didn't enjoy some more feminine habits—fixing my hair being one of them.

Suddenly, someone was knocking on the bathroom door.

I jerked upright and grabbed the closest towel to cover myself. "Who's there?"

"Jenna?" Phillip's voice was muffled by the door.

I deflated. "Go away!"

"Are you all right?"

"I was until you interrupted," I yelled back.

"Maybe I should just come in and make sure ..."

"Gods and Fates, Phillip, if you open that door, I swear I will break your neck."

He was quiet for a moment, and I braced myself in case he really was *that* stupid.

"Seriously, though." His voice had become quieter. "Are you all right?"

I swallowed hard against the thick knot of emotion in my throat. "I'm fine." My voice cracked a bit.

"Really? 'Cause that would be truly astounding if it were true. No one else here is fine right now, Jenna. We're all staring death in the face."

Slowly, I put the towel down and sank back into the tub. I let the hot water rise all the way to my chin. "You don't understand because you're not a soldier. I'm a dragonrider. I can't be afraid of death."

He chuckled. "You're also human. Anyone with a pulse would be afraid—soldier or not."

I watched some of my golden hair swirl in the water around me. For a brief, fleeting moment of pure insanity, I entertained the idea of letting him come in.

What? Was I losing my mind?

"I just don't want you to think you have to do this alone," Phillip said. "I may not be a soldier, but I hope you know I'm your friend. I'm here if you want to, you know, talk."

I laughed out loud. I couldn't help it. "Are you asking me to have a real, adult conversation about feelings with you? I'm not sure you're qualified for that."

"You know I do mean it, right?" His tone was suddenly serious. I didn't like it.

"What?"

"I really do love you, Jenna."

Suddenly, the atmosphere was intensely awkward. It made me wince, and I was thankful he couldn't see it. Why did he always say things like that? What was *I* supposed to say? I … he … argh!

"Go away, Phillip." My tone lacked the authority and

determination I'd been hoping for.

A few more uncomfortable seconds passed. Then, at last, I heard him mutter softly as his footsteps retreated from the door, "As you wish."

The silence that came after wasn't as comforting as it had been before.

**

A sound woke me in the dark. It was the eerie, high-pitched wailing warning sirens.

Panic shot through my body.

I bolted upright in bed and ran to the window, throwing back the heavy drapes to stare into the horror of the night. From where the keep stood high upon the crest of that cone-shaped hill, I could see down across the city, beyond the walls. They were here.

The Tibrans had returned.

I could see them approaching like an encroaching ocean of blazing torches. They were coming at us from every side, stepping over the ash of our dead. I could hear the pulse of their war drums. My own heartbeat raced in that same frantic rhythm.

I took a deep breath.

It took me three minutes to dress for battle. I'd done it so many times now I could manage it without having to concentrate.

As I tied my hair up into a ponytail, I took a few fleeting seconds to stare at my reflection. There were dusky circles under my eyes. I'd lost weight because of the stress, so my cheeks looked sharper. Somehow, it made me look vulnerable despite of the dragonrider armor I had buckled against my body.

I scowled, grabbed an untouched pot of rouge lipstick from the vanity, and drew war lines under my eyes, on my chin, and across my forehead.

Snatching my royal blue cloak off the bedpost, I slung it around my shoulders so that the fur collar was pulled around my neck. I buckled my favorite weapons—a pair of short leaf-shaped blades that Kiran had taught me to use when I was a child—around my hips and grabbed my helmet.

My three remaining dragonrider companions waited for me, already outfitted and ready to go, right outside my bedroom door. Well, most of them. Lieutenant Eirik Lachlan was still buckling his sword-belt and yawning. Eirik had been my friend ever since we began our training as fledgling dragonriders together. We were the same age, and he had taken a liking to me after I dislocated his shoulder during our first sparring match. I guess I had earned his respect then. He was brawny, gruff, and came from a long line of proud dragonriders. I enjoyed his crude, brutal honesty almost as much as he enjoyed ale.

Eirik was the wing end to a man everyone called Haldor, although I'd heard rumors that wasn't his real name. It didn't matter much to us what he called himself—he was a brilliant archer and could speak three or four languages. He'd graduated from the dragonrider academy a class ahead of ours, and while

I'd never dared say a word about it, I found him handsome. His skin was a much darker shade of olive brown than I was used to seeing because his mother had come from one of the eastern desert kingdoms. His hair was as fine as silk, jet-black, and his eyes were a peculiar light amber brown that almost seemed gold in the right light.

The last of our group was Calem. He had been my wing end for some time now, and while he was the youngest and rarely said a word, he was perhaps the most brutal fighter among us. He had a deceptively pretty face for a man—which I'd heard had caused him to be the victim of a fair amount of teasing when he was a student at the academy. He was lean in build and his straight hair was the color of corn-silk. I'd honestly never seen him smile once, but he seemed set on staying at my side as long as I allowed—which I didn't mind considering how well he fought and flew.

We were an odd bunch of misfits. I suppose when they had decided to join me in exile, rather than staying behind in Halfax with the rest of the dragonriders to defend the city, my father probably hadn't considered it much of a loss. But I trusted every one of these men with my life, and I knew they held me in the same regard. They didn't care that I was a woman, or a princess, or anything other than a capable dragonrider.

As I stepped out of my chambers and closed the door, I glanced at their faces. We'd already lost one of our company in the last battle. No one had spoken about him yet. We would, eventually, drink to his honor. Not yet, though. There was still work to be done.

"So? Everyone ready to die?" Eirik chuckled hoarsely. He was finally finished getting dressed.

Haldor rolled his eyes.

Calem just stood there, his wide gray-blue eyes staring into the distance like he was lost in his own private world of thought. It was terrifying how he could go from doing that to cutting someone's head off in about two seconds.

I smirked back at them. My whole body relaxed and all my apprehensions dissolved. Just knowing they were there, watching my back and fighting by my side, gave me all the confidence I needed.

I stuck my helmet under my arm and turned to lead the way, striding down the halls of the keep. "Absolutely. Let's go kill some Tibrans."

THREE

We split off once we reached the lowest level of the keep, where our dragons were housed right next to the launching contraption that would fire us, one by one, into the air like a giant slingshot. I'd balked at the idea when I first saw the launcher. I didn't like the idea of my dragon and I being hurled into the air like a stone from a slingshot. Once I saw the machine in action, though, I had to admit that it was effective. It had the added benefit of catching our enemy off guard.

Well, last time, anyway. Now they'd likely be expecting it.

Phevos raised his head as I came into his stall and he greeted me with anxious chirping. I watched my dragon unfurl himself from the far corner where he'd been crouched, most likely waiting for me to appear. Even down in the bunker beneath the keep, you could hear the warning sirens wailing outside and the distant sound of catapults firing. Battle sounds weren't unfamiliar for either of us. He knew I would be coming.

I rubbed the plated scales on his head as I walked around to check his saddle. I went over every buckle and strap quickly, making sure nothing had been damaged or knocked out of place. Normally, I didn't leave him in it any longer than necessary. At eighteen years old, he was a young dragon, and the weight of it still made him anxious. But I hadn't bothered removing it after the last battle because I knew full well we would be riding back into combat very soon.

"Hello, handsome," I crooned as he pushed his big purple snout against my side. His strong, scaly body was a gorgeous, deep eggplant purple color dappled with vivid, teal-green stripes. The large black horns on his head were curved sort of like those you might see on a ram, and he had smaller jagged black spines running down his spine all the way to the tip of his tail. The leathery membranes of his wings were nearly black, as well, and there was more of that vibrant teal color flecking his legs as though he'd accidentally stepped in paint. He had big, intelligent, golden eyes that tracked my movements around his stall as I buckled down my go bag crammed full of emergency supplies.

Phevos snorted in agreement, blasting my face with moist, smelly dragon breath as he tried licking at my cheek. I smiled and grabbed ahold of one of his ears, giving it a playful tug. "Such a big, beautiful boy. What did I ever do to deserve you, hm?"

"Phillip would be jealous."

I glared over my shoulder to see my older brother, Aubren, standing in the doorway of my stall. Quickly, I turned my back to him so he wouldn't be able to see me blushing with embarrassment. "Phillip is a moron."

"I won't disagree with you there," he said again. His tone carried a heavy tension, as though there was something else he'd come here to say—something much more serious.

"Come to beg me to stay behind?" I muttered as I fidgeted with my saddle straps.

Suddenly, a warm hand fell over mine and held it tightly against the side of my dragon. Aubren was standing right beside me, his presence far more invasive than ever before. It wasn't like him to be so aggressive. Something really was wrong.

"Jenna, please be careful," he said quietly, his tone strange.

I froze, waiting for him to continue.

"I won't ask you not to go. I know you believe you have to. But please, Jenna, please don't let this be the last time I see you. Sometimes it feels like you're all the family I have left in the world."

My stomach twisted into knots. I stared at his hand, much larger and broader mine. I bit down hard because, honestly, I felt the same way. Our mother passed away while laboring to birth a stillborn child. After, our father grew distant. Even Kiran had left us by then. So Aubren and I had been forced to cling to one another. We didn't have anyone else.

His hand slipped away from mine. I felt his presence retreat.

When I dared to turn around, I found him hesitating in the doorway of the stall, his broad back to me and his head bowed slightly like he might be looking down at the tops of his boots. "I'm not evacuating," he said quietly.

I swallowed hard.

"I'm the only one fit to lead the infantrymen who will be

defending this city. So, I intend to stay with them as long as possible and see that every last man, woman, and child have an opportunity to evacuate into the mountain passes."

My body felt strangely cold, even under all my armor.

Aubren looked back at me, flashing a brief, thin smile that had died long before it ever touched his eyes. "I am proud of you, my sister. Perhaps I've never done a very good job of showing it. But of the two of us, you have always been far braver. I am confident you will make a fine queen."

"That's not—"

He cut me off with a wave of his hand before I could finish. "There was something else I came here to tell you in case I don't have the opportunity to tell you later. I think you need to know."

I watched his expression cloud over with a darkness I didn't understand. "What? What is it?"

"The boy I brought back from Luntharda. Reigh—I believe he might be our brother. I'm not sure how, but I think Kiran was up to something. I didn't want to tell you this until I had some real evidence, but now we're out of time."

I struggled with what to do with that information. That boy was my brother? How could that be possible? Did my father had a love affair? When?

I guess Aubren could read my puzzled, frustrated thoughts more easily than I'd anticipated. He smiled, chuckled and waved his hand again like it didn't matter. I guess now, with the city of Barrowton about to be overrun, it really didn't.

"Take care of yourself, Jenna," he said softly. "If not in this lifetime, I'll see you again on the other side."

***

That wasn't how I wanted to leave things with Aubren. I should have said something—anything—to let him know I loved him. Gods and Fates, I loved that idiot more than anything.

But the moment was gone and so was he.

The wind howled past my helmet as Phevos and I were hurled into the sky by the launcher. With his powerful hind legs curled, my dragon waited until the launcher reached the very end of the tunnel to spring forward with the momentum of the wooden sleigh that had flung us out into the air. He spread his mighty wings wide, catching the wind and climbing steeply into the sky.

I moved with him, gripping the handles of my saddle and flexing my legs to lean into his speed. I could feel every one of his powerful muscles working around me, his strong wing arms pumping, his sides swelling with deep breaths, and his tail whipping to counter balance the added weight of me and the saddle.

Overhead, I saw Haldor and Eirik already aligning to begin their first pass. Our plan was simple—we were going to give the Tibrans hell as they approached the city and then keep them pinned between the second and third wall for as long as possible. With so few of us in number, there wasn't much more we could do. Our last act, of course, would be to destroy the entrance to the evacuation tunnels so that the Tibrans couldn't pursue any of the fleeing citizens into the mountains. Until that time came, we had to stall our enemy. Every minute gave someone else a chance to get to safety.

I steered Phevos into a steep turn, looking back as the launcher spat out the last of our company. Calem sat astride his white and silver dragon, a lithe female he called Perish. It was a fitting name. She was known for being extremely high-spirited, temperamental, and had killed the last two riders who had tried to own her. Calem's family had gotten her at a discounted price, both because of that nasty reputation and the fact that her near-albino coloring was less than desirable for most dragonriders. It made her very easy to spot.

Perish swooped into formation behind me like a sterling comet, her scarlet eyes glittering, watching us for cues.

I gave Calem a series of hand signals, communicating to him what we were about to do. He gave me a thumb's up in reply. Time to go.

Below us, the battle was already underway. Maldobarian soldiers on the ramparts fired catapults into the oncoming hoard of Tibran warriors. They'd brought a force larger than I could have imagined in my wildest nightmare. They came like a flood, thousands upon thousands of soldiers carrying bronze shields and pikes. Within minutes they would be at the outermost wall.

I set my jaw and twisted the saddle handles, adding a bit of pressure against Phevos's hide to tell him how to turn and move. He dropped into a steep, blitzing dive. We made a low pass, moving in perfect unison with Calem and Perish, and I gave both handles an inward twist. Immediately, I felt Phevos's sides swell as he took in a deep breath. As soon as we were within range, he opened his mouth and poured out a shower of burning venom upon the first two ranks of Tibran soldiers.

Behind us, I heard Perish doing the same. The sound of the roaring flames from their burning venom mingled with the roar of battle. The wailing sirens. The snap and boom of catapult fire. The cries of men as they burned. The clatter of sword and shield. The pulse of war drums.

This was a dark symphony I knew all too well.

Calem and I made pass after pass, scorching the Tibran ranks until their numbers overwhelmed ours. We couldn't douse them fast enough to stop their progression. They reached the first wall and broke upon it like waves upon a rocky shore. But as Phillip had warned, that outermost wall had taken a real beating in the last battle. The gates were compromised, and they fell quickly to the brunt force of the Tibran army.

Right on cue, Haldor and Eirik fell into formation beside Calem and me. They gave me the signals, gesturing that they were ready. It was time to hold the boundary.

I gave them all a dragonrider salute—clasping my hand into a fist and holding my arm across my chest.

Every one of them saluted back.

Then, as one, we spiraled downward to begin our attack.

Out of the corner of my eye, I saw Haldor reach back and pull his bow from his saddle sleeve and notch an arrow. Not many dragonriders could wield a bow in flight and hit anything with it. He was a crack-shot, though. He rose, standing in the boot-sheaths that held his legs to the saddle, and began firing one shot after another. He picked off a dozen Tibran cavalrymen as they rode in through the gate on ironclad horses.

It was hard not to be impressed.

We dropped in low, flying swift figure-8 patterns around the gate where the bulk of the Tibran soldiers were forced into a bottleneck. We set them ablaze, and they fired volley after volley of projectiles in an attempt stop us. They flung clay orbs filled with dragon venom from slingshot-like contraptions. They also had a rolling, horse-drawn machine that could fire spears like arrows. All of this we had seen before. We knew how to dodge, how to pitch our flight patterns so that we were more difficult to hit.

But when *she* appeared—it was something none of us had ever seen before.

OTHER MONTH9BOOKS TITLES YOU MIGHT LIKE

FLEDGLING
AVIAN
TRAITOR
IMMORTAL
IN THE SHADOW OF THE DRAGON KING

Find more books like this at http://www.Month9Books.com

Connect with Month9Books online:
Facebook: www.Facebook.com/Month9Books
Twitter: https://twitter.com/Month9Books
You Tube: www.youtube.com/user/Month9Books
Blog: www.month9booksblog.com

DRAGONRIDER CHRONICLES 1

Fledgling

NICOLE CONWAY

DRAGONRIDER CHRONICLES 2

Avian

NICOLE CONWAY

DRAGONRIDER CHRONICLES 3

Traitor

NICOLE CONWAY

DRAGONRIDER CHRONICLES 4

Immortal

NICOLE CONWAY

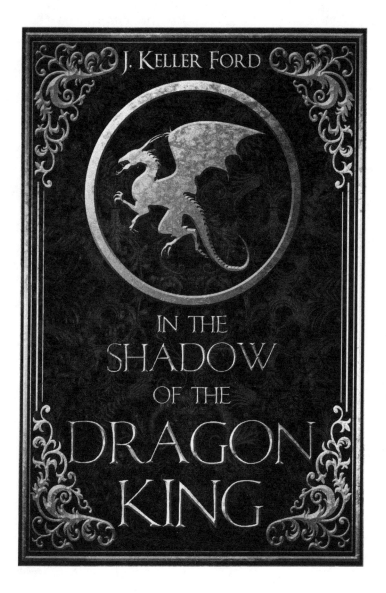

J. KELLER FORD

IN THE
SHADOW
OF THE
DRAGON
KING